Alistair Grim's Odd Aquaticum

Again, for my daughter
—G.F.

For Ben, who explored the old streets of London with me
—V.T.

First Edition, January 2016
1 3 5 7 9 10 8 6 4 2
FAC-020093-15288
Printed in the United States of America

This book is set in Adobe Caslon
Designed by Whitney Manger

Library of Congress Cataloging-in-Publication Data
Funaro, Gregory.
Alistair Grim's odd Aquaticum / Gregory Funaro.—First edition.
pages cm
Sequel to: Alistair Grim's Odditorium.
Summary: With evil Prince Nightshade hot on their trail, Alastair Grim and
his apprentice Grubb and the rest of the crew of the unique mechanical/magical
apparatus known as the Odditorium embark on a perilous underwater adventure
to the otherworldly realm of Avalon, to find the legendary sword Excalibur,
the only weapon capable of penetrating the prince's magical suit of armor.
ISBN 978-1-4847-0007-5
[1. Magic—Fiction. 2. Apprentices—Fiction. 3. Orphans—Fiction.
4. Adventure and adventurers—Fiction.] I. Title.
PZ7.1.F96Ak 2016
[Fic]—dc23   2015006351

Reinforced binding

Visit www.disneyhyperionbooks.com

Alistair Grim's Odd Aquaticum

GREGORY FUNARO

Illustrations by
VIVIENNE TO

Disney • HYPERION

Los Angeles   New York

Table of Contents

From an article in *The Times*, London. October 25, 18—

ALISTAIR GRIM WANTED DEAD OR ALIVE!

In light of the now notorious events in Bloomsbury, The Times has learned that, in response to numerous lawsuits, all liquid assets and material holdings belonging to Mr. Alistair Grim have been ordered seized by the Magistrate's Court and are to be sold at private auction. Although this information seems to corroborate earlier reports that Mr. Grim fled London to evade his creditors, it is the opinion of The Times that, unless the unhappy man and his Odditorium are found, all interested parties will have little to show for their efforts.

Readers of The Times will recall how Alistair Grim—inventor, fortune hunter, and, some say, mad sorcerer—and his long-time associate Lord Dreary partnered with various investors to transform Grim's Antiquities Shop into the aptly named Odditorium: a flying house of mechanical wonders billed as the most spectacular attraction on the planet. After more than five years of construction and countless delays, the Odditorium gave its first public presentation three weeks ago, upon which Grim and his mechanical marvel vanished amidst what can only be described as the most bizarre spectacle our beloved city has ever seen.

Readers of The Times are by now familiar with the numerous eyewitness accounts of how, after an unprecedented demonstration of technical prowess, the much-anticipated preview of Alistair Grim's Odditorium quickly devolved into bedlam. Spectators not only reported seeing a trio of purple-eyed street urchins with superhuman strength, but also a giant, black-winged demon and a flying cavalry of skeleton soldiers—all of which were said to have attacked the Odditorium before its mysterious mid-flight disappearance over the English countryside.

Although these events lend credence to Mr. Grim's reputation as a sorcerer, renowned Cambridge University scholar and Regius Professor of Modern History Oscar Bricklewick believes he has a more scientific explanation. "The only sorcery here is a bit of high-tech flimflam," Bricklewick said upon inquiry from The Times. "Judging from the eyewitness reports of a sparkling green mist emanating from the Odditorium as it took flight, it is clear that Mr. Grim unleashed upon the public a powerful hallucinogenic gas, thus creating both mass hysteria and the perfect cover for his escape."

Indeed, it is the opinion of The Times that, if Professor Bricklewick's hypothesis is correct, it is nothing short of a miracle that no deaths were reported in the wake of Mr. Grim's escape. However, in light of this blatant disregard for the welfare of his fellow man, Scotland Yard has assembled a special task force charged with capturing Alistair Grim, dead or alive.

It is also the opinion of The Times that, with debtors' prisons bursting at the seams, it is inevitable that a few misguided souls will take extreme measures to avoid their financial obligations. However, should one of them possess the criminal genius of an Alistair Grim, Londoners can only hope that he shall refrain from the sort of havoc that the aforementioned has wreaked upon our fair city.

— ONE —

The Sorcerer's Apprentice

G o ahead," Father said, and he passed me the Black Mirror.

The handle was warm to the touch, and I could barely make out my reflection in the mirror's polished black glass. My eyes narrowed and my lips pressed together tightly. This was not the first time I'd gazed upon this strange black mirror. But unlike on previous occasions, I now knew what to say.

"There's nothing to fear," Father said. "All you have to do is ask."

I swallowed hard. "Show me my mother," I said, and the glass burst to life in a swirl of sparkling colors. I gaped in disbelief, my heart hammering as the colors began to churn faster and faster. The mirror flashed, and in its glass appeared the face of a woman weeping. I recognized her from the portrait in the parlor.

Elizabeth O'Grady, the Lady in Black.

"I'm sorry, my love," she said, her voice hollow and distorted. She turned as if something caught her attention, and then her image dissolved and the glass went dark again. A heavy silence hung about the room.

"There, you see?" Father said finally. "Among other things, the Black Mirror is capable of holding the last reflection of anyone who gazes into it, words and all."

"So that's how you knew," I said in amazement. "Because I'd looked into the mirror before, you saw my reflection when you asked to see your son."

"An excellent deduction, my young apprentice." Father took the mirror and slipped it into a wooden case upon the desk. It was nighttime, and yet, in the soft blue glow of the library's lamplight, I could see his eyes had grown misty.

"Begging your pardon, Mr. Grim—"

"Father," he said gently. It had been nearly a month since I learned that the man sitting across the desk from me was my father. But still, I hadn't gotten used to saying it out loud.

"Begging your pardon—Father—but how did you come by this mirror?"

"It was a gift from Elizabeth O'Grady upon our engagement. Legend has it one of her ancestors stole the Black Mirror from a sorceress, after which it was handed down in her family for generations. What you saw was your mother's last message to me before she died."

A long silence passed between us. "I wish I'd known her," I said finally.

"I wish you had too," Father said.

I stared down at my shoes. There were still so many questions I wanted to ask, but Father was not the sort to talk about such things. Besides, we were on an adventure. And when one is on an adventure, there is little time to get gobby-eyed about the past.

"Now, on to more pressing matters," Father said, "the

first of which is preparing you to inherit the Odditorium." He pointed to the notebook of spells on the desk before me. "Let's hear it, then."

"Sumer . . . te . . . sulumor," I read aloud, slowly, and Father snapped his fingers.

"The correct pronunciation is *suh-meer teh suh-loo-mahr*. It's 'Romulus et Remus' in Latin, spelled backward."

"Of course!" I exclaimed, the light dawning, and I uttered the spell again, this time properly.

Father nodded, then crossed to the hearth and pressed a secret button on the mantel. Above it, a large lion's head with glowing red eyes swung open to reveal a hidden compartment in the wall. At the center of the compartment was a small crystal conductor sphere with a tangle of pipes branching out from it in every direction. And inside the sphere floated the light source for the lion's eyes: a fiery glass ball called the Eye of Mars.

Standing on his tippy toes, Father opened the conductor sphere's porthole and removed the Eye.

"There are essentially two types of magical objects in this world," he said. "Ones that are activated by simple physical actions or verbal commands, such as the Black Mirror; and ones that can be activated only by the precise utterance of a magic spell, such as the Eye of Mars."

Father waved his hand over the glowing red ball. "Sumer

te sulumor," he said, and the light went out. I'd seen him do this dozens of times, and yet the simple act of turning the Eye of Mars on and off never ceased to amaze me.

"Go ahead, lad," Father said, passing it to me. I swallowed hard and waved my hand over the Eye.

"Sumer . . . te . . . sulumor," I said—but nothing happened.

"Try it again. A magical spell is only as strong as the belief of the person who utters it."

I took a deep breath. "Sumer te sulumor," I said with conviction, and the Eye of Mars ignited, its red glow warm in my hands.

"I done it, sir!" I cried, and Father mussed my hair.

"That you *did*. Now do it a hundred times more and we'll move on."

"Cor blimey, sir! A hundred times?"

"Consistency is everything in sorcery. Whining is not. Thus, if you wish to inherit the Odditorium someday, I suggest you carry on with your lesson."

Father winked and, raking his fingers back through his long black hair, stepped out through the library's wide-open archway and onto the balcony.

"Sumer te sulumor," I said with a wave of my hand. And as the Eye of Mars went dim again, Father sat down at his pipe organ and began to play. I could barely see him out there in the dark—his long, slender back just a smudge of shadow against the starless sky. And yet the tune he played—"Ode to Joy," I believe it was called—was so festive and cheerful, I could tell how proud of me he was just the same.

My heart swelled, and I tried to carry on with my lesson as best I could, but as Father shifted into a series of expertly fingered flourishes, my eyes began to wander about the library's fantastic contents.

Not much had changed since my arrival at the Odditorium, and yet I could hardly believe that someday it would all be mine. The countless books and clocks and mechanicals. The priceless antiquities. The suits of samurai armor and the lion's head above the hearth—not to mention the Eye of Mars and all the other magical objects about the place.

And yet, for all the wonders I'd encountered, none was nearly so wondrous as the tall, dark man playing the organ out on the balcony.

I suppose every lad thinks his father special—save, of course, for the poor wretch with a father prone to drink and beating him now and then. My father was prone to neither, thank you very much, but to me he was much more than special. In fact, I'd wager there wasn't another father like mine in the whole wide world.

Since when did you become an expert on fathers? you might be asking. And for those of you who know me, I must say I can't blame you. After all, when last we left each other, I'd only known my father a short while—not to mention that I caused him quite a bit of trouble back then. However, for those of you joining me on this adventure for the first time, I suppose a bit of catching up is in order.

You might say that it began with a pocket watch and ended with a prince. And somewhere in the middle, a runaway chimney sweep learned that he was the secret son of an inventor, fortune hunter, and sorcerer all rolled into one. That son, of course, was me, and my name is Grubb. That's right, Grubb. Spelled like the worm but with a double *b*, in case you plan on writing it down. And my father was none other than Alistair Grim.

I say "none other" because, had you lived in London at the time, you no doubt would have heard of Alistair Grim. Had you lived in some other place, you might have heard of him there too. Or at least caught a glimpse of him flying about in his Odditorium—a house of mechanical wonders that looked like a big black spider with a tail of sparkling green smoke.

If you didn't see the Odditorium flying about, you most certainly would have heard it. *Where's that organ music coming from?* you might have remarked, upon which (had I been on the ground with you) I'd have replied, *The Odditorium, of course.* You see, that's how Alistair Grim used to fly his house of mechanical wonders: by playing its pipe organ.

The organ sat upon the Odditorium's balcony and faced

outward so that its massive pipes twisted up and down the front of the building like dozens of hollow-steel tree roots. I must confess, I found it very difficult to play the organ properly at first, but eventually I learned how to make the Odditorium go where I wanted it to—except when traveling underwater.

Good heavens! There I go getting ahead of myself. I suppose if I'm going to tell you about all that underwater business, I best back up and tell you how we got there in the first place. Come to think of it, for those of you unfamiliar with my tale, I best back up to the beginning. Otherwise you might get confused and abandon this adventure altogether.

All right, then: the beginning.

Twelve years before I arrived at the Odditorium, Alistair Grim's bride-to-be, Elizabeth O'Grady, fled London under mysterious circumstances and drowned in the North Country. Before she died, however, Elizabeth gave birth to a son and entrusted him in the care of Gwendolyn, the Yellow Fairy. That son was yours truly, and the Yellow Fairy dropped me off on the doorstep of a kind childless woman by the name of Smears. Unfortunately, she passed away when I was six or thereabouts, and for the next half of my life I had the miserable lot of being apprenticed to her nasty chimney sweep husband, Mr. Smears.

Unbeknownst to me at the time, while I was busy

collecting soot for Mr. Smears, my father, Alistair Grim, was busy gadding about the world collecting Odditoria. Not to be confused with his mechanical marvel the Odditorium (which, as you can see, ends with an *um*), the word *Odditoria*, at once both singular and plural, is used to classify any object—living, inanimate, or otherwise—that's believed to possess magical powers.

In other words, the Odditori*um* is the place, and Odditori*a* are the magical things *inside* the place.

Out of all the Odditoria Alistair Grim collected over the years, there are only three from which he harnesses magical energy to power his Odditorium. The first is none other than the Yellow Fairy herself, whose magic yellow dust enables the Odditorium to fly. The second is the red Eye of Mars, which powers the Odditorium's lightning cannons. The third is a mischievous banshee by the name of Cleona, who provides the Odditorium with a blue spirit energy called animus.

Cleona's animus is by far the most important of Alistair Grim's colored energies; for it's the blue animus that gives life to the Odditorium's various mechanical functions.

However, there was *someone else* gadding about the world collecting Odditoria too: a wicked necromancer by the name of Prince Nightshade. And not only did this Nightshade bloke harness power from his magical objects just as Alistair Grim did, but he'd also gathered about himself an army of nearly every evil creature imaginable: dragons, trolls, goblins, and, most terrifying of all, the Black Fairy.

But for all the prince's success at collecting Odditoria, there remained one magical object that continued to elude him: a source of the animus from which he could create an army of the walking dead.

I suppose that's where I come in. I got into some trouble while sweeping chimneys at an inn with Mr. Smears and, fearing for my life, hid myself in a trunk belonging to one of the guests. That guest turned out to be Alistair Grim, who whisked me away on a flying coach and took me on as his apprentice. My entire life had changed in an instant—not to mention that I made loads of new friends, including Father's right-hand man, Nigel, and an animus-powered pocket watch named Mack (short for McClintock). An odd one, that Mack is, for not only does he never run out of animus, he also stops ticking now and then for no apparent reason.

In fact, it was Mack who kicked off this entire adventure. My first day on the job, I accidentally brought him outside the Odditorium, whereupon Prince Nightshade picked up on his animus and came after us with his army of skeleton Shadesmen. However, Nightshade didn't have many of those bone bags left, so he wanted the animus to turn flesh-and-blood people into Shadesmen too. I'd seen him do it

myself—to Judge Hurst, Father's old enemy from London—
and let me tell you it was not a pretty sight.

So that's the nub of it, and right about where you found
me during my lesson. Cleona and I had narrowly escaped captivity in Nightshade's castle a few weeks earlier, and Father
had since come up with a plan to defeat him. The only
catch? He wouldn't tell anyone except Nigel what he was up
to. The fewer people who knew about his plan the better, in
case the prince caught up to us before we arrived at our final
destination.

Our final destination. I hadn't a clue where it was, but
I got the sense that if we didn't get there quickly, Father's
secret plan to defeat Prince Nightshade would fail. After all,
the evil prince was still out there, plotting his next move
to steal Mack's animus and create his army of purple-eyed
Shadesmen.

Coincidentally, as I was gazing around the library thinking about Mack's animus, the old pocket watch began shaking
in my waistcoat. I'd since traded my raggedy old clothes for
an entire wardrobe that Mr. Grim—er, my *father*—had lying
about since he was a child. If only my mates back in the North
Country could see me now, I thought, they'd think me on my
way to being a right proper gentleman.

I slipped Mack from my pocket and opened his red-and-
gold-checkered case.

"What time is it?" he cried. His mechanical eyes flashed blue, and his thick, curved hands twirled to VIII and IV so they formed a mustache atop his smiling mouth.

"Quiet, Mack," I whispered. "I'm in the midst of my lesson."

"Sorry to disturb ya, laddie," he said. "But if ya wouldn't mind setting me next to me chronometrical cousin there, I'll shut me gob so's ya can carry on."

I glanced over at Father. He was still playing up a storm out on the balcony, so I placed Mack beside the clock on his desk.

"Ten past eight!" Mack exclaimed, and he twirled his hands to the proper time. "I tell ya, Grubb, now that I always know what time it is, I feel like a lad of yer age. Why, I remember when I was—"

"You best quit your jabbering, or Father might ban you from the library again."

"But passing the time with me clock cousins is me reward for helping ya escape Nightshade's castle. Mr. Grim said so himself!"

"I don't mean he'd ban for you good, Mack. Just until my lesson's over. I've got to do this a hundred times, he says."

Waving my hand over the Eye, I spoke the magic spell and the glass ball ignited.

"Well done, laddie," Mack said. "Tell ya what. You do that ninety-nine more times and I'll keep count for ya. After all, what good's the chief of the Chronometrical Clan McClintock if he can't help his best friend become a sorcerer?"

"Why, that's a splendid idea, Mack. I should think it much easier to concentrate on what I'm doing if I don't have to keep track of how many times I'm doing it."

"All right, then, laddie. Off ya go!"

"Sumer te sulumor," I said, waving my hand, and the Eye of Mars went out.

"That's two," Mack said. "Now try again."

"Sumer te sulumor," I repeated—but as the Eye caught fire, it floated out of my hand and hovered in the air just above my head!

"Aye, yer getting good at this sorcery business, laddie," Mack said. "I didn't know you could make things fly."

"But I'm not doing that!" I cried. I rose to my feet and tried to snatch back the Eye, but it darted away from me and began floating toward the hearth—slowly now, as if daring me to follow.

"Father!" I called out in panic. Father ceased his playing at once and came in from the balcony.

"Done already?" he asked, when the sight of the Eye of Mars hovering near the mantel stopped him dead in his tracks. Father's face grew dark and his fists clenched. A long, tense moment of only clock ticking hung about the library, and then Alistair Grim crossed fearlessly to the center of the room.

"Show yourself," he commanded.

And to my horror, someone actually *did*.

— T W O —

A Most Spirited Guest

orcan Dalach," Father said, gritting his teeth, and the spirit smiled.

The young man floating before the hearth was a spirit, all right—and a banshee, to boot. I'd certainly spent enough time around Cleona to know a banshee when I saw one. The spirit had long snow-white hair and ivory skin like Cleona, but instead of a tunic robe he wore a blue cloak trimmed with a glowing white maze pattern. The cloak hung open about his bare chest, below which was a pair of white trousers tucked into a pair of high white boots. In one hand he held the Eye of Mars, and in the other, a length of glowing blue chain.

"Word travels fast in our realm," said Lorcan Dalach. "But I must say I never expected to see you flying about Ireland so soon, Alistair Grim."

"Let me guess," Father said. "You managed to steal on

board as we passed near Dublin. What's it been, nearly an hour you've been sneaking about?"

"Nothing much gets by you, does it, Grim? Except for me. However, someone else knows I've been here the entire time."

"Cleona," I muttered.

"Very good, lad," said Lorcan Dalach. "We banshees can sense each other. But don't be cross with Cleona for not telling you. After all, had she warned you of my presence, she would've exposed herself to these."

The banshee rattled his glowing blue chain.

"I am quite familiar with the Gallownog's spirit shackles,"

Father said. "All you need to do is touch Cleona with them and she's your prisoner, is that it?"

"Aye. But Cleona has always been good at hiding"—Dalach tossed the Eye playfully—"which is why I've had to resort to more drastic measures to flush her out."

"Give that back!" Mack cried. "That's Odditoria what belongs to Mr. Grim!"

"All in good time," said Dalach, and he snickered contemptuously. "That is, if *you* can keep track of it, watch."

"What's that, neep?" Mack said. "Having a laugh at my expense?" Without warning, Mack leaped from the desk. *"MCCLINTOCK!"* he cried, flying straight for the banshee. But Mack passed straight through him, bounced off the mantel, and fell to the floor. Mack sputtered and flashed, and then his bright blue eyes blinked out.

"Mack!" I cried, rushing toward him, but Father held me back.

"You must believe me, Grim," said Lorcan Dalach. "I don't want Prince Nightshade to acquire Mack's animus any more than you do. Both our worlds would suffer greatly should he succeed in creating his army of purple-eyed Shadesmen."

The banshee kicked McClintock across the floor to me. I quickly scooped him up and slipped him back into my pocket.

"Then what *do* you want?" Father asked. "Cleona is now

attached to our family here at the Odditorium and thus is no concern of yours."

"You know very well that banshees are forbidden to interfere in the destinies of the living. And so Cleona must once again stand trial before the Council of Elders."

I understood. Cleona had tried to save my mother from drowning all those years ago. But as banshees are land spirits, they cannot stay over water for very long unless they are protected, and so Cleona failed. Nevertheless, she had broken her clan's sacred law of noninterference and was sentenced to roam the earth in exile. But Alistair Grim rescued her with a magic spell, upon which Cleona attached herself to his family and had since interfered in his destiny heaven knows how many times.

"Cleona is not going anywhere," Father said. "The same law of noninterference that you claim she's broken prevents you from interfering with our destiny here."

Dalach sighed. "You had no business freeing Cleona from exile, Alistair Grim. And so for you that law no longer applies. Therefore, I ask that you command Cleona to go with me. As you are her family's patriarch, she must obey you. However, if you refuse my request, I shall make things very unpleasant for you in England."

"England?" I gasped in astonishment. "You mean we're going back to—"

"Never mind that," Father said. He sat down and turned off his desk lamp. At the same time I noticed him surreptitiously flick the switch to the desk's talkback. I'd helped him install it myself just the day before as part of my technical lesson.

"No, what's more important," Father continued, "is that Gallownogs like yourself cannot fly over large bodies of water. We will be arriving at the English coast within the hour. And so you'll need the protection of the Odditorium's magic paint to get you back across the sea to Ireland. With or without your prisoner."

"Magic paint, eh?" Dalach said, glancing about. "So that's how you keep us land spirits from disintegrating over the sea. Silly me. And I thought you just painted everything black to match your morbid sensibilities."

"The Odditorium has many secrets, Lorcan," Father said, and he leaned back in his chair. "And since I have no intention of transporting you back to Ireland with Cleona, what say you join our happy family here? We could use a banshee of your cunning in our fight against the prince."

Lorcan Dalach sneered. "Have you gone touched in the head, Grim? I've learned much about your Odditorium since I stole on board. It's only a matter of time before your animus reserves are empty and Cleona has to recharge them. And when she does . . ."

The banshee rattled his chain again, but Father appeared unmoved.

"It appears you're the one who's mad, Dalach," he said. "Even if you do capture Cleona, you won't be able to get her back to land without my help. So, what then? You intend to let the Odditorium drift aimlessly over the sea until Prince Nightshade catches up with us? That would mean your end as well as mine."

"And your *son's*," Dalach said, and his cold blue eyes swiveled to look into mine. "Twelve years ago you lost someone you loved. That's right, Grim. I know all about Elizabeth O'Grady. And so I'm wagering you'd do anything to prevent such a tragedy from happening again."

I glanced nervously at Father, and for the first time, I could tell the banshee's words had winged him.

"So you see?" Dalach went on. "I'd wanted to give you and your son a sporting chance. After all, I should think a sorcerer such as yourself could find a way to defeat Prince Nightshade with or without the Odditorium's main power source. And speaking of power sources"—Dalach tossed the Eye again in his hand—"we'll begin by getting rid of this one."

Alarmed, Father rose abruptly from his chair. "Don't be silly, Dalach. The Eye of Mars is extremely powerful. Should you attempt to destroy it, you'll incinerate us all."

"Who says I want to destroy it? I was thinking more of

tossing your precious Odditoria off that balcony there. You'd have a bugger of a time finding it at the bottom of the Irish Sea. Especially without its light"—Dalach passed his hand over the Eye—"Sumer te sulumor," he said, and the Eye's glow went out. "Now hand over Cleona, or the power source for your lightning cannons is gone forever."

"You're quite an expert on the Odditorium's power sources, Dalach," Father said. "But there's one you've forgotten."

"If you're talking about that yellow-bellied fairy down in the engine room, I assure you she's next on my list."

"Who says she's down in the engine room?"

Lorcan Dalach wrinkled his brow in confusion—when suddenly Gwendolyn zoomed in from the parlor and hurled a ball of sparkling fairy dust straight toward him. It exploded on impact, trapping the banshee inside a glowing yellow bubble—but not before the Eye of Mars tumbled from his hand and rolled out onto the balcony.

"The Eye!" I cried, and in a panic, dashed after it.

The banshee howled and whipped his chain at me, striking the insides of the bubble as I ran past. The bubble flashed and fizzled—and somewhere in the back of my mind I feared it might pop—but then I was out on the balcony, gaping in disbelief as the Eye rolled toward an opening in the balustrade.

I dove for it and reached out my hand.

"Sumer te sulumor!" I shouted. The Eye of Mars ignited,

but I was still too far away to catch it, and in the next moment the glowing red ball dropped from the balcony.

My heart froze with horror, and before I realized what I was doing, I leaped over the balustrade and dropped from the balcony too.

The darkness rushed up at me, filling my lungs with icy air as the Eye of Mars plummeted into the black water below. A moment later, I plunged in after it. My entire body felt as if it had been pierced by a thousand red-hot needles, but somehow my arms and legs carried me downward through the frigid waters until finally I felt the Eye's warmth in my hand—more than just my hand, I realized. My *entire body* was now warm, as if I'd fallen into a luxurious bath.

My lungs, on the other hand, were beginning to burn for want of air. I kicked myself upward. I could see the green glow of the Odditorium's exhaust shimmering upon the surface. I kicked harder, the light so close and yet still so far away. My lungs felt on the verge of collapse—I was not going to make it, I thought—when out of nowhere Father dove into the water and pulled me to safety.

Gasping for breath, I offered him the Eye of Mars, but Father only pushed it aside and hugged me. "Thank goodness you're safe!" he said, shivering as he held me tighter than ever before.

"Hold on to the Eye, sir," I said, and I pressed it into his hand. His shivering stopped at once, and we began treading water with the Eye of Mars held between us.

"A job well done, lad," Father said. "But you must promise me you'll never do anything like that again."

I nodded, and Father gazed upward, his face aglow with the light from the Eye. The Odditorium was high above us now. And although I was plenty warm, a chill coursed through my veins when I discovered how far I'd actually jumped.

"Begging your pardon, sir," I said, "but how shall we get back up there?"

At that very moment, Mrs. Pinch, the Odditorium's housekeeper and resident witch, swooped down on her broom and hovered in midair beside us.

"You should have thought about that before you jumped," she said. "Blind me if both your heads don't need oiling!"

"Your advice is duly noted, Mrs. Pinch," Father said. "What say you, Broom? Have you room for two?"

Mrs. Pinch's broom—whose name, by the way, was just that: *Broom*—nodded her stick in the affirmative.

"Up you go, then, Grubb," Father said. "I'll hold on to the Eye while Mrs. Pinch flies you to safety."

Father took the Eye of Mars and instantly I was freezing again.

"Well, climb aboard," said Mrs. Pinch. "I haven't got all night."

Shivering, I hoisted myself onto Broom behind Mrs. Pinch. She flew us up to the Odditorium and deposited me on the balcony. Father's best mate Lord Dreary was there waiting for me, his eyes wide and his mouth gaping below his waxed white mustache. As Mrs. Pinch flew back down to get Father, the old man wrapped me in a blanket.

"Great poppycock, lad!" he exclaimed. "Have you lost your mind?"

I answered him with a *click-click-click* of chattering teeth. Lord Dreary sighed and ushered me into the library, where we found Gwendolyn lounging casually atop a stack of Father's books. Lorcan Dalach, on the other hand, was now in the center of the room, still trapped inside the yellow bubble and struggling to break free. The bubble flashed and fizzled as if it might pop, but Gwendolyn only yawned and hurled another ball of fairy dust to strengthen it.

"You're wasting your time, banshee," she said. "I can go toe-to-toe all night."

Lorcan Dalach growled with frustration.

"Here, lad," Lord Dreary said, and he took off his apron and began drying my hair with it. He'd obviously been in the kitchen helping Mrs. Pinch again. The old woman had been having a hard go of it these past few weeks without her spectacles—which, I'm ashamed to admit, I accidentally squashed during our escape from London.

Father and Mrs. Pinch entered from the balcony with Broom floating in the air behind them. "Well done, everyone," Father said, and he returned the Eye of Mars to its conductor sphere above the hearth. He pressed the secret button on the mantel and the lion's head swung back into place, its eyes ablaze again with light from the red orb hidden in the wall behind them.

"Sorry we didn't get here sooner, Alistair," Lord Dreary said. "But when Mrs. Pinch and I heard you on the talkback, it took us a moment to put it all together."

"Not me," Gwendolyn said. "I know a bully when I hear one."

"A bully, indeed," Father said, locking eyes with the banshee. Then he pressed another button on the mantel and a roaring red fire flooded the hearth. Father motioned for me to join him there, and as soon as I did, my entire body was warm again.

"So what's to be done with this . . . this . . . bounty hunter?" Lord Dreary asked, and Gwendolyn flew off her stack of books and hovered close to the bubble.

"Push him out over the sea," she said. "Leave the bully to the same fate that he would've left for us."

"Come now, we're not barbarians," Father said. "Besides, holding a Gallownog prisoner might come in handy should his comrades come looking for him."

Lord Dreary nervously fingered his collar. "You mean there are others of his kind out there?"

"Most certainly. Our friend Lorcan here is a soldier in the Order of the Gallownog, an elite fighting squad charged with enforcing the banshees' strict code of behavior, as well as the assassination of their enemies."

"Good heavens," Lord Dreary said weakly.

"And speaking of banshees," Father added, gazing round, "you can show yourself anytime now, Cleona."

And with that, Cleona—eyes hard and fists clenched as if readying for a brawl—materialized just outside the doorway to the parlor.

"Nothing to fear, darling," Father said. "You're perfectly safe now that the Gallownog is trapped."

Cleona drifted slowly into the library and Lorcan Dalach stiffened. "We meet again, Cleona of Connacht," he said coldly. The banshees held each other's gaze for a moment, wherein something seemed to pass between them, and then Cleona joined Father and me near the hearth.

"My presence here has compromised our safety," she said.

"That's hardly anything new," Father chuckled. "For twelve years now I've endured the dangers of living with a banshee. I should think Lorcan here would be a stroll in the park compared to you."

"You don't understand," Cleona said. "The Order of the

Gallownog will stop at nothing to bring me back, and they don't care who they hurt in the process. And so we need to turn around at once and return Dalach to Ireland."

"I'm afraid we haven't the time for that, love. We must arrive at our destination before midnight or my plan for defeating Prince Nightshade won't work."

"Hear, hear, now," said Lord Dreary. "I think it's high time you told the rest of us what you're up to, Alistair. Your secrecy on the matter has been quite unsettling these last few weeks."

"All good things to those who wait, old friend. As I've explained, if the prince should learn of my plan before we arrive, I assure you, it will mean the end for us all."

Lord Dreary exchanged an exasperated look with Mrs. Pinch and dragged his handkerchief across his clammy bald head.

"But you can't keep the Gallownog prisoner, Uncle," Cleona said. "Gwendolyn will have to return to the engine room sooner or later. And when she does, her bubble of fairy dust will dissolve and he will escape."

"I am well aware of that, Cleona. Which is why I intend to build a mechanical version of Gwendolyn's prison bubble myself. In fact, ever since Master Grubb told me about your captivity in Nightshade's castle, I've been tinkering with just such a contraption down in the engine room."

"Cor blimey," I gasped. Prince Nightshade had thrown me in a dungeon, but Cleona had been imprisoned in a sphere similar to the ones Father used to harness magical energy from his Odditoria—only the prince's sphere was protected by a purple-and-red force field.

"You really think such a device will work, Alistair?" Lord Dreary asked.

"Of course it will," Father said rather defensively. "If Prince Nightshade can make a spirit prison, so can I."

"Please, Uncle," Cleona said. "You're making a grave mistake."

"I should think if I were, you'd be wailing up a storm by now, wouldn't you?"

Cleona sighed and dropped her eyes to the floor. We all understood what Father meant. As Cleona was a banshee attached to our family, if Father's decision to take Lorcan Dalach prisoner had put our lives in danger, she would have foretold our doom and started wailing at once.

"But, Alistair," said Lord Dreary, "you know better than anyone that the future can be altered by even the most insignificant decisions made in the present. What if the Gallownog's presence here should influence something unforeseen? What if Cleona *does* start wailing?"

"We'll cross that bridge when we come to it."

"You're all a bunch of lily-livered fools," Gwendolyn said.

"The safest course is to push the blighter out over the sea and be done with him."

"Dalach was only doing his job," Father said. "And so I cannot in good conscience destroy him when he could have so easily done the same to us. After all, he was on board for quite some time before he showed himself."

Peeved, Gwendolyn flung more fairy dust at her bubble and then flew up to the lion's head, where she plopped herself down on its nose and began to pout.

"As for you, Cleona," Father said, "how many times these last twelve years have you bewailed my doom only to have it remedied by a simple change of plans?"

Sulking, Cleona turned her back on us, and I glanced over at the Gallownog. Surely, I thought, his animosity would boil over upon learning just how much she had interfered with Alistair Grim's destiny over the years. Curiously, however, Dalach's expression had changed. Gone was the cold hatred from his eyes, and in its place, what I could only describe as pity.

"So it's settled, then," Father said. "We'll drop off the Gallownog on the Irish coast *after* we make our stop in England. Gwendolyn's fairy dust will keep him occupied long enough for us to escape back over the sea. And then Nigel shall proceed with the—" Father glanced about the library. "Hang on. Where *is* Nigel?"

"Begging your pardon, sir," said Mrs. Pinch, and she whispered something in his ear. In all the excitement, I too had failed to notice Nigel's absence. Father was about to whisper something back, but then I sneezed.

"Achoo!"

"Blind me," said Mrs. Pinch. "The Eye of Mars might be good for drying clothes, but it doesn't stand a chance against the sniffles."

Only then did I notice what Mrs. Pinch was talking about. Both Father's clothes and mine were completely dry!

"All right, then," Father said. "Cleona and Gwendolyn shall help me get our prisoner here down to the engine room. Lord Dreary, you accompany Mrs. Pinch and Grubb to the kitchen. I should think a bit of witch's brew is just what the doctor ordered."

And as if on cue, I sneezed again.

"Come along then, Grubb," said Mrs. Pinch.

But as the old woman led me from the library, I glanced over my shoulder just in time to catch Lorcan Dalach smiling fondly at Cleona.

And much to my surprise, Cleona smiled back.

— THREE —

Cheers and Spheres

M rs. Pinch clapped her hands and the kitchen sprang to life. Cupboards swung open of their own accord, pots and pans flew through the air, and all manner of ingredients began mixing themselves into a boiling cauldron upon the stove. Lord Dreary acted as Mrs. Pinch's eyes, nodding his head and barking "too much of this" or "not enough of that," and before I knew it, a bowl of steaming purple stew had been set before me on the table.

"Eat up, lad," said Mrs. Pinch. "Last thing we need is a sick boy on our hands."

The old woman sat down beside me and I spooned myself some stew. As with all of Mrs. Pinch's cooking, it tasted delightful—not to mention that my sniffles disappeared almost at once.

"Well, is it good?" asked Mrs. Pinch. But before I could

answer, Lord Dreary joined us at the table with two more bowls.

"Of course it's good," he said. "What would you expect from Penelope Pinch, Queen of Magical Cuisine?"

Penelope? I said to myself in disbelief. I'd never heard anyone call her *that* before. Mrs. Pinch tried to maintain an air of indifference, but as Lord Dreary smiled and slid her bowl of stew across the table, I could have sworn the old woman was blushing.

"That was a very reckless thing to do, Master Grubb," she said, changing the subject. "Jumping into the water like that."

Lord Dreary chuckled into his spoon. "Well, you know what they say. Like father, like son."

"Blind me," Mrs. Pinch chuckled back. "Heaven forbid Master Grubb should give me so much trouble at his age."

"Begging your pardon, ma'am," I said, "but you knew Father as a child?"

"Of course I did. Why, I've served the Grims in one way or another since I was a girl of seventeen."

"Cor blimey!" I exclaimed. "That must've been ages ago!"

Lord Dreary stifled a giggle, and Mrs. Pinch stiffened and pressed her lips together tightly. Clearly, I'd offended her.

"My apologies, ma'am," I sputtered. "What I meant to say was, you've always been a . . . er, uh . . ." I wanted to say *witch* but was afraid of offending her again. Fortunately, at that moment Broom began tidying up the kitchen, so I just pointed to her instead.

"A witch?" said Mrs. Pinch, and I nodded. "Well, I suppose one is born with a knack for such things, but I didn't formally take up the craft until after my husband died. Hunting accident, it was, not long after we were married."

"I'm very sorry to hear that, ma'am."

"Thank you, lad," said Mrs. Pinch, her expression softening. "But that was a long, long time ago. Back then I was only a chambermaid at the Grims' manor house in Hertfordshire. Mr. Grim's grandfather was a collector of antiquities too, you see; and amongst his things I found a book of spells. Child's play, really—love potions, sleeping charms, and whatnot—but over the years small things led to bigger things, and here I am."

Mrs. Pinch smiled and spooned herself some stew.

"So the Grim gentlemen have always been sorcerers, ma'am?" I asked, and Mrs. Pinch nearly spit out her food.

"Good heavens, no!" she cried. "The Grims were all business back then and had very little regard for magic. Especially your grandfather."

"Indeed," said Lord Dreary. "Alistair's father was a dear friend of mine, Grubb, but a bit too practical for his own good. His mind always on making a profit when it should have been on spending time with his son."

"Yes, a lonely lad poor Alistair was growing up," said Mrs. Pinch. "But, as is often the case, chance intervened for the best. The master was about your age, Grubb, when he stumbled upon me in the midst of one of my spells. Of course, his father would've sacked me had he found out, but young Alistair never told a soul. And in return for his confidence, I took him under my wing and taught him everything I knew."

"Cor blimey, ma'am," I said. "*You* taught Alistair Grim how to do magic?"

"In the beginning, yes. But that was long before he spent his family's fortune building the Odditorium. A model student, he was, dedicating his life to the craft. And very quickly— Well, what's the saying? The student became the master?"

Lord Dreary scoffed. "Rubbish. No one can hold a candle to Penelope Pinch in the kitchen. And in my book, that's the only magic that counts."

The old man winked and toasted her with a spoonful of stew. And even though Mrs. Pinch tried to keep a straight face, she couldn't help but smile.

"Oh, Harry," she said modestly, and my jaw nearly hit the table. *Harry?* I couldn't quite believe it. The old folks must be getting rather chummy to be calling each other by their first names. Lord Dreary had been a trusted friend of the Grims for years, but I wagered he never felt as at home at the

Odditorium as he had these past few weeks in Mrs. Pinch's kitchen.

"Anyhow," she went on, "if there's a lesson in all this, Master Grubb, it's that everything happens for a reason. All those years ago when Mr. Grim began building the Odditorium, I thought he'd gone mad. But now that Prince Nightshade has reared his ugly head, I see that everything was meant to be. After all, who else but Alistair Grim would stand a chance of defeating him?"

"That devil's still out there, and plotting something big, no doubt," said Lord Dreary, and he scraped up the last of his stew.

I, on the other hand, had lost my appetite, for I was thinking about the *real* reason why Alistair Grim had built his Odditorium: to rescue Elizabeth O'Grady's spirit from the Land of the Dead. It was Prince Nightshade, of all people, who let me in on that little secret while I was a prisoner in his castle. And even though Father's plan had been sidetracked, for some reason my guts still twisted at the prospect of one day meeting my mother's spirit face-to-face—either out of anticipation or fear, I couldn't quite tell.

"Eat up, then, lad," said Mrs. Pinch. "If only your old master, Mr. Smears, could see you now, eh? Why, blind me if you haven't grown some flesh on those bones already."

"Thanks to you, ma'am," I said.

"Indeed," said Lord Dreary. "At the rate he's going, I should think our resident grub worm will soon be too fat to fit in his hole."

The old folks chuckled, and then Father's voice crackled into the kitchen.

"Are you there, Mrs. Pinch?" The old woman answered him at the talkback by the door, and a loud *clang!* rang out on the other end, as if someone had knocked over a stack of pipes. "Is Nigel with you?" Father asked, irritated. "He won't answer on his talkback and I require him in the engine room at once."

"I'll fetch him!" I blurted out impulsively. I'd barely seen Nigel over the last week. Since he was the only one privy to Father's plan, he'd been spending a lot of time alone working on something secret in his quarters.

"Oh, very well, then," Father said with a sigh. "But please hurry, lad. Speed is of the essence if we're going to get the Gallownog secured in time."

"I'm on my way!"

And with that I dashed from the kitchen and straight into the Odditorium's lift. I threw the lever and quickly ascended three stories to the upstairs portrait gallery.

Those of you who are familiar with my tale will remember how Cleona, being the trickster that she is, marred the

Grim family portraits with swirly chalk mustaches and nasty comments about Alistair Grim's spotty bottom. Cleona had since erased all that, but as I emerged from the lift and rushed to the other end of the long, blue-lighted hallway, it was the doors, not my clean-faced relatives, that caught my attention.

There were many more secrets at the Odditorium for me to discover, beginning with one of the rooms up here. There were five rooms altogether, as well as a closet and a washroom. Four of the rooms served as quarters for Father, Cleona, Nigel, and the samurai. As for the fifth room, the others refused to tell me what was inside.

As if reading my mind, the door to the mystery room thumped loudly as I passed. It was directly across the hallway from Cleona's quarters and padlocked from the outside. Hanging from the knob was a small sign that read, SILENCE IS GOLDEN. This was not the first time I'd heard thumping on this door, but Father warned me never to tarry too long in front of it. He'd also warned me never to enter. When I asked him why, he said it was none of my concern. Fine by me, as whatever was doing all that thumping didn't seem to want me around anyway.

I hurried down to the end of the hall, and a pair of samurai standing guard at Nigel's door crossed their spears in an X to block my path. Father had a whole regiment of samurai

stationed round and about the Odditorium. And oftentimes late at night I'd hear their animus-powered armor clanking down the hallways as they made their patrols.

"Orders from Mr. Grim, gents," I said. "I'm to fetch Nigel to the engine room."

The eyes of their scowling black face masks brightened, and then the samurai uncrossed their spears to let me pass. I knocked and called out Nigel's name, but upon receiving no reply, I slowly opened the door and crept inside the dimly lit chamber.

Unlike Father's quarters, Nigel's room was sparsely furnished with only a bed, a small desk piled high with books and papers, and a couple of chairs. Covered with a sheet at the center of the chamber was a large, lumpy mass with all manner of tools and mechanical parts scattered on the floor around it. I must admit I was tempted to take a peek—whatever Nigel had been working on this past week was under that sheet— but given Father's demand for secrecy, I resolved to keep my nose out of it.

Besides, something else had caught my attention.

Pinned to the wall above Nigel's desk were over a dozen newspaper articles with titles like, *ABEL WORTLEY'S MURDER MOST FOUL!* and *WILLIAM STOUT SENTENCED TO HANG!*

Now, for anyone unfamiliar with my tale, the names Abel Wortley and William Stout will mean nothing to you. But to Nigel, they were everything.

You see, Abel Wortley, an elderly collector of antiquities and former friend of Father's, was murdered a decade earlier, and William Stout, his sometime coachman, was hanged for the crime. William, however, was innocent, and so Father brought him back from the dead with his animus. William changed his name to Nigel and pretended to be his own twin brother so as not to arouse suspicion. And for the last ten years, in addition to building the Odditorium, he and Father had dedicated themselves to solving Abel Wortley's murder.

Unfortunately, they'd had little to show for their efforts—that is, until Prince Nightshade showed up. Father believed that Prince Nightshade and Abel Wortley's murderer were the same person. As to the *identity* of that person . . . Well, that was the big question, wasn't it?

My heart sank as I gazed at Nigel's things—not because he'd been framed for something he didn't do, but because as a result he'd been separated from his daughter, Maggie. There she was, in miniature portrait upon his desk. The little girl looked much as I'd imagined her—rosy cheeks and yellow ribbons in her curly red hair. She'd be about thirteen now and was living happily with Judge Hurst's sister in the country. Still I could never picture her in my mind as anything but that sad little girl who lost her father ten years earlier.

I soon became aware of a low humming sound behind me. I crept around the covered mass in the center of the room and discovered Nigel standing in the corner with a large, barrel-shaped helmet upon his head. The helmet was attached to the wall by a mechanical arm, along with a jumble of pipes and wires that ran along the length of it. Even though the big man's face was obscured by the helmet's visor, the blue light flashing behind its eyeholes told me at once what I was witnessing.

Nigel Stout was recharging himself with animus.

"Is anyone still there?" Father called on the talkback. Startled, I rushed over and flicked its switch.

"I'm here, sir. But Nigel—er—well, he's still charging himself, sir."

"He should have more than enough power by now," Father shouted—a bunch of hammering was going on behind him. "Just make sure he brings down that large coach wrench I loaned him, will you? And for goodness' sake, chop-chop, lad!"

Father turned off his talkback and I dashed back to Nigel. "Wake up, Nigel!" I hollered, but the big man didn't hear me. For some reason, I felt strange touching him in his present state, so I stepped up onto a chair and tapped gently on his helmet.

Nigel flinched, and then the helmet automatically lifted off his head and retracted back on its mechanical arm into the wall.

"Hallo, Grubb," Nigel said, his eye sockets bright with animus. "Fancy meeting you in here."

"Forgive me for intruding, Nigel," I said, and quickly brought him up to speed on the capture of the Gallownog, as well as Father's request for the coach wrench.

"Oh dear," Nigel said, and he gathered up a handful of wrenches from the floor. "Gallownogs are not to be trifled with. Right-o, then. Let's be off, Grubb."

"Aren't you forgetting something?" I asked, and I pointed to a pair of thick black goggles on his desk. Embarrassed, Nigel pointed to the helmet contraption.

"Head gets a bit loopy after all that," he said, and then his face dropped with alarm. "Er, uh, you didn't by any chance peek under that sheet, did you?"

"No, sir."

"Good lad, Grubb," Nigel said, relieved. He slipped the goggles over his eyes, and without a word more we hurried down the hallway, dropped three floors in the lift, and dashed into the engine room.

The yawning chamber was a bedlam of activity. The furnaces blazed fiercely, bathing the walls in a frenzy of flickering shadow as swarms of giant mechanical wasps buzzed about in every direction. Some hammered and welded, while others crawled along a tangle of pipes that connected the Odditorium's massive flight sphere to a smaller, glowing sphere in the center of the room. Father's spirit prison. I could see Lorcan Dalach pounding on the walls inside, his form hazy and green behind a force field of sparkling yellow fairy dust as he struggled to break free. Gwendolyn spun madly in the flight sphere to keep her dust flowing to the spirit prison—but something was wrong. The force field was flickering and flashing as if it would fizzle out at any moment.

"Thank heaven you've arrived!" Father cried, rushing over. He took the largest of Nigel's wrenches and handed it off to a wasp that was buzzing past. The wasp flew up to the engine room's honeycombed ceiling, where it joined a cluster of other wasps and began tightening a pipe coupling that was leaking great spurts of fairy dust. The problem was clear. If the leak wasn't mended soon, then the Gallownog would escape.

Father screamed, "Now, Gwendolyn!"

In a flash I saw her change into a monstrous, toothy ball of yellow light—the form in which she gobbled up nasty grown-ups—and then a blinding explosion filled the engine room. When next my eyes cleared, the force field around the prison sphere glowed steady and bright.

Nigel and I sighed with relief. Lorcan was secure.

Father raked back his hair. "Well that was a close one," he said, and Number One, the queen of the wasps, flew down to him and handed him the coach wrench. Father thanked her and pressed some buttons on a nearby control panel, upon which all the wasps flew up to the ceiling and settled into their combs—their bulbous blue eyes shining down on us like stars.

"I've never seen a Gallownog before," Nigel said, peering cautiously into the prison sphere. Lorcan Dalach had stopped struggling, and sat slumped in a shadowy green heap inside. "I thought he'd be a lot scarier looking, quite frankly."

"Don't let his appearance fool you," Father said. "A Gallownog is one of the spirit realm's fiercest warriors, and should he escape . . . Well, I don't need to tell you how that would throw a wrench in our works." Father tossed his coach wrench upon a pile of other tools, and a loud *clang!* echoed through the chamber. I flinched.

"I realize that, sir," Nigel said. "But if you use this crystal ball to house the Gallownog, which one will you use to house the—"

Remembering my presence, Nigel caught himself and clamped his lips tight.

House the what? I wanted to ask. I knew it had something to do with Father's secret plan to defeat Prince Nightshade, but I also knew the only way Nigel would ever tell me anything was by a slip of the tongue—which, luckily for me, he was prone to do now and again.

"I appreciate your secrecy on the matter, Nigel," Father said, winding his pocket watch. "But the witching hour is fast approaching, and so the first phase of my plan will be revealed to Grubb very soon." Father inspected a massive gauge at the base of the flight sphere, the needle of which read FULL, and then he hollered up to Gwendolyn to stop spinning.

Dizzy, the Yellow Fairy flew out of her dust-filled sphere and shook the cobwebs from her head. According to the gauge, the Odditorium's flight reserves and its new spirit prison would be charged for quite some time. And as a reward for her hard work, Father tossed Gwendolyn a large chunk of chocolate.

"*Oooh!*" she cooed, and flew up to her dollhouse (which was hung from the ceiling) and began munching away on the front steps. Father crossed over to the talkback and flicked its switch. "Cleona, darling, any sign of our destination?"

"The coordinates indicate we're well over the English countryside now," she replied. "But it's hard to tell our precise location with all this fog."

Father rolled his eyes and sighed. "What next?" he muttered. "Very well. Divert all power from the Eye of Mars to charge the searchlight, will you? We're on our way up now."

"Uncle," Cleona said tentatively, "is Lorcan . . . well, is he all right?"

Father frowned. "You needn't worry about him," he said tersely, and flicked off the talkback. Cleona's question had clearly irritated him. Had he noticed the banshees smiling at each other in the library too?

Father threw a lever on the wall, and the door at the top

of the engine room's stairs slid open. Nigel and I followed him up the stairs and out into the grand reception hall, where we found the Odditorium's giant birdcage waiting for us. We piled in, traveled up through the reception hall's ceiling, and then stepped off into the library. The empty birdcage continued upward, disappearing into the garret above, while at the same time Father's desk slid back over its trapdoor in the floor. The three of us joined Cleona on the balcony—she was right about the fog. It was so thick that I could barely make out my hand in front of my face.

Father pressed some buttons on his pipe organ and a massive beam of bright red light shot out from below the balcony. It seemed to dissolve the fog on contact, cutting through the gloom and forming a sharp circle on the ground below.

"There we are," Father said. He'd trained the searchlight on a ring of tall, standing stone blocks far off in the distance.

"Cor blimey," I said. "Is that where we're headed, sir?"

"But of course," he said with a smile. "What better place than a hell mouth to catch a demon on All Hallows' Eve?"

— F O U R —

The Hell Mouth

The Odditorium hovered high above the circle of stones. I counted at least two dozen of the massive blocks, some of which were joined together by smaller blocks resting across their tops, while others lay tipped over on their sides in the long grass. The searchlight cast the scene in a sinister red glow, but still it was impossible to see anything beyond the outermost stones. And as Lord Dreary joined Father and me on the balcony, Nigel and Cleona hurried off to make the final preparations for the evening's adventure.

"A hell mouth, did you say?" Lord Dreary asked as he peered down over the balustrade. A sense of dread hung over the place, as if the very air here was heavy with fear.

"A hell mouth, yes," Father replied. "Didn't you ever wonder how Prince Nightshade made his castle fly?"

"What are you talking about?" the old man sputtered—he was as anxious about this hell mouth business as I was.

"I must admit, it took me a while to put it together," Father said, thinking. "But those thick black clouds surrounding the castle's foundation are what finally tipped me off. Demon dust, don't you know, expelled from the castle's exhaust vents in very much the same manner as the green mixture of fairy dust and animus is expelled from the Odditorium's."

Lord Dreary gulped and his eyes grew wide. "*Demon* dust?" he said. "You mean to tell me that Prince Nightshade uses a demon to fly his castle?"

Father chuckled and shook his head. "One demon could hardly provide him with enough power to fly something of that size. No, I should think the old devil would need at least a hundred of the little rascals to get his castle off the ground."

"Good heavens!" cried Lord Dreary, and I shivered as I thought back on my imprisonment in Nightshade's castle. Somewhere in its bowels had been an engine room much like the Odditorium's, only instead of a flight sphere powered by a fairy, the prince's engine room had a sphere that contained a hundred demons.

"So that's why you were building a spirit prison," I said in disbelief. "You wanted to capture a demon just like Prince Nightshade done!"

"Grammar notwithstanding, you are correct, my young apprentice. The circle of stones down there marks a hell mouth—a supernatural doorway, if you will, through which demons pass into our world. Problem is, the mouth only opens once a year and for a very short period of time."

"At midnight on All Hallows' Eve!" cried Lord Dreary.

"Which leaves us precisely thirty minutes," Father said, checking his watch. Lord Dreary and I exchanged a terrified glance. There was no denying it now. Alistair Grim actually intended to add a demon to his collection of Odditoria!

"But have you gone mad?" asked Lord Dreary. "Why on earth would you want to bring a demon on board the Odditorium?"

"Do not let the relative calm of these past few weeks lull you into a false sense of security, old friend. You know very well that Prince Nightshade is out there plotting his revenge. Thus, if we are going to defeat him, we must go on the offensive and fight fire with fire—or in this case, a demon with a demon."

"You can count on me, sir," I said, trying to be brave, and Lord Dreary nodded reluctantly.

"Very well, then," Father said. "Prepare the Odditorium for landing, Grubb." I gaped at him as if to say, *Now?* But he just winked and motioned for me to take my seat at the organ. And with a deep breath, I did.

I began to play slowly—a simple tune that Father had taught me to unfold the Odditorium's spider leg–like buttresses and activate its vertical thrusters. I'd only been playing for less than a month, but Father said I was a chip off the old block. And as the massive mechanical limbs groaned loudly under my command, Lord Dreary patted me on the back and said:

"You're a regular prodigy, Grubb Grim." I didn't know what the word *prodigy* meant, but it sounded good, so I changed my tune to make the legs crawl in midair.

"Show-off," Father said with a chuckle. "Nevertheless, I better take over from here. We don't want you growing up too fast."

Father took my place at the organ, played a quick flourish, and we began to descend. Gazing out over the balcony, I could hardly believe my eyes. Father meant to land the Odditorium directly over the hell mouth.

Lord Dreary and I watched in awe as the Odditorium's legs touched down in a perfect ring around the outermost stones. Father flicked on the energy shield, sealing off the balcony in a sweeping halo of blue, and the three of us hurried through the library and into the parlor, where Father summoned the lift. As we waited, I gazed up at the portrait of Elizabeth O'Grady above the hearth. How many hours had I passed studying it since my arrival? So many that, when I closed my eyes, I could still see every curl of my mother's hair beneath her hat—every stone in her necklace, every twist in her flowing black gown. And yet, now that I'd seen her in the

Black Mirror, for the first time her expression in the portrait struck me as frightened—her eyes brimming with some terrible secret that drove her away from Alistair Grim.

The lift arrived, startling me from my thoughts, and we all dropped down to the floor below and dashed into the Odditorium's main gallery, where Father led us through a dizzying maze of magical objects—giant statues, piles of armor, cauldrons, goblets, and brooms—as well as towers of wooden crates, the tops of which vanished among the shadows near the ceiling. Many of the crates had been recently opened, their fantastical contents spilling out onto the floor in haphazard heaps of wonder.

It was in one of these heaps that Father began searching through a wide assortment of chests, some of which were gilded and adorned with precious jewels. Finally, he settled on an old wooden box about the size of a breadbasket. Compared to all the other boxes, it wasn't much to look at. Then again, if there was one thing I'd learned in my time at Alistair Grim's, it was that the most powerful Odditoria were most often things that, on the surface at least, appeared to be ordinary.

"You're going to catch a demon with that box, aren't you?" Lord Dreary said as we followed Father to the gallery's main door.

"An excellent deduction, old friend," Father replied. "And so it should come as no surprise to you that this box is called just that: a demon catcher. Used for centuries by sorcerers to rid themselves of evil spirits and whatnot."

"The operative word being *rid*, Alistair!"

"Well, either way, let's just hope it works."

Lord Dreary gasped. "You mean you've never tried it?"

Father shrugged and unbolted the door, and the three of us spilled out onto the reception hall's upper landing. A curved staircase stretched down from either side of the landing to the floor below; and as we descended the stairs on the left, I was distracted for a moment by the life-size portrait of Father on the lower wall between the two staircases. It showed him holding a bright blue orb of animus, but I knew the portrait doubled as a secret panel that hid the entrance to the engine room behind it.

A loud clanking sound echoed through the chamber. And had I not been so preoccupied with Father's portrait, I might have seen the secret button he'd pressed to activate the large, chain-wrapped winch that was now rising up from the floor. I'd seen winches like it before at the coal mines back home, but still, my eyes grew wide in amazement. Was there no end to the secrets hidden within these walls?

Father pressed a button next to the front door and it slid open. Outside, I could see the Odditorium's front steps silhouetted against the soft red glow of the searchlight reflecting up from below.

"The winch connects to an emergency escape ladder at

the base of the front steps," Father said, cranking away. "Once we're safely on the ground, Lord Dreary, you'll crank the ladder back up and close the front door. The Odditorium's magic paint should repel any evil spirits that may try to sneak on board, but better safe than sorry."

Lord Dreary's face dropped with fear, but Father just smiled at him and exited through the front door with the demon catcher tucked snugly under his arm.

"Come along then, Grubb," he called from the bottom of the steps.

"You mean I'm going with you, sir?" I asked in amazement.

"Of course," Father said as he disappeared down the escape ladder. "Dangerous as it may be, this *is* your first quest for Odditoria."

My heart began to hammer—in all the excitement, it never once occurred to me that I would actually be *accompanying* Father on his demon quest—but as I slowly made my way to the door, I remembered that Mack was still in my pocket.

"Better safe than sorry, sir," I said, echoing Father's words, and I handed Mack to Lord Dreary. It was common knowledge now that Mack was forbidden to go outside. Unlike the Odditorium, Mack's animus was not protected by magic paint, which meant the doom dogs—vicious shadow hounds charged with fetching escaped spirits back to the Land of the Dead—would come after him.

"I don't like this business one bit, lad," Lord Dreary said with his hands on my shoulders. "Promise me you'll take care?"

"I promise, sir."

"We haven't got all night!" Father called, unseen from below, and I bounded down the front steps to meet him.

Although the Odditorium's spider legs had landed outside the circle of stones, the Odditorium itself was still suspended a good ten yards off the ground directly above its center. I slid down the metal escape ladder, and as soon as my feet hit the grass, Father called up to Lord Dreary and the escape ladder folded back into the front steps. Next, we heard the front door slide shut above us and all was deathly silent. I shivered.

"It's good that you're afraid," Father said, reading my thoughts. "Fear keeps the senses sharp. And in time you'll learn to channel that fear into something sharper."

"If you say so, sir," I said, and we sat down upon one of the fallen stones. The wind hissed eerily through the grass and a crow cawed far off in the distance. My heart skipped a beat. Crows never caw at night, I thought—not to mention that Prince Nightshade had an entire flock of them trained to track doom dogs. What if the prince was watching us now?

I closed my eyes and tried to push the idea from my mind.

"Are you happy here, son?" Father asked, and I glanced around, confused. Who could be happy in such a dreadful

place? "At the Odditorium," Father added. "With *me*."

"But of course, sir. I haven't been this happy since before Mrs. Smears died."

"You still miss her, don't you?"

"Yes, sir," I said—then added quickly, "But not nearly as much as I did before I come to live with you, sir."

Father smiled, but I could see in his eyes that he'd grown sad. He often looked that way when I talked about my life with the Smearses. It was more than pity. Alistair Grim felt guilty about all the time lost between us, and nothing I ever said seemed to make it better for him. But still, I always tried.

"You know," Father said, changing the subject, "when I was your age, one of my favorite things to do was fish. You ever been? Fishing?"

"I'm afraid not, sir."

"I'm sorry to hear that. A delightful experience, really— the silence, the anticipation. Much like this, in a way. One of our grooms—this was at the old manor house, of course—he taught me how to catch the big ones. Showed me a secret spot and used to lend me his pole when my father was away. He thought fishing an idle pastime, my father. A waste of mental energy, he called it. But still, I always wished he would join me. Magic is much more fun when you've got someone to share it with, don't you think? And to be sure, there was nothing quite so magical to me back then as fishing. The mystery lurking there unseen beneath the water, the excitement of that first nibble on your line."

Father squinted up at the Odditorium. "It's strange, isn't it?" he said. "In spite of all the Odditoria I've collected over the years, deep down I've always known there's more magic in things like that—simple things, like a lad with his fishing pole—than anything up there."

Father seemed lost in thought for a moment, and then, as if remembering my presence, he abruptly cleared his throat and said, "I suppose what I'm trying to say is, when all this is over—and I promise you, one day it will be—well . . . I'd like to take you. Fishing, that is. Would you like to go, Grubb?"

"I should like that very much, sir," I said, and as if by magic, all my fear seemed to vanish in an instant.

Father sighed with relief and raked his fingers through his hair. "So it's settled, then," he said. "And please forgive my lack of eloquence on the subject. All this father business is still quite new to me."

"I understand, sir. All this son business is new to me too."

Father chuckled and checked his watch. "All right, then. Time to cast our line."

And just like that my fear returned in a rush. We stood up on the stone and Father slipped a small bottle of white powder from his coat pocket.

"As with most evil spirits," he said, handing me the bottle, "your standard demon will only manifest itself in visible form if sufficiently provoked. The itching powder in this bottle should annoy them enough to do just that."

"Itching powder, sir?"

"Upon my command, you're to fling some down there at the opening of the hell mouth. I'll take care of the rest with the demon catcher."

"But I don't see any opening, sir. Just the grass and a patch of dirt."

"Evil most often enters our world unseen to the naked eye. You may feel a sudden drop in temperature, and may perhaps hear a ringing in your ears, but I'm afraid that's the only warning you'll get that the hell mouth has opened."

I swallowed hard, and Father produced from the demon catcher a pair of necklaces, each of which held a large milky-green stone. Father slipped one of the necklaces around my neck, and then the other around his own.

"Now take heed, lad," he said. "The warding stones on these necklaces should protect us from demonic possession. However, in the unlikely event one of us does become possessed, the other is to knock him squarely on the head with the demon catcher. That should set things right again. Understand?"

"You mean, a demon can actually get inside a bloke's body?"

"Unfortunately, yes. And if that happens, believe me, a thump on the noggin will be the least of your worries."

Summoning my courage, I took a deep breath and stiffened my spine.

"That's a good lad," Father said. "Now uncork that bottle and get ready to toss the itching powder at the hell mouth upon my command."

Father minded his watch as I stared unblinkingly at the ground. "Nibble, nibble," he whispered finally, and a cold, moaning breeze wove its way among the stones. At the same time, my ears began to ring so loudly that I could barely hear Father when he said, *"Now!"*

I flung a dash of itching powder at the desired spot, and a low, inhuman whine began rising up all around us.

"What's happening?" I cried. If the hell mouth had opened, I certainly couldn't tell by looking at the ground.

"There," Father said, and a handful of demons materialized in the grass at the base of the stone. Their pint-size bodies were entirely black, but their eyes and the insides of their black-fanged mouths blazed with orange fire as they squirmed about, frantically scratching themselves all over.

Suddenly, one of the demons cried, *"It's the boy what done this!"* Upon which the whole lot of them turned their orange eyes on me. After all, I was the one standing there with the bottle of itching powder.

The demons howled with rage and flew up at me in a single mass—their hideous, snarling faces hovering just inches away from my own. My entire body froze—and I tried in vain to scream—but then the demons caught sight of the amulet about my neck, and they shrank back in terror.

"The stone!" they cried as one, and in a great, sweeping *whoosh* flew off shrieking into the night.

Before the last of them could escape, however, Father opened his box and shouted, *"Demonicus expugno!"* A giant skeleton hand sprang forth from the box and snatched one of the demons from the air. The inky black spirit howled in anguish, and then the skeleton hand withdrew again into the box with the demon in its clutches.

"Well, that was easy," Father said, latching closed the lid. But then I noticed an orange-eyed shadow descending upon him from behind.

"Father, look out!"

It was too late. And before Alistair Grim even knew what hit him, a demon tore off his warding stone and tossed it into the surrounding darkness.

I gasped in horror. Father was no longer protected!

Struggling with the evil spirit on his back, Father dropped the demon catcher and tumbled from the stone. A second later, the demon vanished and Father began writhing on the ground with a chorus of horrible animal noises coming from his mouth.

I jumped down into the grass beside him. Father whirled

around on all fours to face me. His eyes blazed with orange fire, and his snarling mouth was filled with fangs. I screamed.

The demon had taken possession of Alistair Grim's body!

"Die, boy!" he growled, and with a terrifying roar he swung his fist at me. I ducked and, scrambling around behind him, picked up the demon catcher and thumped it on his head.

Dazed, Father teetered for a moment on his knees and then fell over face-first in the grass. At the same time, the shadowy figure of the demon seeped out from his ear and, like a drunken bullfinch, zigzagged its way out of the stone circle and into the darkness beyond.

"Are you all right, Father?" I said, turning him over, and he blinked open his eyes.

"That was quite a wallop, lad," he said, rubbing his head. "Nevertheless, I thank you for it."

The demon catcher shook violently in my hands.

"We better get our newest Odditoria back on board," Father said, taking it from me. He called up for Lord Dreary to lower the ladder, and in no time we were back inside the reception hall, demon and all.

"What happened?" Lord Dreary cried, but then he saw the demon catcher shaking under Father's arm, and the old man's face blanched with fear. "Is that the—"

"You needn't worry," Father said. "The demon is perfectly secure, and thus the first phase of my plan is complete."

"Yes, but—"

"I'm also proud to announce that Grubb proved himself a worthy apprentice on my latest quest. In fact, I couldn't have captured the demon without him."

Father mussed my hair, but Lord Dreary appeared unconvinced.

"Jolly good, then," the old man said. "Now that you have your demon, would you mind telling me what you plan on doing with it?"

"I'm afraid that will have to wait until morning."

Lord Dreary gasped in disbelief. "Alistair, how could you!"

"Please try to understand," he said, and he put his hand on the old man's shoulder. "As is most often the case here at the Odditorium, any attempt to explain my endeavors without an accompanying demonstration would prove futile. And in order for that demonstration to work, Nigel and I have a long night of tinkering ahead of us."

"Yes, but—"

"I promise you, Lord Dreary, all will be revealed tomorrow after breakfast. So until then, I ask that you and Grubb get a good night's sleep. We still have quite a journey ahead of us, and I'll need you both to be sharp and well rested for the next phase of my plan. Please, old friend. For me."

Lord Dreary heaved a heavy sigh and reluctantly nodded, upon which Father crossed to the wall and twisted one of the animus-burning sconces. The winch immediately retracted back into the floor, while at the same time the giant birdcage dropped down from above. Father stepped inside, bade us good night, and promptly disappeared up into the ceiling. Lord Dreary was about to leave too, when something in his waistcoat pocket began to tremble. It was McClintock.

"I believe this belongs to you," he said, handing him to me.

"Thank you," I said. "And chin up, sir. I haven't a clue what Alistair Grim's up to either."

A smile hovered upon the old man's waxy white mustache. "Story of my life," he said, and then Lord Dreary took his leave through the adjoining parlor.

"What time is it?" Mack cried as I opened him. "Hang on"—he spun round in my hand—"what are we doing down here? And where's that scaffy banshee what took the Eye of Mars?"

Mack had been dead to the world for quite some time, I realized—not to mention that, in all the excitement, I'd completely forgotten about Lorcan Dalach.

"A lot has happened since you fizzled out back in the library, Mack. I'll explain it to you on the way to the shop."

As I passed through the dining room and kitchen and down the servants' hallway, I brought Mack up to speed on the evening's events. Once we were back in the shop, I set him down amongst the clutter on Father's worktable and readied myself for bed. However, as I was still anxious from my encounter with the demons, I decided to leave the warding stone on.

Just then, I heard the muffled sound of organ music, and the entire Odditorium began to shake. We were on the move again, blasting off into the air as Father set course for our next destination. I closed my eyes and imagined myself at the organ in his place, my fingers moving along the proper keys to control the Odditorium's spider legs.

Soon, however, the organ music stopped and everything grew still. We had reached the desired height—or "altitude," as Father called it—and the helm was now set to follow his course automatically. And so it was that the Odditorium drifted off into the night while Alistair Grim went to work on the next phase of his plan.

And so it was that I too drifted off to sleep with the warding stone about my neck.

Had I known how much trouble it would bring, I'd have left the cursed bauble back at the hell mouth where it belonged.

Dreams, Asleep and Waking

In my dream, I was lost in the dungeons of Prince Nightshade's castle, dashing this way and that through a murky-red maze of corridors and staircases. I pushed open a large iron door and stumbled into the prince's throne room. Great stone pillars rose up around me as shafts of bright red light cut downward through the dark. But instead of a throne, hovering there in midair above the dais was an enormous, glowing green eye.

I froze and trembled under its gaze.

"Aye, that's him," echoed a gruff and growly voice. I recognized its owner at once. Mr. Smears.

"Are you certain?" asked a woman, unknown to me.

"For twelve years I fed and clothed him, and what've I got to show for it? Nothing but ruin and a bad reputation."

"It is destiny that brought us together," said the woman. *"And so together we shall have our revenge."*

"You hear that? I'm coming to get you, Grubb!"

And with that, the eye transformed into the hulking figure of Mr. Smears—his snarling, scarred face twisting with fury as he sprang forth from the gloom and made to strangle me.

Terrified, I bolted upright—my nightshirt soaked with sweat, my eyes darting over unfamiliar shapes and shadows. Where was I? The dark chamber in which I'd awakened looked nothing like the stable. For the briefest of moments I thought I saw a green light flash beneath my nose, but then I caught sight of Mack, asleep on the worktable, and everything came back to me.

"The shop," I sighed with relief.

Yes, I was safe in my bed at the Odditorium, far away from Mr. Smears and all the other demons in my life.

Demons.

Instinctively, I grasped the warding stone. The bauble felt warm, almost hot to the touch. Odd, I thought as I gazed around the room, and all at once I had the gnawing sensation that someone was watching me.

It's just the dream, I told myself. *Just that glowing green eye and Mr. Smears what's put you out of sorts.*

The animus in the wall sconces burned bright enough for me to see that I was alone. But this was the Odditorium, and appearances could be deceiving—not to mention that, in this very room, Cleona once played a trick on me by slipping Mack into my pocket while she was invisible.

"Is that you, Cleona?" I whispered. No reply except for Mack ticking softly on the worktable. Even Cleona knew it wasn't proper to play tricks on people when they were asleep, and after what happened as a result of her last trick, no doubt she'd think twice about pulling a stunt like that again. However, come to think of it, Cleona had been acting strange lately—distant and gloomy—ever since the Gallownog stole on board.

"Dalach!" I gasped, and Mack stirred.

"Heh-heh, silly bam," he muttered in his sleep, and then he began to snore.

I, on the other hand, had begun to panic. Yes, there was now *another* spirit at the Odditorium who could make himself invisible. And if Lorcan Dalach had escaped from his prison sphere, the sort of tricks he might play would be far worse for us than anything Cleona might dream up.

You're just being foolish, I told myself. *After all, who wouldn't wake up feeling watched after dreaming about a big green eye?* But still, I couldn't shake the feeling that something was wrong. Then, through the crack under the door, I saw a blue light pass by in the hallway outside.

My heart began to hammer. The light was too strong to have come from a samurai on patrol. No, the only things at the Odditorium that glowed like that were banshees.

I donned my slippers and crept silently from the shop so

as not to wake Mack. I tiptoed down the hallway and came to the engine room's big red door. Listening there for a moment, I could hear only the low hum of the flight sphere within, so I cracked open the door and peered inside.

As I expected, the flight sphere was aglow with fairy dust, the gauge above it reading more than three-quarters full. Attached to the gauge was an alarm clock that would wake Gwendolyn should the reserves run low. I couldn't see her from the hallway, but the yellow light coming from her doll-house told me she was fast asleep in her bed. The force field around the prison sphere also glowed bright with fairy dust, and a wave of relief washed over me upon seeing the hazy figure of Lorcan Dalach still inside.

Much to my surprise, however, there was now someone *outside* the sphere too.

"Cleona!" I gasped, and quickly clamped my hand over my mouth. Thankfully, she didn't hear me.

"Please, forgive me," Cleona was saying, with her hand upon the sphere. "There's nothing I can do."

"You can still come home," Dalach replied. "If you help me escape, I'll bear witness for you at the trial."

"You did that once before, remember? And look where it got me: eternal banishment."

"Things were different then. You were my betrothed, and so my word carried little weight with the Council."

My jaw dropped. Did I really just hear that? Cleona and Lorcan Dalach were to have been married?

"And now?" Cleona asked. "Have your feelings changed so much these last twelve years?"

"Time passes much more slowly for us banshees."

"You haven't answered my question."

Lorcan Dalach pressed his hand against the inside of the sphere, opposite Cleona's.

"Every second away from you has been an eternity," he said, and Cleona rested her head against the glass. "Please, my love," Dalach said, his voice heavy with emotion. "I beg of you, come with me. I am now a captain in the Gallownog, and I've gained influence with the Council. If only you'll tell them how you were bound to the Grims by sorcery, they will no doubt pardon your transgressions here."

"And those of twelve years ago? You forget that I tried to save Elizabeth O'Grady of my own free will."

"You're wrong. Elizabeth O'Grady was versed in the art of sorcery too. Don't you see? She slipped and fell off that cliff and conjured you in a panic. There was nothing you could do to resist her. You were bewitched then just as you are now."

"That isn't true," Cleona said, recoiling from the sphere. "You are a Gallownog—solitary by nature and incapable of attaching yourself to any family. As such, you cannot possibly fathom my bond with the Grims."

"Cleona, my love, you're in too deep to recognize them for what they are. There's a reason we banshees are forbidden to interfere in human destiny. It goes against the natural order of things. You understood that before you fell under these sorcerers' spells. And once you're back amongst your kind, you'll see just how badly you've been bewitched. So will the Council of Elders, I promise you that."

"What I do, I do of my own free will. Just as you do now."

"What do you mean?"

"The Order of the Gallownog doesn't know you're here, do they?" Cleona asked, and Lorcan Dalach bowed his head.

"I know your heart better than anyone. You came for me of your own accord, but the question is will you tell the Order you found me when I refuse to return with you?"

"Cleona, listen to me!"

"Quiet, you'll wake Gwendolyn!"

Dalach lowered his voice, but it grew tight with anger. "What I do, Cleona, I do out of honor for us both. I am a captain of the Gallownog first, and your one true love second. You best remember that should you seek to test me."

"I don't believe you," Cleona said, stepping away from him. "I am not bewitched now and I never was. And should the Council take me at my word, would you really risk losing me again to eternal banishment? Could you live with yourself knowing it was you alone who sent me there?"

Lorcan Dalach was silent for a long time. "You underestimate both my love for you and my resolve," he said finally. "But hear me, Cleona of Connacht: By hook or by crook you *will* come back with me, upon which I shall prove that you are just another victim of Alistair Grim's sorcery."

Cleona was about to reply, but then Gwendolyn poked her head out of her bedroom window.

"What's all that jabbering down there?" she called. From where the dollhouse was hanging, she could not see Cleona on the other side of the prison sphere, but just to be safe Cleona made herself invisible. "You better shut your gob,

Gallownog," Gwendolyn said, "or I'll come down there and shut it for you!"

I didn't stick around to hear any more, and quickly padded back down to the shop. I climbed into bed and pretended to be asleep just in case Cleona decided to check up on me. My mind was spinning, however, and I lay awake for hours, consumed by what I'd just witnessed. More than the revelation of the banshees' betrothal, I couldn't help but wonder if there was any truth to Dalach's tale. Was my mother really a sorceress? And if so, had both she and Father bewitched Cleona into helping them?

If sleep came to me at all that night, it came dreamless and only for minutes at a time. And in the morning, when Mrs. Pinch summoned me for breakfast on the talkback, I quickly dressed, slipped Mack into my waistcoat, and joined the grown-ups at the dining room table, happy to be free from the prison of my thoughts.

"Expecting another demon, are we?" Father said, and he pointed to the warding stone about my neck. I hadn't even realized I was still wearing it.

"Begging your pardon, sir," I said. "Should I take it off?"

"Not if it makes you feel safer. In fact, I'm happy to see it finally getting some use. The demon catcher and its contents have been in storage for— What's it been, Nigel? Four, five months since our last trip to Scotland?"

"Six, actually," Nigel said, nibbling at his sausage. "Nasty business, that quest. Never forget it. Neither will that daft witch from what you stole—er, uh—*acquired* all them things."

"Now, now, Nigel, you know very well I won the demon catcher fair and square. Besides, Mad Malmuirie was up to no good with it anyway."

"Mad Malmuirie, sir?" I asked.

"A beautiful but deadly witch who lives in a cave along the North Sea. Stumbled upon her quite by accident, if you want to know the truth. The demon catcher was merely the price she paid for picking a fight with me."

"You fought a lady, sir?"

"A battle of wits is more like it. Riddles, dueling spells— that sort of thing. It'll all be second nature to you by the time we're done with your training."

Father winked and sliced into his sausage.

"Just be thankful your Father goes about his quests incognito," said Mrs. Pinch. "Had Mad Malmuirie known it was Alistair Grim who took her Odditoria . . . Well, I shudder to think what might have happened had she tracked him back to London."

"Who knows?" Father said, munching away. "Should Prince Nightshade pay her a visit, she may yet have her revenge."

"Cor blimey, sir," I said. "You don't think that witch might've joined up with the prince, do you?"

"I sincerely doubt it, Grubb. Even though the old devil has managed to gather about himself quite a menagerie of Odditoria, Mad Malmuirie doesn't strike me as the sort who'd share her power with anyone. Not willingly, that is. Come to think of it, you didn't see any highly fetching, mentally imbalanced ladies during your captivity in Nightshade's castle, did you?"

"Only goblins and trolls and whatnot. And all of them were quite ugly, sir."

Father chuckled. "Well there you are, then. Nothing to worry about, see?"

I nodded, but my mind began to wander. There was something familiar in Father's tale—something that made me think back on my dreams from the night before—but all I could see were flickering images of Mr. Smears and the banshees in the engine room. Yes, all that business with Cleona and Dalach was beginning to seem like a dream too—the whole night was becoming just one big blur of confusion.

"Now eat up, Grubb," said Mrs. Pinch, startling me from my thoughts. "Blind me if I should heat your sausages only for you to eat them cold."

"Yes, ma'am," I said, and I dug in.

"Now see here, Alistair," said Lord Dreary. "Before we leave the subject of Mad Malmuirie's demon catcher, what say you make good on your promise from last night?"

"Very well, then." Father rose from his chair and spoke into the talkback beside the dining room's massive, china-filled breakfront. "If you're within the sound of my voice, Cleona, please join us in Nigel's quarters at your earliest convenience, will you?" Father switched off the talkback and sat back down at the table. "Eat up, then, all of you," he said. "You'll want a full stomach for the day I've got in store."

We quickly finished our breakfast and followed Father upstairs into Nigel's chambers. Cleona was there waiting for us, hovering beside the heap in the center of the room. But when she smiled and wished me good morning, I could hardly meet her eyes. I felt guilty about spying on her the night before, but I also felt suspicious. Was Cleona really bewitched? And if so, would she ever leave if Dalach broke Father's spell?

Rubbish, I told myself. Father loved Cleona, and he would never bewitch her into doing anything against her will.

"Isn't that right, Grubb?" Father asked, and I shook off my thoughts to find everyone staring at me.

"Er, uh," I stammered. "Isn't what right, sir?"

"I was explaining the events of last night, and looked to you for confirmation." My heart froze and I just stood there gaping. Did Father know about my spying on the banshees? "You *do* remember helping me catch a demon, don't you?" he added.

I sighed with relief. "Oh, *that*—yes, sir."

"You feeling all right, Grubb?" Nigel asked. "Your head's been in the clouds all morning."

"Still a bit shaken, I suppose. Nasty business, that demon catching."

"Speaking of clouds," Father said. "Nigel, would you care to do the honors?"

And without further ado, Nigel tore off the sheet, exposing his secret project underneath. The old folks gasped, and my jaw nearly hit the floor.

There in the center of the room was a black open-air carriage with a small crystal conductor sphere attached to its back end. Inside the sphere, a cloud of black smoke churned violently; outside, pipes connected in all directions to steering mechanisms and exhaust vents similar to the Odditorium's. Attached to the front of the carriage was some sort of furnace contraption loaded with gears and pistons, and from which a long cable plugged into Nigel's charging station.

"Behold my latest invention," Father said. "I call it a demon buggy. Named, of course, after its main power source."

"Great poppycock!" Lord Dreary cried. "You mean the demon you captured last night is inside that sphere?"

As if in reply, the conductor sphere began to tremble and a pair of glowing orange eyes snapped open amidst the smoke within. I jumped back in fear.

"The demon buggy works exactly the same as the

Odditorium," Father said. "Under the protection of my magic paint, Cleona's animus safely controls its mechanical functions, while the dust harnessed from our demonic friend enables the buggy to fly."

Lord Dreary gulped and fingered his collar, and Mack began to rumble in my waistcoat. "What time is it?" he cried as I opened him, but upon seeing the demon in the conductor sphere, he let out a loud *"Ach!"* and closed his case again. Cleona, on the other hand, was unafraid, and drifted over to the demon.

"I should think it'd go mad in there," she said sadly.

"Unfortunately, madness and evil often go hand in hand," Father replied.

"It's just that, evil spirit or not, I can't see taking part in torturing it."

Father raised his voice. "Any discomfort this servant of evil might experience in the conductor sphere pales in comparison to that which it would inflict upon mankind. And once the foul creature has served its purpose, we shall send it into oblivion over the sea, thus ridding the world of untold pain and suffering. I should think, however unjust you find its temporary imprisonment, you'd be happy to have a hand in that. And so this discussion is closed."

Frowning, Cleona heaved a heavy sigh and floated from the room. I felt sorry for her, but at the same time couldn't help but wonder if she wasn't on her way to see someone else who she thought had been unjustly imprisoned—someone who, only a matter of hours ago, called himself her one true love.

"Very well. Who's up for a little jaunt about town?" Father asked, lightening the mood, and he disconnected the cable from the buggy's front furnace—which, judging by its location and its coating of magic paint, I understood to be charged with animus.

"You mean you're going to fly that thing *now*?" Lord Dreary cried.

"My entire plan to defeat Prince Nightshade hinges upon it," Father said. He threw a nearby lever and the Odditorium's outer wall split apart like a set of jaws preparing to chomp the sky. A cold wind swirled through the chamber and rustled the newspaper articles on the wall above Nigel's desk. Father climbed into the demon buggy and, donning a pair of goggles, sat down behind the steering wheel and cranked on the ignition. The buggy's engine roared to life, and tendrils of black and blue smoke began seeping out of the rear exhaust vents.

I shivered. The blue smoke was obviously expelled animus. And if Father was planning on taking the buggy outside, unprotected by the Odditorium's magic paint, the doom dogs would most certainly pick up on it.

Father read the fear on my face. "You needn't worry about the doom dogs!" he hollered above the din. "The demon's dust renders the animus harmless, just like Gwendolyn's! Who's with me?"

Father held up another pair of goggles, and before I realized my feet were moving, I tossed Mack onto Nigel's desk and sat down next to Father with the goggles over my eyes. Nigel strapped a large leather cowl onto his head and climbed into the seat behind us, but Lord Dreary and Mrs. Pinch remained where they stood.

"Blind me if I ever set foot in that thing!" Mrs. Pinch shouted. "Your heads need oiling, the lot of you!" Lord Dreary nodded in agreement.

"We should be back by noon!" Father called. "Have the hangar doors open and lunch waiting, will you, Mrs. Pinch? We won't have time to dillydally!"

And with that, Father threw the demon buggy into gear.

In one moment we were rolling toward the opening in the wall, and in the next the sky was all around us—the cold wind whipping at my hair as we plummeted toward an endless blanket of sun-frosted clouds.

My heart leaped into my throat. The demon buggy wasn't flying, it was falling—and falling fast!

I screamed and grabbed hold of my seat.

"Not to worry!" Father shouted. He pressed some buttons on the buggy's instrument panel, but still we continued to drop like a stone. Finally, Father pushed and pulled a collection of levers that stuck up between our seats. Gears clanked and dampers flapped, and then the demon buggy leveled off and began soaring upward into the air.

"It works, sir!" Nigel cried out behind me, and I gazed past him to find a massive plume of black and blue smoke billowing out of the buggy's exhaust. The demon inside the conductor sphere was spinning madly, its eyes and black-fanged mouth just a blur of orange amidst its whirling black dust. Father tapped me on the shoulder and pointed to a bright red button on the instrument panel.

"This knob releases itching powder into the conductor sphere!" he shouted. "Just one pull will keep that demon back there churning out dust for hours!"

I nodded, speechless, and Father plunged the buggy into the clouds. A thick gray fog enveloped us at once as beads of water rippled across my goggles and chilled my cheeks. I could barely see the buggy's controls in front of me. It seemed as if our descent would go on forever—when finally we emerged from the clouds high above the countryside. Rolling patches of farmland dotted the landscape in every direction, and in the misty distance I could see a large, rambling town of majestic stone buildings.

Father flew straight for it, descending quickly and landing the demon buggy on one of the outlying country roads. He flicked some switches and pulled some levers, and soon we were rolling along, kicking up dust and drawing strange looks from people we passed.

"Aren't you afraid we'll be spotted, sir?" Nigel asked. "After that scene in London, lots of people will be looking for us, not to mention Prince Nightshade."

"The town you see before you is Cambridge, home to the esteemed university of the same name and some of the most brilliant minds in the world. Residents in these parts are used to seeing mechanical wonders, and will undoubtedly think our demon buggy just another one of those steam-powered carriages that have become so popular of late."

"If you say so, sir."

"Nevertheless, your point is well taken, Nigel." Father pulled a yellow knob on his instrument panel and a metal canopy folded down over the rear conductor sphere, shielding the entire contraption from view. "We'll find a place to hide the buggy too. Hope you don't mind standing guard over it until Grubb and I return."

"Right-o, sir," Nigel said, and upon reaching the outskirts of town, Father parked the demon buggy behind a large clump of trees. He gave some final instructions to Nigel, and then Father and I set off across a bridge toward the town on the opposite side of the river.

"Begging your pardon, sir," I said, "but may I ask where we're going?"

"To visit someone who, quite literally, holds the key to my plan."

My heart nearly burst with excitement. "You mean we're going after some more Odditoria to defeat Prince Nightshade?"

Father stopped and held me by the shoulders. "You must never say his name in public, son," he whispered. "One never knows where his spies might be perched." Father glanced up at some nearby trees, and I understood. Crows. Prince Nightshade used his flock mainly to locate animus, but who knew what other tricks those crafty birds were capable of? I swallowed hard and nodded, and then we were on our way again.

After winding our way through a labyrinth of cobblestone streets, Father and I eventually came upon the soaring edifices of the university. Carriages rattled and horses clopped as crowds of scholarly gentlemen milled about, many in strange square hats and hooded robes that appeared much too big for them. Father paid them no mind, but would often pause to look at something and mutter to himself, "Ah, that's new," or, "I don't remember that." He knew where he was going, and just as a bell began to toll, we passed through a wide stone archway and into a squarely groomed courtyard.

"Right on schedule," Father said, gazing up at the clock tower, and a mob of students began pouring out of the surrounding buildings. Father quickly led me into one of them, where we climbed a narrow staircase and shut ourselves inside

a cluttered study. Books and manuscripts were piled everywhere, and portraits of sour-faced gentlemen stared back at us as if irritated by our presence.

"Please, have a seat, Grubb," Father said, and he plopped down behind the desk and began perusing a newspaper. I cleared off a stack of books from an armchair, and then the two of us just sat there waiting, the ticking of the clock on the mantelpiece the only sound. My curiosity quickly turned to impatience. *Who are we meeting and why?* I kept asking myself, and then a muffled voice startled me from my thoughts.

"I'll expect your rebuttal by noon tomorrow," a man said just outside the door, and the knob began to turn. My body tensed, but Father seemed unconcerned, and just carried on with his reading.

A tall red-haired gentleman with ruddy cheeks and wire spectacles entered the study. He did not see us at first, and tossed a large leather volume upon a table by the door. He then hung up his robe on a nearby coatrack and, catching sight of Father in a mirror upon the wall, wheeled around with surprise.

"You!" was all he could manage, and Father folded his newspaper and smiled.

"Hello, Oscar. Long time no see."

— S I X —

The Rival Bricklewick

Father and I rose slowly to our feet, and a long, tense silence passed in which the three of us just stood there, sizing each other up. The red-haired gentleman looked terribly anxious. For a moment, I was certain he would bolt, but then, with a heavy sigh, he appeared to resign himself to our presence. He thrust his hands into his pockets and said, "But you're a cheeky blighter, aren't you?"

"I believe some introductions are in order," Father replied. "Grubb, I'd like you to meet Oscar Bricklewick, world-renowned scholar and Regius Professor of Modern History. Oscar, this is my son, Grubb."

"Grubb, did you say?"

"That I did. Spelled like the worm but with a double *b*, should you care to write it down."

"Is he . . . ?" Bricklewick asked, giving me the once-over, and Father nodded.

"It's a long story, but yes."

"Then the rumors were true. All those years ago—Elizabeth *was* with child."

"It appears you're an expert on rumors as of late," Father said, and he read from the newspaper. "'"The only sorcery here is a bit of high-tech flimflam," Bricklewick said upon inquiry from *The Times*. "Judging from the eyewitness reports of a sparkling green mist emanating from the Odditorium as it took flight, it is clear that Grim unleashed upon the public a powerful hallucinogenic gas—"'"

"That's enough," Professor Bricklewick said. He grabbed the newspaper and tossed it in the dustbin. Father sat on the edge of the desk and shook his head, *tsk–tsk*.

"Really now, Oscar," he said. "Hallucinogenic gas? Mass hysteria? Is that the best you can do?"

"What should I have told them? That Alistair Grim, my once closest friend, is indeed a sorcerer? Capable of feats of magic far beyond the evasion of his creditors?"

"Someone must've gotten word that we went to school together," Father said. "Why else would they consult a history professor about something so clearly outside his area of expertise? Unless, of course, the professor in question approached *The Times* himself for a bit of publicity."

Professor Bricklewick's cheeks grew red. "What are you doing here, Alistair? I should think being wanted dead or alive would discourage a scoundrel of your repute from making social calls."

"You know very well this isn't a social call. Therefore, let's dispense with the chitchat and get to the point. I need your help."

Professor Bricklewick gasped in astonishment. "My *help*? Surely you must be joking." Father shrugged. The professor appeared on the verge of a tirade, but upon seeing my confusion, stopped himself and said, "You haven't told him, have you?"

"Told him what?" Father replied.

"About your betrayal."

"That's a bit strong, Oscar, don't you think? *Betrayal?*"

Professor Bricklewick sneered and began frantically pacing the room. "Your insolence truly knows no bounds," he said, incredulous. "Let me tell you something about your father—Grubb, right? It is Grubb, isn't it?"

"Yes, sir."

"What your father here has neglected to tell you is that Elizabeth O'Grady and I were once engaged to be married. And that Alistair Grim, my closest and most trusted friend, stole her from me behind my back. Now, you look like a fairly intelligent lad. You tell me. If that doesn't qualify as betrayal, what does?"

Speechless, I turned to Father, expecting him to protest,

but he just stood there, arms folded and eyes on the floor.

"And now," Bricklewick said, "nearly a decade and a half later, this same Alistair Grim has the audacity to barge into my place of employment asking for my help. You'll have to forgive my lack of objectivity on the matter, but does anyone else see a problem here?"

"I do not wish to rehash old rivalries, Oscar," Father said quietly. "Nor do I wish to pour salt on old wounds."

"Oh, but you're a sanctimonious little twit, aren't you?" Professor Bricklewick said bitterly. "How dare you come here trying to make amends, after all these years."

"I didn't come to make amends. I came seeking help."

"Grubbing for money, no doubt—pardon the expression, lad," he added, and then made for the door. "Now if you'll excuse me while I alert the authorities of your presence."

"I can get you Excalibur," Father said quickly, and Bricklewick froze with his hand upon the doorknob.

"What did you say?"

"You heard me. Excalibur, the legendary sword of King Arthur, and perhaps the most powerful weapon ever created. I can get it for you, but I'll need your help in return."

Of course! Excalibur! If there was one Odditoria I'd heard of before my arrival at Alistair Grim's, it was the sword Excalibur. In fact, I'd have wagered that every lad in Britain had at some point or another played at King Arthur and his

Knights of the Round Table. And as I gazed round again at the countless books and manuscripts, all of which had something to do with Arthurian legend, I felt foolish for not having realized why we were here sooner.

"Have you gone mad, Alistair?" Bricklewick said, but the bitterness was gone now from his voice, and in its place a sort of cautious wonder.

"You see, Grubb," Father said, "despite what he told *The Times*, what very few people know about Oscar Bricklewick is that he was once a sorcerer like me, but abandoned the art soon after the love spell he cast on Elizabeth O'Grady wore off."

Professor Bricklewick's eyes became like saucers behind his spectacles. "How dare you accuse me of such a thing!"

"And since that time," Father went on, "in addition to his academic endeavors, Oscar Bricklewick has devoted his life to the search for Excalibur. Thus, out of professional courtesy, as well as a lack of necessity on my part, I never pursued Excalibur for myself. Until *now*, that is."

"I wouldn't expect anything less," Bricklewick said contemptuously. "You're an expert on that, aren't you? Stealing things from your friends? Why should Excalibur be any different?"

"Nevertheless," Father said, ignoring him, "as any quest for Odditoria takes significant preparation, given our present state of affairs, there is simply no time for me to carry out the proper research. Fortunately, Professor Bricklewick knows the precise location of Excalibur already. Problem is, he doesn't have the means to get there. I, on the other hand, have the means but not the location. You see where this is going, Oscar?"

"You really have gone mad, haven't you?" Bricklewick said. "Even if I believed you, which I don't, after everything you've done, how could you possibly think that I would turn over my life's work to my most hated rival?"

"Because, like it or not, we've run into something much bigger than you and me—something so dangerous that, if you refuse to help me, the world as we know it will cease to exist."

"What in heaven's name are you talking about?"

"An evil, magic-absorbing necromancer bent on world domination. His name is Prince Nightshade, and he is more powerful than anything you could possibly imagine—so powerful, in fact, that only Excalibur can defeat him."

The professor's mouth hung open, and Father proceeded to give him a brief summary of the events leading up to our arrival in Cambridge, including Nightshade's attack on the Odditorium, his quest for the animus, and his plan to create an army of purple-eyed Shadesmen. And when he'd finished, a stunned Professor Bricklewick sank down into an armchair and rubbed his forehead.

"Good heavens, Alistair," he said weakly. "What have you done?"

"You see, Oscar, although I've known about Prince Nightshade for quite some time, the old devil had been entirely unaware of my quests for magical objects until his discovery of the animus at the Odditorium last month. However, I am convinced that we first crossed paths a decade earlier—unbeknownst to one another, in the wake of Abel Wortley's murder. You remember old man Wortley, don't you?"

"Of course. He was my family's friend as well as yours."

"Well, it is my belief that Prince Nightshade murdered Abel Wortley all those years ago for his Odditoria. And since that time, not only has he managed to keep his true identity secret, but he's also ensconced himself in a suit of magical armor that is virtually impenetrable to both conventional and magical weapons alike."

"But, Alistair, if what you say is true and this necromancer is capable of absorbing magical power, I should think Excalibur would be useless against him."

"Unlike most magical weapons, Excalibur does not require a spell to activate it. The sword's power lies simply in the strength of the blade itself. Therefore, it would be able to cut through the prince's armor without him absorbing its magical properties."

Professor Bricklewick thought for a moment. "Indulge me.

Let's suppose that I agree to hand over my dreams to the man who betrayed me. Surely you must remember your history. Excalibur was forged for the Pendragons, the ancestral line of King Arthur, and thus, theoretically, can only be recovered by a descendant of the royal bloodline."

"I am well aware of that, yes, but I thank you for the refresher."

"So tell me," Bricklewick said, leaning back in his chair. "Unless that cold black heart of yours beats with Pendragon blood, just how do you propose to get your grubby little hands on Excalibur?" Again, he added for me, "No offense, lad."

"None taken, sir."

"You know me better than anyone, Oscar," Father said sincerely. "And given the substantial risk I've taken by coming here, do you think I'd put the success of my quest entirely in your hands if I wasn't certain I could make good on my promise?"

Professor Bricklewick held Father's eyes for a long time, wherein the air between them seemed to change. Then he rose from his chair and crossed to the study window.

"Tell me," he said, gazing out at the courtyard. "Do you really still believe, after all these years, that I cast a love spell on Elizabeth O'Grady?"

"In truth, no," Father replied. "But looking back, I suppose

I wanted to believe it. Eased my conscience somewhat, made things simpler."

"Why did she choose you over me?"

"Perhaps she didn't see it as a choice, Oscar. After all, we'd only known her a short time. And once you told me of your feelings, I stepped aside so that you might court Elizabeth unburdened by the knowledge that I too had been in love with her from the beginning. How she found out, I never knew, for upon my honor I never spoke a word of it to her. But once she opened her heart to me . . . well . . . I hope someday you can forgive me, old friend."

"I hated you so much," Bricklewick said, thinking. "But more so I hated myself, in part because, somewhere deep down, I'd known all along that the two of you were better suited for one another. Ah, but this stubborn British pride, you see—honor and all that. Not to mention that I *am* much smarter than you."

Father smiled wryly. "No argument there."

Bricklewick turned from the window. "But you must believe me: when I heard what happened, never once did I gloat or rejoice in your loss."

"Thank you."

"Her leaving you like that—so unexpectedly, rumor had it—was it something you said, something you did?"

"I don't know. All she left me was this." Father produced

the Black Mirror from inside his coat and handed it to Bricklewick. "Show me Elizabeth O'Grady," Father said, and the Black Mirror flashed and filled the professor's spectacles with sparkling swirls of reflected color. From where I was standing, I could not see the glass itself, but judging from Bricklewick's stunned expression, I knew when the image of my mother appeared.

"I'm sorry, my love," she said, her tearful voice far away; and then the glass in both the mirror and the professor's spectacles went dark again.

Professor Bricklewick, deeply moved, swallowed hard and handed the mirror back to Father. "I want no part of your magic, Alistair Grim," he said. "It has brought me nothing but pain and suffering."

"I understand, old friend. However, if I am going to get Excalibur and defeat Prince Nightshade, I'm afraid you have no other choice but to endure it one last time."

"What do you mean?"

"I want you to go with me, of course. To find Excalibur and save the world."

Bricklewick's mouth dropped open in shock. "You can't be serious."

"Oh, but I am. After all, even a sanctimonious twit such as me wouldn't expect you to take me at my word."

"But, Alistair, my work here—my career, my students—"

"We're not getting any younger, Oscar," Father said with a hand on the professor's shoulder. "Don't you see? I'm giving you the chance to realize your life's ambition: to not only hold Excalibur in your hands, but also to be part of something much greater—a quest worthy of King Arthur himself." The professor's eyes dropped to the floor. "Please, Oscar. Come with me. The future of mankind depends on it."

Bricklewick fumbled for a reply, but then quickly turned his attention on me.

"That amulet about your neck," he said. "Is it glowing?"

"Sir?" I replied, confused. The warding stone looked the same to me as it always had—milky green—but it did feel warmer to the touch. As to whether or not it had been glowing, well that was just silly, now, wasn't it?

"Never mind," said the professor, blinking. "Just a trick of the light, I suppose."

"Yes, never mind," Father muttered, eyeing the stone suspiciously; then he turned back to Bricklewick and, with a smile, said, "Well, Oscar, what do you say? Are we a team again or not?"

Bricklewick took a deep breath and adjusted his spectacles. "Very well, then. Give me an hour or two to prepare and gather my things."

"Splendid!" Father exclaimed, and he looked at his watch. "We'll rendezvous near the old Mill Pond at noon. Come along then, Grubb."

Father and I took our leave and began our journey back through the town. There were so many questions I wanted to ask him, but I was so bewildered by what I'd just learned—the least of which being our quest for Excalibur—that I couldn't speak. Indeed, the surprise of the love triangle between my mother and father and Oscar Bricklewick weighed much more heavily on my mind—so much so that I found myself siding with the professor. Had Father really gone behind his best mate's back and stolen his girl?

I must have been wearing my thoughts on my face, for out of the blue Father said, "I should think you'd be more interested in our quest for Excalibur than my rivalry with Oscar Bricklewick." I stared down uncomfortably at my shoes. "Just remember, son, there are three sides to every story: yours, the other bloke's, and the truth. Unfortunately, the latter is not always crystal clear."

"If you say so, sir."

"Oscar Bricklewick was once my apprentice, you see. I was young, barely a competent sorcerer myself, when I took him under my wing here at Cambridge. A bit of a weed Oscar was back then, and perhaps it was out of arrogance that I made it my mission to change him. And I did, for that matter. Stiffened the space between his shoulder blades, built up his confidence and all that.

"At any rate, we met Elizabeth O'Grady in the fall of our final year—at a reception honoring her father, who was a professor here before he died. We both fell head over heels, of course, but when Oscar revealed his feelings to me, I suppressed my own so that he should carry the day. They courted for nearly a year before . . . well, before your mother confessed that it was I she loved all along."

"Poor Oscar," I said quietly.

"Your mother didn't think so. She felt as if she'd been under some sort of love spell—her words, not mine—and would never have allowed things to go so far had she not been blinded so. Naturally, we both suspected the spell had come from Oscar. However, afterward I learned that the O'Gradys themselves came from a long line of sorcerers, and I began to wonder if the spell hadn't come from one of Elizabeth's relatives. Anyhow, that's the nub of it. And once I learned of your mother's love for me, I was helpless to resist my own heart. For as you know, love is the most powerful Odditoria of them all."

I nodded, but my mind was racing. All this talk of sorcery surrounding the O'Gradys had got me thinking again about what I'd overheard in the engine room the night before. Did Father know that the Cleona was once betrothed too? And should I tell him that Dalach had accused him of bewitching her into joining him at the Odditorium?

If I do, I thought, Cleona might get into trouble. After all, she shouldn't have been down in the engine room talking to the Gallownog in the first place.

"And speaking of Odditoria," Father said, stopping me in the street, "let's have another look at that warding stone."

He lifted the necklace off my neck and rolled the amulet between his fingers. "Nothing glowing as far as I can tell," he said as he inspected it. "Nevertheless, best get this back into the demon catcher where it belongs."

Father made to stow the necklace in his pocket when, unexpectedly, it slipped from his fingers and tumbled down through a sewer grate nearby.

"Oh no!" I cried. I dropped to my knees and peered down through the grate, but all I could see was a black pool of water far below.

The warding stone was gone.

"Oh dear, clumsy me," Father said with a sigh. "Yet, not to worry. Should we encounter any more demons on our quest, I'm certain we can find something else back home with which to defend ourselves. Come along then, Grubb."

As we set off again down the bustling street, Father began to whistle a happy tune. He certainly seemed to be taking the loss of his Odditoria quite well.

So well, in fact, that if I hadn't known better, I would have sworn he dropped the warding stone into the sewer on purpose.

SEVEN

A Sticky Situation

xcalibur!

Just saying that name over and over again to myself quickly pushed all thoughts of Father's rivalry from my mind, and soon I began peppering him with questions about his plan—Where *was* Excalibur? And how did he intend to get it?—but Father put an end to my interrogation almost immediately. We were not to speak of such things in public, he said. If word of our quest ever got back to Prince Nightshade, well that would certainly put a damper on things, now wouldn't it?

And so Father and I spent the rest of our morning running errands about town. We bought some chocolates for Gwendolyn, a box of colored chalk for Cleona, some herbs for Mrs. Pinch, and an expensive cigar for Lord Dreary. A clock somewhere was just chiming noon when we returned to our hiding spot at the edge of town. Professor Bricklewick arrived in a hired coach soon after, upon which Nigel gave him a pair of goggles and loaded his bags into the demon buggy. A moment later, we were speeding off into the country.

Father tried to prepare the professor for our flight, explaining the technical aspects of his demon buggy as he drove along, but as soon as we took to the air, Professor Bricklewick's entire body went rigid with fear. Sitting behind him as I was, I could not see his face, but his ears flushed as red as his hair—not to mention that he hadn't said a word since his introduction to Nigel. It was as if every wonder he encountered only made it harder for him to speak—so much so that, by the time Father flew us up through the clouds and back inside the Odditorium, I was convinced the poor professor would never speak again.

"Well, blind me if that isn't Oscar Bricklewick!" said Mrs. Pinch, squinting as we piled out of the demon buggy. She and Lord Dreary were waiting for us in Nigel's quarters with a serving cart full of food.

"Great poppycock!" the old man cried. "Don't tell me Alistair Grim's convinced you to come along with us too!"

Professor Bricklewick removed his goggles. He made to speak, but when he caught sight of McClintock smiling up from where I'd left him on Nigel's desk, once again his tongue got stuck.

"Never heard of a Clan Bricklewick," Mack said. "But any friend of the Grims is a friend of mine. So, as chief of the

Chronometrical Clan McClintock, allow me to welcome you to—"

Nigel tapped Mack on his XII, knocking him out, and handed him to me.

"Don't mind him, Professor," Nigel said. "Never stops jabbering, that one."

Professor Bricklewick swallowed hard and finally managed to speak. "Is that the—the pocket watch that caused all the trouble?"

"I'm afraid so, sir," I replied, and I slipped him into my waistcoat.

"Oscar comes bearing gifts," Father said, and he handed the sack of herbs to Mrs. Pinch. "There's something in there for you too, Lord Dreary."

There was a brief round of "thank yous" and "good to see you agains" (in which I learned that Lord Dreary was best mates with Oscar Bricklewick's uncle) and then Father passed the professor a plate of food.

"I don't mean to be impolite," he said, "but we need to take our lunch on the run. Lots to see and so little time. Oscar can have my room, and I'll sleep on the sofa in the library. Grubb, if you wouldn't mind helping Nigel with the professor's things, I shall give our newest guest a brief tour of our humble abode."

Plates in hand, Father and Professor Bricklewick set off on

their tour of the Odditorium. And after a quick lunch there in Nigel's quarters, the big man and I delivered the professor's bags across the hallway as instructed. Nigel had known about all that Excalibur business for weeks now, he confessed, and was visibly relieved when I told him that I was now in on the plan. It felt good to have no secrets between us again. However, as we were leaving Father's room, I noticed a large pistol and holster under Nigel's coat. I'd never seen them before.

"Cor blimey, Nigel, since when did you start carrying a barker?"

"Since we all became wanted men," he replied. "However, this is no ordinary gun, Grubb." Nigel slipped the pistol from its holster. The brass barrel and cylinder were much wider than any I'd ever seen, and sticking up from the top of the pistol was a tangle of thin copper tubing. "This here's called an egg blaster. One shot, and your target is stuck in a mess of goo."

"An egg blaster, did you say?"

"That's right." Nigel flipped open the gun's cylinder, revealing four chambers, each containing a different colored egg. "And just as this is no ordinary pistol, these are no ordinary eggs." The big man stifled a giggle. "The orange ones are the messiest. I've got four more in my ammo case." Nigel pulled back his coat to reveal a square leather pouch attached to his belt.

"Are those eggs Odditoria, then?"

"I suppose they are in a way, but . . ." Nigel glanced back cautiously over his shoulder, and then, with a mischievous smile, whispered, "Care for a bit of fun?"

"Fun? But shouldn't we be preparing to search for Excalibur?"

"I'd say this qualifies as preparation," Nigel said slyly. "I should think knowing how to use the egg blaster might come in handy on our quest, wouldn't you?"

"Very well, then—fun it is!"

"Right-o! You fetch Cleona and meet me on the roof. I'll see about getting us some more ammo."

I rushed down to Cleona's quarters while Nigel stopped at the door directly across the hallway—the door with the SILENCE IS GOLDEN sign hanging from its knob. Nigel made to enter, but then snatched back his hand upon remembering Father's instructions.

"Oh dear," he said. "You're not supposed to know what's inside here, are you?"

"No, but if I'm to inherit the Odditorium someday, I don't see why not."

"It's a bit complicated to explain, but—"

Thump! went the door, and Nigel jumped.

"Er—uh," he stammered. "Eight eggs should be more than enough." Nigel twisted a nearby sconce, and a secret panel opened to reveal a spiral staircase hidden in the wall beside the lift. "Right-o, then. See you on the roof!"

The big man shot me a nervous smile and then hurried up the stairs. The panel closed again behind him—so much for there being no secrets between us, I thought—and my eyes wandered back to the door. *What's hiding in there?* I wondered. *And why can't I know what it is?*

"Is someone there?" Cleona called from within her quarters. I announced myself and was given permission to enter.

The large porthole in the wall opposite me stood open, and Cleona's mirror-paneled chamber shone brilliantly in a bright mosaic of reflected blue sky. Hanging from a mechanical arm near the porthole was Father's Sky Ripper—a massive, somewhat intimidating contraption that looked like a giant silver egg sawed in half lengthwise. Pipes and wires zigzagged from it in every direction, and sticking out from the egg's belly was a wide, stubby cannon.

"Well, what do you want?" Cleona asked. She was sitting up in her bed, which was similar in appearance to the Sky Ripper, but much smaller and minus a cannon. A mechanical arm connected it to the wall on one side, while a dozen or so pipes connected it to the wall on the other. It was from this strange-looking bed that Cleona charged the Odditorium with her animus, and the mirrors on the wall held the reserves.

"Sorry to bother you, miss. But Nigel asked me to fetch you."

"What for?"

"A bit of fun with the egg blaster, I think."

"Pshaw," Cleona scoffed, and I noticed her gift of colored chalk on the floor beside her bed. "Don't tell me Uncle's showing off again for his friend? Professor Ticklewick, is it?"

"Bricklewick, miss," I replied. "And as a matter of fact, Mr. Grim doesn't know a thing about it. Looks like a bit of mischief, if you ask me."

Cleona's eyes flickered with excitement—yes, I thought, if there was one thing she couldn't resist, it was a bit of mischief behind Alistair Grim's back—but then, much to my surprise, Cleona sighed and gazed gloomily out the porthole.

"You go on without me," she said. "I'm afraid I won't be much fun today."

"If I may be so bold, miss, what's bothering you? You haven't been yourself since the Gallownog came on board."

"You wouldn't understand, Grubb."

"I should think I would," I said defensively, and before I realized my lips were moving, I blurted out what I'd overheard Cleona and Lorcan Dalach talking about in the engine room—that they still loved each other, and that the Gallownog believed Cleona was bewitched. Cleona's eyes grew wide with horror. "Don't worry, miss," I said quickly. "I haven't spoken a word of it to Father."

"Oh, Grubb, you mustn't! If Uncle thought for one moment that I was unhappy here . . . Well, I couldn't bear the idea of him feeling guilty on my account."

"Then you are unhappy here, miss?"

"Of course not!" Cleona cried. "Granted, I'm feeling a bit glum at present, but it's not because I believe what Lorcan said. It's because I don't."

"Miss?"

"He's the one who's bewitched, Grubb. He's convinced himself that I'm under some sort of spell because he doesn't want to believe that I can think for myself. How'd you like it if the person you loved thought so little of you? Not to mention that he was willing to risk my banishment all over again just to prove it to himself."

"I suppose I never thought of it like that."

"Pshaw," Cleona said with her arms folded. "As if I'd want to go back to my clan anyway. Not after what they pulled. Banishment is not a pleasant experience, Grubb. I wouldn't wish it on anyone."

"Well, I must confess that I'm relieved to hear that, miss. I was worried you were thinking about leaving us."

"Me? Leave the Odditorium? What sort of banshee do

you take me for? Why, I'd sooner go back into banishment than abandon my family."

"I'm glad, miss. I mean, I know this whole family business is new to me, but I can't think of anyone else I'd rather have attached to mine than you."

Cleona smiled. "Pshaw, look at us, talking nonsense. If this is what having an old flame on board brings you, I don't mind saying that I'm looking forward to the day we're rid of him."

"Me too, miss."

"Come to think of it, now that everything's out in the open, I don't feel nearly as glum as I did before." Cleona raised an eyebrow and smiled slyly. "A bit of mischief, you say? Behind Uncle's back?"

"That's right."

In a streaking flash of blue, Cleona flew up to the port-hole, slammed it shut, and then snatched her box of chalk from the floor. "Come on, then," she said, beaming. "Let's get to blasting!"

Cleona and I rushed down the hallway, through the secret panel, and up the spiral staircase that led to the garret. Inside, the porthole to the roof was open, bathing the cramped cluster of clockwork gears in a shaft of yellow sunlight, but still the farthest recesses of the garret were dark enough for us to see the beady blue eyes of Nigel's bats glowing back at us. Cleona flew up through the porthole, and I clambered up the ladder and onto the roof behind her.

We found Nigel waiting for us beside the upper gunnery with his coat draped over one of the cannons, and farther away, propped up against the battlements, was an enormous wooden shield.

"Glad you could join us, Cleona," Nigel said. Cleona slipped out a piece of chalk from her box and flew over to the shield, where she drew two concentric rings and a bright red bull's-eye in the center.

"So it's a bit of target practice, eh?" I asked, and Nigel smiled.

"Should one of Nightshade's minions ever come after you, an egg blaster won't do you any good if you can't hit him with it."

Cleona joined us again by the gunnery. "Game's simple, really," she said. "Any eggs outside the bull's-eye don't count, and the person with the most bull's-eyes wins. You're up first, Nigel."

Nigel leveled the egg blaster at the target, and after a long, tense silence, squeezed the trigger. *Thwiiip!* the muzzle rasped, and a bright pink egg whizzed across the roof and hit the outer ring with a *splat!* Bits of pink eggshell sprayed everywhere, and a load of pink goo covered half the shield.

Nigel frowned—no bull's-eye—so he handed the blaster to Cleona. A moment later, *thwiip-splat!* It was a purple egg this time, but her shot missed the target entirely and splattered the battlements behind it. Cleona sighed and gave me the blaster.

"Perhaps you'll have better luck, Grubb," she said.

"I'll do my best, miss."

With a deep breath I aimed the egg blaster at the target, when out of nowhere a black-robed figure rose up on a broomstick and hovered in midair above the battlements. I couldn't see the figure's face, but assumed it was a lady by the ringlets of bright red hair tumbling out from under her hood.

I gasped, and my entire body froze.

"Defense! Defense!" Nigel cried, running for the gunnery. A load of samurai scrambled up onto the roof from the garret, but the hooded lady was already moving. She darted quickly over our heads and drew a magic wand from her robes.

"Run, Grubb!" Cleona screamed. She tried to disappear down through the roof, but the lady on the broomstick fired a blast of lightning from her wand and struck the banshee down.

"No!" I cried. Cleona's eyes were closed, her glowing, transparent body motionless. More blasts of lightning rained down around me and I took cover on the opposite side of the gunnery. At the same time, I heard Nigel cry out from within. He didn't get the gunnery's shield up, I realized in horror.

Four more blasts exploded unseen behind me, each accompanied by the sound of a samurai's armor clunking heavily upon the roof. And then all was silent.

I sat there panting in terror. My only hope of escape now was the porthole to the garret, but that was on the other side of the gunnery. I gripped the egg blaster tightly with both hands, and without thinking, scrambled back around the turret, ready to fire. As I expected, Cleona and the samurai lay sprawled out across the roof, but the lady on the broomstick was nowhere to be seen.

Just then, I felt a rush of wind behind me. Before I could turn around, a strong hand clamped down on my collar and yanked me off my feet. I screamed, and in a panic, dropped the egg blaster as I was whisked away off the roof—my legs pedaling frantically at the air as the hooded lady flew me up and over the battlements.

"Let me go!" I cried. The lady plopped me down face-forward on the broomstick. With a viselike arm around my waist she pulled me so close that I could barely breathe.

We flew out from the Odditorium in a wide, swooping arc, doubling back and coming to a stop in midair only a few yards from the balcony.

"I know who you are, Alistair Grim!" the lady called out from behind me. "Show yourself or your son gets dropped!"

Father rushed out onto the balcony with Professor
Bricklewick following close behind.

"Mad Malmuirie," Father said, splaying his fingers upon
the balustrade. His voice was calm, but his eyes were all fear.
My captor's grip loosened some and I turned to find a beautiful yet slightly crazed-looking young woman smiling back
at me.

"The boy has your eyes, Alistair Grim," she said. "And you have mine."

"The warding stones," Father said flatly, his face tight. "You've been watching us in your crystal ball ever since I removed them from the demon catcher, haven't you?"

I gasped. Father had lost his warding stone at the hell mouth, but I'd kept mine around my neck—and in doing so, I had led the witch straight to us!

But there's something else too, a voice said inside my head. Yes, it was all coming back to me now. The dream I'd had about the big green eye the night before. The woman's voice I'd heard along with Mr. Smears's—it had belonged to Mad Malmuirie!

"I arrived in London soon after I saw your likeness in the papers," she said. "Indeed, I suspect other victims of your quests will be coming after you too, now that they know the identity of the man who robbed them of their treasures. But they've got to find you first. Fortunately for me, the enchantment I placed on the warding stones still worked. Too bad you didn't take them out of the demon catcher sooner."

"I won the demon catcher from you fair and square, Malmuirie. However, as a show of faith, if you return the boy I'll give it back to you. No questions asked."

Mad Malmuirie scoffed. "Keep it. A demon catcher is much too dangerous a toy without its warding stones. Besides, you have something *else* that belongs to me." The witch affected a thick, Scottish brogue: "Something much more powerful, laddie. *Ticktock, ticktock, ticktock.*"

Mad Malmuirie cackled loudly and my heart leaped into my throat. The witch hadn't come for the demon catcher at all. She had come for Mack!

"I know he's in there, Grim," she said. "I saw him myself with the stone."

My eyes darted down to my pocket. Mad Malmuirie had no idea that Mack was sitting right there on the broom in front of her.

Of course, I thought. The last time she could have seen him through my warding stone was before we left in the demon buggy, when I tossed him on Nigel's desk. And as Father had since dropped my warding stone in the Cambridge sewers, Mad Malmuirie obviously thought Mack was still inside the Odditorium.

"How do I put this?" Father said with a smile. "Dougal McClintock has . . . *changed* since last you saw him. You wouldn't want him back, I assure you."

"Tut-tut, you expect me to fall for a trick like that? You don't know what you've got there, Alistair Grim."

"Oh, believe me, I do."

At that moment, one of the upper gunnery cannons locked into place above the battlements, the swell of its muzzle pointing straight at us. Behind the turret's energy shield I could see Lord Dreary and Mrs. Pinch with Nigel slumped over behind them.

"We've got her in our sights!" Lord Dreary's voice crackled from the organ's talkback, and Mad Malmuirie pulled me close.

"Call them off, Grim," she said, "or I swear I'll snap his neck!"

"You heard her," Father said into the talkback. "Pull back, Mrs. Pinch."

The old woman complied, and the cannon retracted out of sight behind the battlements.

"Tut-tut, Alistair Grim," said Mad Malmuirie. "I showed mercy to the others on the roof. They shall awaken from their slumber shortly. However, if you don't return my pocket watch, I'll put your son to sleep *permanently*."

"If I give you McClintock," Father said, "you shall return the boy unharmed?"

Mad Malmuirie smirked and raised her right hand in oath. "You have my word, Alistair Grim. I shall return the boy unharmed."

"Very well," Father said. "You'll find what you seek in the boy's waistcoat."

"Father, no!" I cried—but Mad Malmuirie's hand was already in my pocket.

"Ah!" she sighed, holding up McClintock in triumph.

"All right, then, Malmuirie," Father said. "You've got what you came for, now keep your word and return the boy."

"Oh, I *shall* return the boy, Alistair Grim," she said. "I just won't return him to *you!*"

And with that, Mad Malmuirie steered her broomstick away from the Odditorium and dove straight for the clouds.

"Grubb!" Father cried, but then everything went gray, and all I could hear was the witch's laughter behind me.

EIGHT

Playing with Fire

A thick forest canopy rushed up at us through the misty air, and then all at once we were swallowed up in a sea of yellow and orange branches. The witch flew close to the ground and wove her broomstick amongst the trees at frightening speed—the autumn leaves twisting after us like a fiery serpent's tail. Soon, we emerged at the foot of a small hill, on top of which stood the walls of a tumbledown church.

Dismounting, Mad Malmuirie shoved me off her broomstick. With its tip lodged in my back, she marched me up the hill and into the heart of the crumbling ruins. A brooding figure dressed in black emerged from around a pile of stones inside. My feet rooted where I stood. I could hardly believe my eyes.

I gasped in terror. "Mr. Smears!"

The hulking man with the scar on his cheek sneered

hatefully. "We've got a score to settle, Grubb," he growled, lumbering toward me, but Mad Malmuirie drew her wand and stopped him in his tracks.

"Tut-tut, Smears," she said. "I returned the boy as promised. Now you keep your end of the bargain and tell me where to find the map you stole from Alistair Grim."

Mr. Smears smiled slyly and scratched his scar. My entire body was pounding with fear, but my brain felt nimbler than ever. *Map?* I said to myself. *Mr. Smears never stole a map from Alistair Grim.*

And suddenly I understood what my old master had done. He'd somehow crossed paths with Mad Malmuirie and promised her a fictitious map in exchange for me. However, as Mr. Smears was rash and rarely looked beyond his next beer, I also understood that he hadn't figured out yet what to do when it came time to make good on his promise.

"Well?" Mad Malmuirie said, and Mr. Smears narrowed his eyes suspiciously.

"You witches with your spells and trickery," he said. "How do I know the boy is genuine? How do I know he's not some demon what you conjured up to look like him?"

Even though he was reckless by nature, Mr. Smears could be crafty when he put his mind to it—especially when off the drink. He was buying time, which is exactly what I needed to do too, because now that Mad Malmuirie had McClintock, she most certainly would kill us both if I exposed Mr. Smears's deception.

McClintock, I said to myself, glancing down at him—he was still in Mad Malmuirie's hand. He should be waking up any moment now, I thought. But if the witch opens him outside the Odditorium, unprotected by its magic paint . . .

I shivered at the thought of the doom dogs coming for Mack's animus, but at the same time an idea began bubbling in my brain.

"How dare you question my word, Smears!" said Mad Malmuirie, her emerald-green eyes flashing with fury.

"Begging your pardon, ma'am," said Mr. Smears, "but look what your word's got Alistair Grim: a stolen watch and a son what's about to get himself kidnapped."

"I should have known better than to trust a ruffian such as you," the witch said, and she readied her wand to strike. Without thinking, I leaped between them.

"I know where it is!" I cried.

Mad Malmuirie lowered her wand and bore her eyes into mine. "Where?" she asked, and I glanced at Mr. Smears. His face was all puckered with confusion.

"Er—well—I can't be *certain*," I said, lying, "but I know where Mr. Smears hides things what's valuable. I can show you, ma'am—but you must promise not to hurt him."

Mad Malmuirie smiled. "But you're a curious lad, aren't you? Why on earth would you want to protect a man bent on kidnapping you?"

"Well, ma'am, if you kill him, what use would you have for me?" Mad Malmuirie chuckled at my candor. "Besides, I should think this map must be very valuable should a lady of your breeding traffic with the likes of Mr. Smears."

"Indeed," said the witch. "And I suppose that, if you have a hand in delivering the map, you'll want something in return?"

"Just my life, ma'am, if you please. And Mr. Smears's. And perhaps a ride on that broomstick of yours back to the Odditorium."

"How about I just kill him now for you? From what I gather, this blackguard didn't show you much kindness over the years."

"No, he didn't, I'm afraid. But please don't kill him, ma'am. He can't help what he is no more than a rat can. If you spare us both, I'll lead you to his hiding place. I can't promise the map will be there, but if you kill us, I can promise you'll never find it."

Mad Malmuirie eyed Mr. Smears suspiciously. "You're awfully quiet, Smears, given that the lad is campaigning on your behalf."

Mr. Smears scratched his scar. "Never you mind about him," he said. "I believe the boy's genuine now. Hand him over and I'll bring you to the map myself."

Mad Malmuirie laughed. "Not on your life, villain," she said, mounting her broomstick. "Now climb aboard, fetch me the map, and the two of you shall live."

My eyes dropped again to McClintock. Why wasn't he waking up?

"Er, begging your pardon, ma'am," I said, thinking quickly. "If I'm to help you, I should probably know what this map is. Mr. Grim never mentioned a stolen map, but then again he's quite fond of keeping secrets from me."

"Especially secrets about swords," whispered Mad Malmuirie, and my heart nearly stopped. She knew about

Excalibur. Of course she did. I had been wearing the warding stone in Professor Bricklewick's study. And hadn't he asked me if it was glowing?

"You needn't worry, lad," said the witch. "I have no use for silly swords. But *maps*, on the other hand . . ." She flitted her eyes at Mr. Smears. "Your former master claims he stole Alistair Grim's map at the Lamb's Inn. But poor Mr. Smears can't read—not to mention that he was much more interested in finding *you*."

Mad Malmuirie smiled, and I glanced over at Mr. Smears. He just stood there silent and stone-faced, but I could see in his eyes that his mind was racing a mile a minute. Mine was too. Even if Mad Malmuirie was telling the truth about having no use for Excalibur, should she alert Prince Nightshade to our quest . . .

I needed to escape straightaway and tell Father—but before I could do that, I needed to wake up Mack!

"You see, Grubb," the witch went on, "I too am a seeker of Odditoria. And from what little I know of Alistair Grim, this map of his must lead to a magical object of great power— something useless to a chimney sweep, but priceless to a lady of my talents."

Come on, Mack, wake up! I screamed in my head, but my mouth said, "Er, uh, speaking of chimney sweeps, ma'am, how did you wind up with Mr. Smears here?"

"Word of Alistair Grim's Odditorium and its mysterious disappearance traveled fast. I recognized your Father's likeness in the newspapers and came to London with the hopes of tracking him down. Mr. Smears did the same."

"Put two and two together, I did," he said. "Only way you could've escaped from us that night was in that fancy black coach. Of course, Grim used a phony name at the Lamb, but when I saw his mug in them papers, I knew I had my man."

"Our paths crossed purely by chance while making inquiries in London," said Mad Malmuirie. "Mr. Smears told me he was in search of a boy who Alistair Grim had stolen from him. And once the warding stones confirmed his tale, I agreed to an even trade for your father's map."

"My livelihood is ruined on account of you, Grubb," said Mr. Smears. "And so I've taken up life as a villain. My first offense? Holding you for ransom. I wager a man like Alistair Grim would pay handsomely to have his son back. And if he refuses? Well, I needn't mention what's in store for you then."

Mr. Smears cracked his knuckles.

"Tut-tut, Smears," said Mad Malmuirie. "On second thought, I've decided to amend our deal. You shall not lay a finger on the lad. I've grown fond of him."

Mr. Smears gasped. "But you gave me your word!"

"Your reward in exchange for the map shall be your life. Count yourself lucky you're getting that."

Mr. Smears's face flushed red, and he clenched his fists so tightly that his knuckles grew white.

"As for you, young Grubb," said the witch, "now that Prince Nightshade is onto your father, I should think the sooner we get moving the better. Wouldn't want him to get his dirty little hands on Excalibur, would we?"

Mad Malmuirie chuckled, slipped McClintock into her robes, and donned her hood. Despite everything that was happening, I was relieved to learn that, as Father had suspected, the witch was not in league with Prince Nightshade. At the same time, I decided I couldn't wait any longer for Mack to wake up on his own. I needed to act fast.

"Begging your pardon again, ma'am," I said. "What Father said back there on the balcony—about McClintock having changed and whatnot—well, you may want to look for yourself. He's prone to fizzling out from time to time."

"Fizzling out?"

"Yes, ma'am. I'm afraid he just stops ticking now and then for no reason."

"Well of course he does. He's a time stopper, is he not?"

"A time stopper, ma'am?"

"A watch that stops time. You mean your father never told you?" I shook my head. "McClintock has the unique ability to freeze time for as long as one full minute, enabling whoever holds him to move about undetected by others. Why else would your father want a magical pocket watch on his quests if not to freeze the beings from whom he stole his Odditoria?"

The witch's explanation made perfect sense to me, and yet now I was confused. How come Mack never told me he could stop time? We certainly could have used such a trick during our escape from Nightshade's castle. And furthermore, if Father had planned on using Mack on his quests, surely he would have needed to coat him with magic paint to conceal his animus.

Unless, of course, Mack didn't have animus until he came to the Odditorium.

That's it! I said to myself. Mad Malmuirie didn't seem the least bit concerned about the doom dogs, so she must be unaware of Mack's animus. Perhaps that's what Father meant when he said Mack had changed. Could he have broken McClintock and then tried to repair him with the animus? Could that be the reason why Mack was always in the shop—because Alistair Grim was trying to mend his time stopper?

"Your doubts are in your eyes, Master Grubb," said Mad Malmuirie. "However, because I've grown fond of you, I shall show you how the time stopper works."

The witch removed McClintock from her robes and my heart began to hammer. I'd been lucky once playing with fire—during my escape from Nightshade's castle, when I opened Mack and sicced the doom dogs on the prince's minions. My present plan was something similar. However, being as it was cloudy today, there was no sunlight to protect me. Meaning, when Mad Malmuirie opened Mack and summoned the doom dogs, I would have to snatch him back immediately and make a run for it through the forest. I'd spotted a narrow river on our flight here. If I could reach it in time, I thought, I might be able to wash off my scent and lose the doom dogs on the other side.

That was my plan, anyway. And yet, now that the moment of truth had arrived, the whole lot of it suddenly seemed quite daft.

Mad Malmuirie opened Mack, gave him a quick shake, and then frowned when his face remained dark. "Odd. The time stopper is supposed to awaken when opened."

"If you tap him on his twelve, ma'am, that usually does the trick."

Mad Malmuirie obliged, and with a crackle and a flash, Mack came alive at once. Mr. Smears let out a gasp, and the witch smiled wide.

"What time is it?" Mack cried, mustache twirling, his eyes bright with animus. But when he saw who was holding him, he let out a shriek and said, "Ach! Not you!"

"Welcome back, old friend," said Mad Malmuirie, and Mack began struggling to break free.

"Let me go, ya barmy witch!" he cried. "I belong to Mr. Grim now!"

"Tut-tut, is that any way to greet your old mistress? And what's with this blue light of yours?"

"That's what I'm tryin' to tell ya. I'm of no use to ya anymore. Me time stopper is broken. Been that way ever since Mr. Grim rescued me!"

"*Rescued* you?" Mad Malmuirie laughed. "Alistair Grim has taught you well. If you were broken, you couldn't go on jabbering such. And now I'll show your friend Grubb just what a little liar you are."

Mad Malmuirie thrust McClintock out before her and pressed her thumb down on his winding knob—but nothing happened.

"I tried to tell ya!" Mack cried. "Me time stopper's broken!"

"It can't be!" Mad Malmuirie hissed, instantly furious. She pressed down on Mack's knob again, and again nothing happened.

"I'm afraid Father was telling the truth, ma'am. Mack's never been able to stop time as long as I've known him."

The witch began to tremble, her eyes lolled in their sockets, and her lips curled back from her teeth.

"Uh-oh," Mack said, and Mad Malmuirie let out a shriek that shook the very walls of the tumbledown church.

"Take, take, take, that's all you humans do!" she cried, wheeling on me. "And now I shall take something from Alistair Grim!"

Mad Malmuirie raised her magic wand to strike, when without warning Mack leaped from her hand. *"MCCLINTOCK!"* he cried, and slammed hard into the witch's brow. Mad Malmuirie yelped and tumbled off her broomstick into the dirt. Before I had time to fathom what was happening, out of the corner of my eye I saw Mr. Smears swinging for my head.

"Why, you little worm!" he growled. But the clumsy brute was as slow as ever and I easily ducked his blow. Mack flew up from the ground just in time and smacked Mr. Smears between the eyes, then bounced off right into my hands. Dazed, Mr. Smears staggered back and plopped down heavily onto his bottom.

"Nothin' like a good brawl now and then, eh, mate?" Mack chuckled.

Just then I saw the first of the doom dogs taking shape in a darkened corner of the church—only a billow of black smoke at first—but I didn't stick around to see any more. I closed Mack's case, slipped him into my pocket, and dashed for the nearest opening in the crumbling ruins.

"Stop him!" cried Mad Malmuirie. I was already halfway down the hill when I spotted the glowing red eyes of another doom dog blinking open in a hollow nearby.

My breath froze in my chest, but thankfully my legs kept moving, darting this way and that down the craggy slope until finally I reached the edge of the forest. Glancing back over my shoulder, I saw a series of bright white flashes coming from inside the church. A doom dog leaped out from the entrance. Mad Malmuirie appeared close behind it, and with a lightning blast from her magic wand, she reduced the beast to a scattering cloud of thick black smoke.

Despite my fear, I couldn't help but gape in wonder at Mad Malmuirie's power—the daft enchantress could destroy doom dogs. But more were coming. The hound I'd seen taking shape on the hill tore off after me.

I ran through the forest as fast as I could, my feet barely touching the leaf-covered ground. The *crunch, crunch, crunch* of the shadow hound's paws drew closer and closer behind me. I dared not look over my shoulder again. The river was just beyond the rise ahead of me, I remembered, and in no time I reached its banks and splashed across to the other side. The doom dog howled, and I whirled round to find the beast pacing frantically back and forth along the opposite bank.

Why wasn't it coming after me?

The doom dog touched a tentative paw at the river's edge and immediately shrank back, squealing in pain as if the water had burned it.

"You're like any other spirit, aren't you?" I said, breathless. "You can't travel over water!"

The doom dog snarled and barked at me. Seconds later, Mad Malmuirie and Mr. Smears emerged from the forest on her broomstick, and the creature set its glowing red sights on them. The doom dog gnashed its teeth and leaped into the air, and once again Mad Malmuirie fired a bolt of lightning from her wand, reducing the beast to smoke.

Panicking, I took to my heels, my lungs burning as I ran for my life. And yet, deep down, I knew there was no way I could escape. The witch's broomstick was much too fast. And sure enough, when I looked back over my shoulder Mad Malmuirie and Mr. Smears were almost upon me.

The witch, her eyes crazed with hatred, raised her wand and fired. I dove out of the way, and her lightning bolt streaked past me, missing my head by inches and striking the forest bed in a spray of dirt and burning leaves.

Mad Malmuirie zoomed over me, circled her broomstick back through the trees, and then raised her wand again.

"Now I've got you!" she hissed.

But then, with a loud *thwiiip*, something whizzed across

the air and splattered her from head to toe in a blanket of orange goo.

"*Argh!*" she cried, losing control, and her broomstick veered sharply toward a large oak tree. Mr. Smears jumped off just in time, but Mad Malmuirie, covered as she was in orange goo, smacked into the tree with a loud *splat!* She was stuck there—out cold and halfway up the trunk—like a redheaded wasp caught in a glob of honey.

I scrambled to my feet to find Nigel's egg blaster hovering by itself in midair only a few yards away from me. My jaw dropped—I could hardly believe my eyes—when a glowing blue hand materialized around the egg blaster's handle.

"Cleona!" I cried, and the rest of her body quickly followed.

"Sorry it took so long for me to find you," she said. "I must say, however, this saving-your-life business is getting to be a full-time job."

My heart swelled with relief. "Thank goodness you're all right," I said. "And Nigel, the others . . . ?"

"Everyone's fine," Cleona said, when suddenly her eyes grew wide. "Look out, Grubb!" she shouted.

Cleona fired the blaster again and the egg whizzed past my head. Spinning round, I found Mr. Smears falling backward onto the ground in a massive blob of purple goo. He had tried to sneak up on me.

"I'll get you for this, Grubb!" Mr. Smears growled, struggling. But the more he struggled, the more the forest bed stuck to him, and soon he looked like some enchanted leaf man that Alistair Grim might like to have at his Odditorium.

"That should keep them both busy for a while," Cleona said. "Now we best get you back home before Uncle sends everyone out looking for you."

"McClintock," I said. "Mad Malmuirie opened him, which means—"

Just then a crow cawed loudly above our heads, and I gazed up to find at least a hundred of the big black birds staring down at us from amongst the trees. Crows can naturally sense when doom dogs enter our world, and Prince Nightshade had trained his flock to alert him of their presence in the event they were tracking animus. It was impossible to tell whether or not any of these crows belonged to the prince, but one thing was certain: we needed to get away from them just in case.

Caw! another of the birds called, and Cleona made a fist at it.

"Caw yourself!" she called back defiantly. I threw my arms around her neck, and in a flash Cleona took flight, soaring up through the clouds and straight for the Odditorium with me hanging on.

As we drew nearer, I discovered that Father's mechanical wonder had been readied for battle. The blue energy shields

were up, the gunneries engaged, and the wasps were buzzing round and round outside. The hangar doors to Nigel's quarters were open, and as Cleona flew us inside, we found Father preparing to take off in the demon buggy.

"Hold your horses," Cleona said. "I told you I'd bring him back."

Father leaped from his seat and hugged me tight, upon which Cleona rushed over to the talkback and announced to everyone that I'd been rescued.

"Are you all right?" Father cried. "Did Mad Malmuirie hurt you?"

"No, sir, but she knows about Excalibur. The warding stone . . . She—"

"I assumed as much, yes."

"And you were right, sir. She wants nothing to do with Prince Nightshade. But Mr. Smears, he's in league with her too."

Father raised a quizzical eyebrow, and I promptly related how Mad Malmuirie and Mr. Smears teamed up after tracking him to London. I told him about the stolen map (which, as I suspected, turned out to be untrue) and Mr. Smears's plan to hold me for ransom. I also gave a brief account of my escape and how the witch destroyed the doom dogs with her magic wand. However, before I could broach the subject of

McClintock being a time stopper, Cleona jumped in about the crows and said, "You needn't worry about them tracking us, Uncle. We flew out of that forest so quickly, those dopey birds didn't know what hit them."

Father rushed over to the hangar doors and gazed down at the clouds. "No sign of them," he muttered to himself. "We're too high for crows to fly, I should think."

"Pshaw, I told you. It's not like I've never shaken off a flock of crows before."

"Nonetheless, we need to get moving. Should one of those crows lead Prince Nightshade to us before we acquire Excalibur . . ."

Father shuddered, then threw the lever on the wall, and the hangar doors closed behind him with a hiss.

"Pardon me, Uncle," Cleona said, "but did you say Excalibur?"

"That I did. We shall journey to the magical realm of Avalon on a quest for the sword of King Arthur himself."

"Avalon?" Cleona gasped. "But that means—"

"Precisely, my love. Therefore, I suggest you charge the reserves, batten down the hatches, and prepare yourself for what shall henceforth be known as Alistair Grim's Odd Aquaticum!"

Maps and Mothers

"An *Aquaticum*, did you say?" Lord Dreary asked.

The old man sat openmouthed in an armchair. Professor Bricklewick, his face frozen in a similar expression, stood by his side. For some time now the gentlemen had been peppering Father with questions as he combed the bookshelves from atop one of the library ladders. I had loads of questions too—mainly about all that time stopper business—but with Lord Dreary and the professor jabbering on such, I didn't think it my place to interrupt.

"Yes, an Aquaticum," Father replied. "A term I coined to mean a sea, lake, or river voyage in search of Odditoria."

"Well, I gathered that," said Lord Dreary. "Legend has it that Excalibur is bestowed upon King Arthur's descendants by Queen Nimue of Avalon, who thrusts up the sword from an enchanted lake—hence her title, the Lady of the Lake."

"An excellent summation, old friend," Father said. "There-fore, anyone with half a brain would deduce that Excalibur presently resides in Avalon, the entrance to which must be underwater."

"Exactly. So unless you plan on growing a pair of gills, would you care to explain just how you intend to embark on this Aquaticum of yours?"

"I should think that'd be quite obvious," Father said, and he made a sweeping gesture indicating the Odditorium.

"Great poppycock!" Lord Dreary exclaimed. "You mean to tell me this mechanical wonder of yours is capable of trav-eling underwater?"

"In theory," Father said, more to himself. "And with some slight modifications. Then again, we won't know for certain until we give it a go, now will we?"

Lord Dreary gulped and dragged his handkerchief across his head. The Odditorium was now flying above the clouds at full speed, shields up with the helm set on "autopilot," as Father called it. Nigel and the others were busy somewhere making the final preparations for our journey, but Father insisted that I be present in the library for what he called "a lesson in magical cartography." I had no idea what that meant but, what with everything else going on, thought it odd that he should be worried about my studies.

Then again, if there was one thing I'd learned during my

brief residence at the Odditorium, it was that the odd was the ordinary at Alistair Grim's.

"Ah, here we are," Father said, snatching a book from its shelf. "*The Legend of Excalibur* by Oscar P. Bricklewick. Wonder what that *P* stands for. Prickly, perhaps?"

"Very funny," the professor said, and Father tossed him the book.

"You'll be sure to sign it for me at some point, won't you?"

Father slid down the ladder where he was perched and crossed to his desk, on top of which was an old map of England belonging to Professor Bricklewick. I'd spread it out earlier for him at his request—a strange coincidence that, given Mr. Smears's phony map story, was not lost on me.

"Now, Oscar," Father said, scanning the map, "would you be so kind as to open that book of yours to the chapter on Avalon?"

Professor Bricklewick obliged. And as we all gathered round Father's desk, I noticed that the page to which the professor had turned bore a map similar to the one spread out before us.

"If memory serves me," Father began, "this map of England was passed down to you from your father. At least, that's what you claim in your book. Am I correct?"

"I'm surprised you read it," the professor said dryly. "But in answer to your question, that was a bit of a fib. The map was actually given to me by none other than our old professor at Cambridge, Doctor Shamus O'Grady."

Lord Dreary's eyes darted apprehensively to Father.

"Come again?" Father asked.

The professor cleared his throat. "Knowing my obsession with Arthurian legend, Elizabeth's father gave me the map as a gift upon our engagement. The Map of Merlin, he called it. From what she told me, he'd won it years earlier in a wager with none other than Abel Wortley. Curiously, for all his knowledge of antiquities, it appears old Wortley had no idea what it was."

"An intriguing turn of events," Father said, looking quizzical. My mind too was spinning. There was that name again: Abel Wortley. The man whom Nigel had been framed for murdering. His presence always seemed to be lurking in the background of our adventure like a specter in the dark.

"I beg your pardon, Professor," said Lord Dreary. "Notwithstanding this map's connection to our dearly departed friend, are you implying that it also once belonged to Merlin the Magician, the legendary wizard and mentor of King Arthur?"

"According to the legends," the professor began, "Merlin the Magician drew a map showing the location of the Gates of Avalon. To the untrained eye, the map before you appears to be just a crude, ninth-century rendering of Britannia and its surrounding waters—valuable in its own right as an antiquity, yes—but to someone with a knowledge of Odditoria, it is nothing short of a key to another world."

"Well, other than its age, I see nothing out of the ordinary with this map," said Lord Dreary.

"I needn't remind you that the most powerful Odditoria are often things that appear to be ordinary," Father said, and Lord Dreary rolled his eyes. "Go on, Oscar."

Professor Bricklewick pointed to the map in his book. "As you can see, there are a number of theories as to where the magical realm of Avalon is located. I've highlighted many of them here in my book. Curiously, the one thing that all these theories have in common is that Avalon is always referred to as an island. However, as I conveniently fail to mention in my book, *my* theory is that Avalon is not an island at all—at least not in the physical sense—but another dimension floating amidst our own. Thus, in order to get there, one would need the ability to space jump."

"But you also think there is an actual entrance into Avalon underwater?" Lord Dreary asked.

"I do not think, old friend, I *know*."

With a wave of his hand, Professor Bricklewick uttered a strange incantation, whereupon the map flashed and exploded into a luminous blue mist that filled the entire chamber. A grid of white navigational lines stretched out to the walls,

and hovering in midair among them was a colorful three-dimensional image of the British Isles. A glowing white compass floated nearby too—just east of London, from what I could tell.

"Good heavens!" Lord Dreary cried, and he steadied himself against Father's desk. "Oscar Bricklewick is a sorcerer too!"

The professor shrugged, and Father gave him a pat on the back. "Glad to see you've still got it, old friend," he said with a wink, and Professor Bricklewick began madly swiping his hands along the grid. The entire map scrolled through the air, while at the same time the British Isles grew larger, as if we were swooping down on them from above. I could see castles and farms, even the leaves on the trees, until finally the professor moved the map out to sea off the coast of northwest England. He parted the imaginary waters with his hands, and there before our eyes appeared a pair of sparkling blue gates bearing the letter *A*.

"Great poppycock!" cried Lord Dreary. "It's the Gates of Avalon!"

"Yes, but watch closely," said Professor Bricklewick. He swiped the map so that we were looking down over Great Britain again, and a dozen or so glowing stained-glass windows materialized above the same number of corresponding lakes in the North Country.

"As I suspected," Father said. "There are other entrances to Avalon beside the main gates—shortcuts, if you will—that Queen Nimue must have used in her dealings with King Arthur. Thus the varying claims as to Avalon's location."

"And yet, as Avalon is located in another dimension," said the professor, "not even a necromancer of Merlin's power could travel there. Only an Avalonian could pass back and forth between our two worlds—most often, as you can see, through a handful of shortcuts located in shallower water throughout the old kingdom."

"So, if I follow you, professor," said Lord Dreary, "you think Merlin made this map so he could travel to Avalon?"

"I do. Merlin no doubt kept a record of where the Lady of the Lake appeared and then plotted those locations on his map, hoping in vain that one of them might lead him into Avalon. Unfortunately, legend has it that only the heart of an Avalonian can get you through these entrances—unless, of course, you have a Sky Ripper, eh, Alistair?"

"That's the idea, yes," Father said, and my mouth fell open. So that was it! Alistair Grim was planning on using his interdimensional Sky Ripper to get into Avalon. I'd seen the mechanical marvel in action only once—a few weeks earlier, when we escaped from Prince Nightshade through a hole in the sky over London—but I never imagined it might work underwater!

"But, Professor," said Lord Dreary, "if memory serves me, after King Arthur was wounded in battle, didn't the Lady of the Lake take him to heal in Avalon?"

"Bravo, Lord Dreary. Your knowledge of Arthurian lore is impressive. King Arthur *did* travel to Avalon. Which means that it is possible not only for a human to travel there with an Avalonian companion, but also for him to stay in Avalon for an extended period of time."

"However," Father said, "since the Lady of the Lake has no intention of taking us to Avalon herself, we must space jump there via the Sky Ripper."

A heavy silence fell over the room as the gentlemen

pondered this. I too was thinking about spending time in another dimension, but not Avalon. No, what occupied my thoughts at present was our brief excursion into the Land of the Dead when we used the Sky Ripper before. For some reason, unbeknownst even to Alistair Grim, the Odditorium had only been able to stay there for a few seconds before being spit out again like a cherry pit. If the same thing should happen to us in Avalon, then our entire quest for Excalibur would have been for naught.

Apparently, Lord Dreary was thinking the same thing. "But, Alistair, let's say we can stay in Avalon without being expelled as we were during our last space jump. Will we need to use the Sky Ripper again to leave?"

"I should think traveling back to our own dimension would work roughly the same way as last time. Indeed, if we take the legend literally, one needs only the heart of an Avalonian to get in. It says nothing about needing one to get out."

Lord Dreary sighed and dragged his handkerchief across his head.

"And yet," Father went on, studying the terrain, "as this map is over a thousand years old, many of these lakes have either disappeared or are too shallow for the Odditorium to navigate—which means the only way for us to get to Avalon is through the main gates."

"I'm afraid so," said Professor Bricklewick, swiping the map back to its original position over the Irish Sea. "Perhaps there are other gateways into Avalon of which Merlin was unaware, but unless we find an Avalonian to accompany us, our surest bet is the main gates roughly five miles off the coast of Blackpool."

Father raised an eyebrow. "Blackpool, did you say?" he asked, and the professor nodded. I knew what Father was thinking. Elizabeth O'Grady's body had washed up on a beach near Blackpool. Cleona had told me so herself. What a strange coincidence. . . .

"Hallo, hallo?" Nigel called from the talkback, startling us. "Are you there, sir?"

Father flicked the switch upon his desk. "What is it, Nigel?"

"Sorry to bother you, sir, but it appears we've got a bit of a jam in the lower gunnery—rotary gears, directly under the gyro-seat. Nothing major, but I'm afraid my hands are too big to reach it. Was hoping you could spare Grubb for a moment, otherwise the wasps will have to tear everything apart."

"No need for that," Father said. "You heard him, my young apprentice. Your presence is needed down below."

"Begging your pardon, sir," I said, "but what about my lesson in magical cart . . . er, uh . . . cart—"

"Cartography," Father said. "And I'm happy to report that you just completed it."

I stood there, gaping in confusion, upon which Father winked and motioned for me to be on my way. I dashed from the library, through the parlor, and into the lift, where I threw the lever and began my descent. Cartography lessons aside, at this rate, I thought, I might never find out about Mack being a time stopper. Unless, of course, I asked the time stopper *himself.*

I slipped McClintock from my pocket and tapped him on his XII.

"What time is it?" Mack cried, flashing to life with animus. But upon seeing me, he shouted, "Run, Grubb! That scaffy witch'll fry yer hide!"

Poor Mack, I thought. With all the commotion in preparation for Father's Aquaticum, I hadn't had the chance to inform him of our escape from Mad Malmuirie.

"It's all right, Mack," I said. "We're home safe and sound now."

Mack spun round in my hands. "Ah, so we are, laddie," he said, glancing about. "How'd ya give that nut bag the slip?"

"I'll fill you in about all that later. But first, you need to tell me about being a time stopper that once belonged to her."

"I was telling the truth back there, laddie. Me time

stopper's been broken ever since I came to the Odditorium—just before ya arrived, come to think of it."

"Nigel told me at breakfast you've been here nearly six months now."

"Has it really been that long?" Mack asked in amazement. I nodded, and Mack sighed sadly. "Ah, laddie, what I wouldn't give to keep me proper time again."

"You mean there was a time when you didn't fizzle out?"

"That's right, Grubb. Ya see, I was made chief of the Chronometrical Clan McClintock because I never stopped ticking—never needed winding nor repairing neither. Those were the days when the Clan McClintock lived in Edinburgh—in a shop belonging to an old clockmaker what protected me. However, me time stopper was damaged during Mr. Grim's battle with Mad Malmuirie. I've no memory of what happened, but from what I gather, Mr. Grim tried to repair me with his animus and . . . Well, ya get the idea."

"So you really could stop time, Mack?"

"I suppose that's a way of looking at it, but what I'm really doing is speeding up time for the person holding me."

"I don't follow you."

"Think of it this way, lad. If you were to use me time stopper, everything around you would appear to freeze because time is passing normally for the rest of the world while *your* time is ticking away faster—so fast, in fact, that you become invisible to everyone else. You can do things and go places without others seeing you, as if you've stepped out of time for a bit but haven't left the world in which it's ticking. Understand?"

"I think so. And what was it Mad Malmuirie said? You could only do this for a minute or so?"

"Stopping time takes a lot outta ya—like Cleona firing the Sky Ripper—so after about a minute, I get tired and need to rest a spell before doing it again. Thankfully, me old master was a good man, and only used me to play tricks on his wife now and then."

"And let me guess: it was Mad Malmuirie who stole you from him?"

"Aye, laddie," Mack said with a sigh. "Done away with him, she did, along with the rest of me clan. Far as I can tell, I'm the only one what survived. Mad Malmuirie is a lot like the prince, ya see. Always up to no good and looking for Odditoria, and I'm ashamed to say that I was forced to help her on her quests before Mr. Grim rescued me."

"I'm very sorry about your family, Mack. I had no idea about all that. In fact, all this time I just assumed it was Father who made you."

Mack chuckled. "That's understandable, mate. But there's no use getting all gobby-eyed about it—not when we're on an adventure. Ain't that what Mr. Grim says?"

"That he does, old friend."

The lift had already come to a stop on the bottom floor, but I'd been so wrapped up in Mack's story that I hadn't noticed. Remembering that Nigel had called for me, I dashed down the servants' hallway and into the engine room.

As expected, I found Gwendolyn in the flight conductor. She was spinning overtime, Father had said—something about needing extra fairy dust for the levitation shields—but still, I hadn't a clue what that had to do with our Aquaticum. Indeed, as far as I could tell, Father had used the levitation shields only once before—during our escape from London, when he buzzed off a load of Shadesmen that had been climbing about outside.

"Might I have a word with you, Grubb?" someone said, and I spun round to find Lorcan Dalach standing with his hands pressed against the insides of his prison sphere. Only a hazy outline of him was visible through the shield of fairy dust, but still, I felt as if I could see the Gallownog's cold blue eyes boring into me just the same.

"Mind yer gob, neep," Mack said. "We've got nothing to say to the likes of you."

"When I want commentary from a sputtering Scotsman, I'll ask for it."

"Why you little—tick—tick—!" Mack trembled and

flashed, and then his eyes went dark. Just as well, I thought, as this wasn't the time for brawling. I slipped him in my pocket, and realized my heart was pounding.

"A word, Grubb, please," Dalach said. "You needn't be afraid."

Cautious, I stepped closer to the prison sphere, and the Gallownog pressed up against the glass so that I might see him better. His normally blue face, coming into focus, looked green now behind the shield of sparkling yellow light that surrounded him.

"I wanted to thank you for being such a good friend to Cleona," he said. "She told me of your escape from Nightshade's castle, and how you risked your life to save her."

I didn't quite know how to reply, and just stood there, eyes hard, staring back at him suspiciously.

"I was able to watch you for a bit when I first came on board," Dalach went on. "I hope you don't mind my saying so, but you remind me of your mother."

"It's not polite to spy on people," I said. "Especially in the midst of their lessons."

Dalach smiled. "You misunderstand me, lad. I'd seen your mother once before I spied her in that mirror. Only from a distance, of course, but enough to know that your heart beats with the same courage and character."

"But how—"

"We Gallownog are capable of things that other banshees are not."

"I don't believe you," I said. "My mother died in England. Banshees cannot cross over the Irish Sea unless they're protected, so you couldn't have seen her."

"If banshees can't cross over the Irish Sea, then how did Cleona get to England to wail your mother's death?"

I fumbled for an answer, but when I couldn't find one, Lorcan Dalach found it for me. "Love," he said simply, and I just stared back at him, confused. "It's as simple as that, Grubb. A banshee's love for her family is so powerful that it can carry her across entire oceans to wail for them at the moment of death. However, if a banshee tries to interfere, as Cleona did, she is banished to Tir Na Mairg."

"Tir Na Mairg?"

"It means Land of Sorrow—an afterlife where evil spirits and the damned dwell in eternal torment. Tir Na Mairg exists between this world and the Land of the Dead."

"I don't understand."

"Think of Tir Na Mairg as if it were the shield of fairy dust around this sphere. Inside, where I am, is the Land of the Dead. The fairy dust is the Land of Sorrow, and where you are is the Land of the Living. But Tir Na Mairg is by far the worst of the three. It's the in-between. I've seen it with my own eyes, Grubb—a terrible, desolate place of untold pain and suffering, for Tir Na Mairg is home to the doom dogs."

I took a sharp breath in. "You mean you've traveled there?"

Lorcan Dalach held up his spirit shackles. "Aye, lad. It is the unhappy lot of the Gallownog to escort banished banshees into Tir Na Mairg, for only a Gallownog has the fortitude to endure the horrors that dwell there." Dalach leaned in closer and held my gaze. "And so it was, Grubb, that on one such journey I saw your mother in the Land of the Dead." My eyes grew wide and my jaw hung slack. "I saw her in much the same way as you see me now"—he gestured at the force field of fairy dust—"from a distance, through the mists of Tir Na Mairg."

"You're lying," I said, my voice small, but I could tell by the look in his eyes that the Gallownog spoke the truth.

"I swear it on my love for Cleona," he said, raising his hand in oath. "I saw your mother, Grubb; and from what I've seen of the Odditorium, I'll wager Alistair Grim intends to find her by using Cleona's spirit energy to take him into the Land of the Dead."

I averted my eyes. This bloke doesn't miss a trick, I thought, and the Gallownog smiled as if he'd read my mind.

"Then what I say is true," he said. "But take heed, lad. Cleona is a banshee, a spirit meant only for this world unless banished to the Land of Sorrow. And so her energy will transport Alistair Grim not to the Land of the Dead, but to Tir Na

Mairg—and only for a moment, because love and goodness cannot exist there."

"So, the first time Father used his Sky Ripper, it was the Land of Sorrow what spit us out?"

"Ah, so you've tried already," Dalach said, and I dropped my eyes. Once again, I'd revealed too much. "Then you know I speak the truth. Alistair Grim will never reach the Land of the Dead through Tir Na Mairg. The evil that dwells there, repelled by the love in Cleona's energy, will cast out his Odditorium in the blink of an eye."

My heart sank. "Poor Father," I muttered. "It's all for naught."

"No, there is hope, lad," Dalach said, and he rattled his spirit shackles. "As a Gallownog, I can take your father into Tir Na Mairg. Once he's chained to me he can remain as long as I do. After that, well, I should think if anyone could find a way from there into the Land of the Dead, it'd be Alistair Grim."

"You mean, you'd help Father find his lost love?"

"Aye, lad. I've had a change of heart. My love for Cleona has made me see the error of my ways. But in order to help your father, you have to get me out of this sphere."

"Perhaps you should tell him of this change of heart yourself."

"He won't believe me. Besides, I imagine your father's preoccupied at present, what with Prince Nightshade on his tail. *You*, on the other hand—if you let me out of this prison, I can take you into Tir Na Mairg. Then you can tell your father what I say is true. You can tell him you saw Elizabeth O'Grady's spirit for yourself."

"If you think I'm going to set you free, you're even dafter than this witch I know."

"But don't you want to meet your mother, Grubb? Don't you want to ask her why she abandoned you all those years ago to a life of misery?"

The banshee's words cut me to the quick. It was as if he'd read my innermost thoughts—thoughts that, until now, I'd been afraid to admit even to myself. For although I desperately wanted to know what drove Elizabeth O'Grady away from Father, even more so I wanted to know why she kept my birth a secret from him. Unfortunately, there was only one person who knew the answer to that question, and she presently resided in the Land of the Dead.

"All your questions shall be answered in Tir Na Mairg," Dalach said. "I can show you your mother. I can show you how to talk to her, and then—"

"That's enough!" someone shouted, and I spun round to find Nigel poking his head up from the porthole to the lower gunnery. His face was cast in shadow, his eyes hidden behind his goggles, but it was clear from the tone of his voice that he was cross.

I glanced back at the Gallownog. "Tir Na Mairg, lad," he whispered. "Tir Na Mairg." And then Lorcan Dalach withdrew into the sphere, his shape becoming just a fuzzy green shadow amidst the glow of fairy dust.

"Come along, Grubb," Nigel said, and when I joined him down in the gunnery, he lifted me up by the shoulders so that our noses were nearly touching. "The Gallownog speaks with a silver tongue," he said with quiet anger. "Should I catch you with him again, the boss's son or not, it'll be my hand you feel across your mouth. Understand?"

I nodded, terrified, and Nigel set me down. I'd only seen him like this once before—all those weeks ago when I first blurted out the prince's surname in the marketplace. And yet, despite my present fear of him, I knew deep down that the big man's anger stemmed only from his love for me.

"Carry on, then," he said, handing me a wrench. A panel in the floor had been removed and an oil can sat nearby. I shimmied into the cramped crawl space beneath the gyro-seat and set to work on the jammed rotary gear. I tried hard not to think about my conversation with the Gallownog—I truly did—but once the gear was oiled and moving freely again, I lay there on my back for a long time afterward with Lorcan Dalach's words echoing in my head.

"*Tir Na Mairg, lad . . . Tir Na Mairg . . .*"

TEN

The Moral of the Story

ll through the afternoon and well into the evening Nigel and I labored feverishly, oiling gears and rerouting pipes in nearly every room of the Odditorium. We spoke very little during our work. As the evening wore on, I sensed that the big man had grown sad—so much so that, when he asked to be left alone in his quarters to charge himself, I felt the need to apologize for speaking with the Gallownog.

"Trouble yourself no more about it, lad," Nigel said with a smile. Nevertheless, I could tell something was still bothering him, and as he removed his goggles and made to lower the charging helmet upon his head, I saw that his animus-filled eyes were rimmed with tears.

My heart squeezed, and without thinking, I rushed over and hugged his leg. "Oh, don't despair, Nigel!" I cried as my own tears began to flow. "I'd never set Dalach free—no matter what he promised!"

Nigel chuckled and placed a beefy hand upon my shoulder. "I know that, Grubb."

"Please forgive me, then, won't you? I didn't mean to make you cry."

"Now, now, lad. It's not your fault. All that talk about seeing people what's passed on . . . Well, I suppose we all have someone we'd like to talk to again, eh?"

At first I thought Nigel meant his daughter, Maggie. After all, he was always so jolly except when missing her. But Maggie was alive and well and residing in the country with Judge Hurst's sister, so Nigel couldn't possibly hope to see her from Tir Na Mairg.

But Maggie's *mother*, on the other hand . . .

The light suddenly dawning, I gazed up at Nigel to find him smiling. *I best not press him about it tonight,* I said to myself. *Don't want to upset him further.*

"You run along to bed now, Grubb," Nigel said. "We've got a big day ahead of us tomorrow. Which reminds me: you better see if Professor Bricklewick needs anything before you turn in."

Without a word, I hugged Nigel's leg one last time and dashed from the room. And after checking in on Professor Bricklewick, who had retired for the evening with his map in Father's quarters, I headed down the hallway toward the lift. However, as I passed by the door across from Cleona's room,

I noticed that the SILENCE IS GOLDEN sign had been replaced with one that read, ENTER, PLEASE.

"That's odd," I muttered. "I wonder who it's for."

The sign let out a puff of shimmering sparkles, and then the words transformed themselves into, YOU, DUMMY!

"Cor!" I gasped in amazement when I realized I'd just been insulted. "Hang on. It's not polite to call people names."

Another puff of sparkles, and the sign again said, ENTER, PLEASE.

I must confess that I was tempted, but Father had been

very clear in his instructions: under no circumstances was I to enter this room. True, I thought it very strange that no one, not even Nigel, would tell me what was inside. But as I'd quickly learned in my time at the Odditorium, Father had his reasons for everything. And, like it or not, those reasons were always sound. Well, *almost* always.

"I most certainly will *not* enter," I said. "That'll be the day I listen to an ill-mannered sign over Father."

I was answered with a loud *thump!* on the door. Startled, I jumped back and waited for the sign to insult me again, but nothing happened. I hurried downstairs to report to Father what I'd seen. The clocks were just chiming ten as I stepped off the lift and into the parlor. A heated discussion was taking place in the library.

"But, Uncle," Cleona said, "you assured us that you'd return Lorcan to Ireland after we left the circle of stones."

Father mumbled something unintelligible, and I crept closer to the pocket doors, which were cracked open just enough for me to get a clear view of him reading at his cluttered desk. Cleona hovered above Father's shoulder, staring down at him with her eyes narrowed and her arms crossed. I knew I shouldn't spy on them, but I also knew I shouldn't interrupt them either.

"Don't change the subject," Cleona said. "You know very

well that Nigel connected the Sky Ripper's induction unit to the flight sphere last night."

"I'm sorry, love, but I simply don't have the time to argue with you."

"But surely—"

"Furthermore, this Aquaticum is sizing up to be my most dangerous quest yet, not the least of which has to do with our traveling underwater. Who knows how the interdimensional space jump will affect the Odditorium's systems once we pass into Avalon. Therefore, I suggest you get some rest in the event you need to charge the reserves in a hurry."

Cleona began gliding back and forth, pacing in mid-air. "That's exactly my point. It's too dangerous to have the Gallownog on board for the space jump. What if something *does* happen to the Odditorium's systems? What if we have another animus drain like last time and Lorcan escapes?"

"If you'll recall, both the flight sphere and Gwendolyn's fairy dust were unaffected by our last space jump. Thus, I am quite confident that the Gallownog will be perfectly secure inside his prison."

"Pshaw. Say your silly Aquaticum pans out and we do reach Avalon, what next? You don't very well think you can just walk up to Queen Nimue and ask her to borrow Excalibur, do you?"

"Well, if you have a better idea, I'm all ears." Father tossed aside the book he was reading and opened another.

"But, Uncle—"

Father pounded his fist on the desk. "Cleona, please!" he thundered. "Need I remind you that the prince and Mad Malmuirie are still on our tail?"

Cleona bowed her head and bit her lip. Father's outburst had clearly winged her.

"Forgive me, love," he said, softening. "But as far as I'm concerned this matter is closed until we gain possession of Excalibur."

Cleona descended slowly to the floor so that her eyes were even with Father's.

"I know why you want to keep him here," she said. "Your little plan of rerouting the Sky Ripper's induction unit—you're thinking about using Lorcan's energy to take you through Tir Na Mairg, aren't you?"

I gasped, and my heart began to hammer. "Have you gone mad?" Father said. But from the way his voice went up in pitch, I couldn't help but wonder whether or not he was bluffing.

"I'm not mad and neither are you," Cleona said. "You know very well why our space jump didn't work last time. You thought my love would transport you across Tir Na Mairg and into the Land of the Dead the same way it transported me across the ocean to wail Elizabeth's death."

"Cleona—"

"But you miscalculated. My love was too strong, and so we were cast out of Tir Na Mairg at once. A Gallownog, on the other hand, can remain there as long as he pleases. You think that if you were to use Lorcan's energy in the Sky Ripper instead of mine, you could stay in Tir Na Mairg long enough to find a way to Elizabeth!"

Father fixed his eyes on Cleona's, and a heavy silence hung between them. "Well?" Cleona asked. "Am I right?"

"Go to bed," Father said, and Cleona dropped to her knees.

"I beg of you, Uncle. It's called the Land of Sorrow for a reason—a realm of unspeakable torment and pain. The Gallownog can negotiate its horrors because they are a different breed entirely—fierce warriors who are trained from birth to endure severe hardship and suffering. Without one of them to protect and guide you through Tir Na Mairg, your spirit will become just another one of the damned walking between this world and the next."

"Listen to me, Cleona," Father said, taking her hands. "I am engaged at present on one mission and one mission only: to find Excalibur and defeat Prince Nightshade. Until then, everything else is irrelevant."

"Promise me, then, will you? Promise me you'll never journey into Tir Na Mairg."

Father heaved a heavy sigh. "I promise," he said quietly, and a wave of relief washed over Cleona's face.

"Thank you," she said, hugging him. Without a word more Cleona floated upward and disappeared through the ceiling. Father sighed and removed the Black Mirror from its case.

"Will you show me now what I wish to know?" he asked. The mirror flashed ever so briefly and Father frowned. "Temperamental as always." He tossed the mirror back into its case and hung his head in his hands.

My heart sank in pity, and yet I just stood there watching, searching for a sign that Father's promise to Cleona had been insincere. I hated myself for being suspicious of him; but more so, I hated myself because, despite everything I'd heard about Tir Na Mairg, part of me hoped that Alistair Grim was planning on traveling there after all.

I gazed up at the portrait of my mother above the hearth and a sea of questions began tossing about in my head. *Why did you run away and leave me with the Yellow Fairy? Why didn't you tell Father of my birth? Didn't you realize what both our lives might have been like had I lived with him instead of Mr. Smears?*

"*Tir Na Mairg, lad,*" I heard Lorcan Dalach say in my mind. "*All your questions shall be answered in Tir Na Mairg.*"

Just then, the secret panel to the spiral staircase opened in the wall beside the lift. I darted back into the shadows, and a pair of samurai stepped out—coming down from the roof, I knew, to make their nightly report. Since our flight from London, the samurai had been keeping watch round the clock in the event the prince should try to sneak up on us—not to mention Mad Malmuirie and Mr. Smears and anyone else who might be looking for Alistair Grim now that his likeness had been in the papers.

I moved aside to let them pass, and the samurai marched into the library without acknowledging me.

"Everything all right?" Father asked. I could not see them from my new position, but the samurai must have nodded yes, for a moment later they marched back through the parlor and out the secret panel.

"You may enter, Grubb," Father called. My stomach lurched—the samurai must have told him that I was waiting outside. "Please, son, I haven't got all night."

"Sorry to disturb you, sir," I said as I stepped into the library. "But I thought it best to inform you that the sign on the door across from Cleona's room bade me enter."

Father looked up from his work. "Come again?"

"After checking in with Professor Bricklewick, I noticed that the 'Silence Is Golden' sign had changed to 'Enter, Please.'

I wondered aloud who it might be for, and the sign said, 'You, Dummy,' and again bade me enter."

Father's face flickered with alarm. "And did you?"

"Why no, sir. I didn't want to disobey your wishes."

"An intriguing turn of events," Father said, and he seemed to become lost in thought.

"Something the matter, sir?" I asked after a moment. Father looked startled, as if he'd forgotten I was there.

"Very well, then," he said, rising. "I suggest we take her up on her offer before she changes her mind."

"Take up who, sir?"

"Er—uh," Father stammered, and he grabbed a samurai helmet that was lying nearby. "You know the saying. Silence is golden and all that. Come along then, Grubb."

I followed Father back upstairs. The sign still said, ENTER, PLEASE. Father took a deep breath, unlocked the door, and was about to enter when, in a puff of sparkles, the words transformed into, NOT YOU, DUMMY!

Father snatched back his hand and moved me in front of him. The sign immediately changed back to, ENTER, PLEASE.

"I thought as much," Father muttered, and he plopped the samurai helmet on my head. "All right, then. You're on your own now, Grubb. Remember, silence is golden, so don't speak unless spoken to. Should you feel the need to run for the door, by all means see if you can grab a half dozen or so eggs on your way out, will you?"

I gulped. "Sir?"

"Carry on, then—I'll be right here waiting for you."

Father smiled nervously, opened the door, and pushed me inside. My fear, pounding in my ears, was all but deafening inside the helmet, but as soon as I saw what lay before me, I was overcome with wonder.

The room into which I'd stepped looked like an ancient forest. Large, knotted trees stretched from the floor to the ceiling, their leafy branches twisting about so thickly that barely a single patch of blue-painted sky was visible between them. The walls themselves were textured and painted to look like trees too—so expertly, in fact, that I couldn't tell where the real trees ended and the painted ones began.

As Father closed the door behind me, I noticed that it too was fashioned to look like a tree. Rocks and splinters lay scattered about on the floor nearby, and were it not for the gouges and chips in its bark, I would have lost the door completely amidst its lifelike surroundings.

So that's what all the thumping was about, I said to myself. *Whatever lives in here fancies throwing rocks at this door!*

Moving farther into the room, there were even more rocks—large moss-covered boulders, some of which were draped with tree roots, while others glistened with rivulets of water that trickled down into a pond filled with water lilies. Across the pond was a path of stepping-stones that led to a grassy grove. In the middle of the grove was a giant bird's nest, on top of which sat the largest goose I'd ever seen—a truly magnificent creature, with bright golden feathers that glowed like a halo of sunshine.

The goose honked and flapped her wings. I took this to mean that I should come closer; and as I stepped across the pond and into the grove, I noticed a silver tray of colored eggs resting on the edge of the goose's nest.

So this is where Nigel gets his eggs, I thought, and the goose honked again.

"Everything all right?" Father called from outside in the hallway—when quick as a flash, the goose dipped her bill into her nest, snatched up a rock, and hurled it at the door—*thump!*

"Don't speak unless spoken to," I heard Father cautioning in my head. But then again, I wondered, how else would a goose speak if not by honking?

"I'm fine, sir," I called back, and the goose bobbed her head at the tray of eggs. "Begging your pardon—er, uh—ma'am, but do you mean for me to take those eggs?"

The goose nodded and flapped her wings, and as I bent down to pick up the tray, I noticed that one egg was different from the others.

"It's gold," I muttered, holding the egg in my hand—it felt much heavier than the other eggs—and all at once I understood. "Odditoria!" I gasped, and the goose cocked her head and blinked her eyes quizzically. "What I mean, ma'am, is that you're magical. You're the goose what laid the golden eggs, aren't you?"

The goose sighed, turned her back on me, and, with a quiet honk, settled down into her nest to sleep—my cue to exit, I assumed. And so, with the tray of colored eggs in hand, I left the goose in her forest lair and stepped back out into the hall.

"Well, well," Father said, examining the golden egg. "Silence *is* golden after all."

"Cor blimey, sir. You found the goose what laid the golden eggs!"

"*That* laid the golden eggs," Father corrected me. "And so you're familiar with the story?"

"Mrs. Smears told it to me once. A farmer had a goose what—I mean, that—laid one golden egg every day. He reckoned there must be even more gold inside her, so he cut her open for it, only to find the poor bird was no different than any other goose."

"Thus, the Moral of the story," Father said, jerking his thumb at the door.

"Well," I said, thinking. "The farmer wanted to get rich

quickly and ended up robbing himself of all that gold he might've gotten had he been patient. Patience is a virtue, Mrs. Smears used to say. So I'd say the moral of the story is to be patient."

"Yes, of course," Father said with a smile. "But I was referring to the goose herself. Her *name* is Moral."

"Moral, sir?"

"That's right. However, unlike the goose in the story, Moral doesn't lay golden eggs for just anybody. She is very temperamental, often rude, and exceedingly judgmental. Meaning she won't lay a golden egg for someone unless she thinks he'll use it honorably. In fact, this is the first golden egg Moral's laid in over a year"—Father handed it back to me—"and she laid it for you."

"For me, sir?"

"You saw the sign, didn't you? Moral can control it with her mind, and it was you she bade enter."

I glanced down at the sign, which now read, SILENCE IS GOLDEN.

"Cor," I whispered. "But where—how did you find her, sir?"

"Oh, that's another story for another time," Father said, looking at his watch. "Someone needs to get to bed."

"But why now, Father?"

"Because it's late, I should think."

"No, sir, what I mean is, why did Moral lay a golden egg for me now? I've passed by this door many times, and all I ever got for it was rocks thrown at me—not to mention that the sign has said 'Silence Is Golden' ever since I got here."

"And long before that, I'm afraid. Moral requires peace and quiet to lay her eggs. Hence the 'Silence Is Golden' proverb. It must be heeded quite strictly, which is why we had to keep her a secret. Silence about her existence, both in and out of her presence, is what Moral requires to lay her golden eggs."

I held up the egg to one of the animus-burning sconces. "It truly is beautiful, sir. But why me?"

"Your guess is as good as mine. There are a lot of things about our friend in there that I don't understand, including how she works that sign. However, as Moral laid the golden egg for you, it's up to you to use it honorably."

At that moment, Mrs. Pinch stepped off the lift with a bowl of beans. "Blind me," she said, squinting as she approached. "Is that what I think it is?"

"Yes, ma'am," I said. "Moral laid it for me."

"Humph, well it's about time. And I do hope you'll put it to good use, Master Grubb. Unlike someone else I know."

Mrs. Pinch glared at Father, who smiled back at her sheepishly. I didn't need to ask what she was implying. What with all his Odditoria, no doubt Alistair Grim used a golden egg or two to pay for some of it.

"I don't suppose Moral honked if she was hungry?" Mrs. Pinch asked.

"On the contrary, ma'am," I said. "She seemed quite sleepy."

"Well, blind me if I take any more rocks to the noggin."

Mrs. Pinch removed the samurai helmet from my head, placed it on her own, and then slipped quietly into Moral's room with her bowl of beans.

"Very well, then," Father said, indicating the tray of colored eggs. "Drop those off in the kitchen on your way to bed, and in the morning I'll find you a box in which to keep your golden egg. I'm sure I've got something around here."

Father winked and then, without warning, kissed me good night on the forehead. It was the first time he'd ever done so—in fact, it was the first time *anyone* had kissed me good night since Mrs. Smears died—and I just stood there, gaping up at him in shock.

"I'm sorry, son," he said. "But if you were hoping for one of those stereotypical unaffectionate British fathers, I'm afraid you're out of luck. Too much time has passed for me to stand on paternal awkwardness. Besides, before you know it, you'll be too old for such things."

Father smiled—somewhat sadly, I thought—and I wished him good night. I made my way downstairs in the lift, dropped off the tray of colored eggs in the kitchen, and after I'd washed and settled into the shop, I lay in bed for a long time, studying my golden egg and replaying the day's events in my mind. And what a day, indeed! A flight in a demon buggy, an escape from a mad witch, and a golden egg all rolled into one.

Then again, such days were becoming quite commonplace here at the Odditorium. And yet, for all the amazing things that had happened to me since I awoke this morning, none at present seemed more amazing than that kiss from Father.

If only I'd known what was coming, I most certainly would have kissed him back.

—ELEVEN—

The Guardian at the Gates

After an uneventful morning of last-minute preparations, we were finally about to embark on our Aquaticum. The gentlemen and I stood on the balcony, gazing out across an endless sea of rolling whitecaps, while the others manned their stations: Nigel in the lower gunnery, Mrs. Pinch in the upper (Professor Bricklewick had loaned her an extra pair of his spectacles), Gwendolyn in the flight sphere, and Cleona in the Sky Ripper.

According to the Map of Merlin, the Gates of Avalon were somewhere about two hundred feet below—one hundred feet to the surface of the water, and then another one hundred feet below that. However, as the good professor kept reminding us, we would not be able to pinpoint the precise location of the gates until we were undersea—after which, he said, the map would do the rest.

"That's all very well," said Lord Dreary, "but I still don't understand how Alistair is going to keep this mechanical monstrosity from leaking." The old man's handkerchief had been plastered to his head for the greater part of the morning, his brow perpetually flushed and glistening with sweat.

"As I've explained to you already," Father said, "as a result of rerouting the flight sphere's induction unit, I've reduced the output ratio for the levitation shield while at the same time increasing the duration of its expulsion parameters, thus creating a steady flow of fairy dust that will not only repel the water at the molecular level, but will also create an anti-gravitational shell in which the Odditorium can submerge without the need for pressurization or the flooding of its lower compartments."

"Good heavens, man, speak English!" Lord Dreary sputtered in frustration.

Professor Bricklewick, who had been observing the horizon through a sextant, put a hand on Lord Dreary's shoulder. "What our long-winded friend means to say is that we shall travel underwater in a giant bubble of yellow fairy dust."

"Great poppycock!" Lord Dreary cried, and once again he dragged his handkerchief across his head.

"All systems check out fine below, sir," Nigel called from the organ's talkback, and then Mrs. Pinch chimed in from the upper gunnery too.

"Same up here, sir," she said. "And blind me if I don't feel twenty years younger thanks to the professor's spectacles."

"Cleona, are you in position?" Father asked.

"Yes, Uncle," she replied on the talkback. "But I must confess, I'm somewhat vexed as to how I shall open the Sky Ripper's porthole without letting in all that water."

"The bubble of fairy dust will take care of that. But you will let me know if you feel the urge to start wailing, won't you?"

"Bubble or no bubble, I should think you'd be able to hear that for yourself."

"All right, then, everyone," Father said, flicking some switches. "I wish we had time for a test run, but if for some reason we don't make it, let me just say what a privilege it has been—"

"You're not going to start with that gloom-and-doom speech again, are you?" Cleona asked, and Nigel giggled.

"Very well, then, I'm activating the levitation shields," Father said into the talkback. "Let me know if you sense anything unusual happening with the animus reserves, will you, Cleona?"

"Pshaw, even the most amateur of sorcerers wouldn't worry about a thing like that."

"Well," Father said, "at the risk of déjà vu, here goes nothing."

As Lord Dreary and Professor Bricklewick steadied themselves on either side of the pipe organ, Father pressed a button and the control room's normally blue defense shield wiped across the balcony in a window of glowing yellow fairy dust. I could barely make out anything beyond its haze, but as Father played his pipe organ and we began our descent, I imagined the Odditorium looked like a giant spider caught in a drop of tree sap.

Father changed his tune and I felt a rumbling beneath my feet. Judging from the position of his hands on the keyboard, I knew he was managing the vertical thrusters. And as if reading my mind, Father said, "Go ahead, son, give it a try."

"But I've never landed, sir," I said. "I don't even know the proper tune."

Father shrugged. "I should think being above water the safest place to learn." And before I could think twice about it, I was sitting at the organ and fingering the tune I'd watched him play countless times. The Odditorium wobbled for a moment, but once I got the notes right, we quickly leveled off and began to descend faster.

"A regular prodigy, I tell you," Lord Dreary said. But then we hit the water and the Odditorium listed sharply. I snatched back my hands, and Father squeezed in front of me and took over at the organ.

"An excellent landing, son," he said, changing the tune. "But traveling underwater is a different kettle of fish altogether."

The Odditorium leveled off again, and all at once the world outside was swallowed up in a rising curtain of frothy green bubbles.

"It works!" Father cried. "The shield of fairy dust is the perfect submersible!"

And with a loud *whoosh* the Odditorium was completely underwater.

My body trembled with fear. After all, the only thing standing between us and certain drowning was a thin yellow window across the balcony. And yet, once the curtain of bubbles dissolved and the water around the Odditorium became clear, I was overcome with a quiet sense of awe. Indeed, not a word was spoken as we descended to the sound of Father's organ, the whole lot of us struck dumb by the sheer wonder of this, our first Aquaticum.

For some reason we could see much better now that we were underwater. And although there was plenty of sunshine there beneath the waves, Father turned on the searchlight. The sea ignited all around us in a wall of luminous orange—a mixture of red from the Eye of Mars and yellow from the dust bubble—and with it came even greater visibility. In fact, it appeared as if we could see for miles, the water bright and shimmering with what looked like sheets of crystal-clear fire.

"The searchlight may help illuminate the gates," Father said. "Look for any irregularities in the water ahead—strange ripple effects, shadows and whatnot that seem out of place."

"But how do you even know you're going in the right direction?" Lord Dreary asked. "Your compass appears to be malfunctioning."

I gazed down at the compass on Father's organ. Its needle was spinning madly.

"It's the dust bubble's antigravitational properties," Father said. "You'll have to take it from here, Oscar."

Professor Bricklewick stepped into the library and once again brought the Map of Merlin to life. However, this time when the professor swiped his hands, the blue mist and navigational lines disappeared so that only the map's glowing compass remained. The professor snatched it from the air and joined us again on the balcony, where he hung the compass in midair just above the pipe organ.

"As I suspected," the professor said. "Merlin's compass only works underwater."

Father flicked some switches and changed his tune. As the Odditorium began to move forward as well as down, I took a closer look at this strange white compass. Not only did it have a directional needle like the compass on Father's organ, but also a glowing blue ruler around its dial that Professor Bricklewick said measured depth. Hence, the farther down we traveled, the more of the compass's perimeter glowed blue.

Very soon, however, my eyes were drawn back to the fiery depths beyond the balcony. And the quiet awe that had previously rendered us speechless quickly turned to excited chatter as we marveled at all the undersea creatures that dared to approach us on our journey. Even Gwendolyn took a break from the flight sphere to join Nigel in the lower gunnery, her "Oohs!" and "Ahs!" mixing with the others' as she beheld what Lord Dreary classified as a pod of bottlenose dolphins.

Come to find out, Lord Dreary was quite an expert on marine life, and as we traveled on, the old man named for us all sorts of species, each one more wondrous than the next. There were dazzling schools of trout and salmon; slender, pointy-nosed blue sharks; razor-toothed conger eels; and a jolly-looking creature that Lord Dreary called a long-finned pilot whale. There were many other types of fish too—the names of which I quickly forgot—all of them drawn to the yellow light surrounding us, the old man explained.

"We should be arriving at the gates any moment now," Father said. I noticed that the needle on Merlin's compass was blinking—faster and faster—until the blinks became a continuous glow that swelled and brightened like an ember that had been blown upon. Father ceased his playing, and as the

Odditorium slowed to a halt, he left us to consult his navigational charts in the library.

"I don't understand," said Lord Dreary, searching the waters. "What are we looking for, again? Are the gates nearby?"

"You didn't very well think they'd look like actual gates, now, did you?" asked Professor Bricklewick, and the gentlemen and I joined Father at his desk.

"Listen up, everyone," he said into the talkback. "According to my calculations, the Gates of Avalon should be approximately one hundred yards directly ahead of us. Please stand by for further instructions."

Father flicked off the talkback and raked his fingers through his hair. Something was bothering him.

"What is it, Alistair?" asked Professor Bricklewick.

"Given everything that I've told you about Prince Nightshade, doesn't it seem odd to you that, for nearly a month now, we've seen neither hide nor hair of him?"

"I'm afraid I don't follow you."

Father crossed to a chessboard that he kept on one of his bookshelves. The pieces, I noticed, were in the same position as they were the day before—a game between Father and Lord Dreary, Nigel had informed me, that had been going on for ages. I hadn't the foggiest idea how to play chess, but I gathered it took a lot of strategy—especially when it came to guessing your opponent's next move. On the other hand, I couldn't imagine that the game was much fun, what with all the time it took to play it.

"We've been running from Prince Nightshade for weeks," Father said, fingering one of the pieces, "but what if he hasn't been chasing us?"

"I'm afraid I'm with the professor," said Lord Dreary. "What are you talking about?"

"If you'll recall, given the fact that the Thunderbirds played a pivotal role in our rescue of Grubb and Cleona, Prince Nightshade most certainly would've gone looking for their lair once he regrouped his forces. Fortunately, as you know, the Thunderbirds migrated to another location immediately after our departure, so what do you think the prince did when he found them gone? What would have been his next move?"

"I should think he had only *one* move: to come looking for us."

"I thought so too at the time, Lord Dreary. And yet, as it's been nearly twenty-four hours since Mad Malmuirie opened McClintock—an event that, in theory, would not only attract the doom dogs but Prince Nightshade himself—don't you think it odd that we haven't run into any of his minions? Not a single Shadesman or even one of those bloody doom-dog-tracking crows?"

"You almost sound disappointed," said Professor Bricklewick.

"On the contrary, old friend. However, I just can't shake this nagging suspicion that I've missed something."

"Good heavens, Alistair," said Lord Dreary. "Don't tell me you're having second thoughts about this Aquaticum of yours."

"Certainly not," Father said, and he replaced the chess piece on the board. "However, doesn't it seem just a bit too easy? After all, one blast from the Sky Ripper and"—Father snapped his fingers—"just like that we're in Avalon."

"Might I remind you that you still have to convince the Lady of the Lake to give you Excalibur once you get there," said Professor Bricklewick. "I guarantee you there'll be nothing easy about that. Not only is she a sorceress, but also, according to legend, one who has lived for over a thousand years."

"To be sure," said Lord Dreary. "From what I remember, even Merlin the Magician was no match for her. Queen Nimue is said to have imprisoned him in a tree when he tried to take Excalibur for himself."

"Once again, your knowledge of Arthurian lore is impressive, old friend," said Professor Bricklewick. "However, if you'll recall, the nature of the relationship between Nimue and Merlin differs greatly from one legend to the next. For instance, in the Lancelot Grail Cycle, the Lady of the Lake actually *learns* the art of sorcery from Merlin, who in turn falls in love with her."

"True," said Lord Dreary. "However, if *you'll* recall, in Sir Thomas Malory's version of events, there are actually *two* Ladies of the Lake, the first of whom . . ."

As the gentlemen entered into a lively debate, Father sighed and went back to his charts. Clearly, the exchange with his friends had done little to ease his mind. And I suppose I couldn't blame him. After all, I too often wondered what exactly had become of the prince following his fall from the sky. Given the strength of his armor, there was no doubt in any of our minds that he had survived, as well as no doubt that the shinobi warrior who'd fallen with him had not.

Kiyoko, I said to myself, and a wave of sadness gripped my heart. I'd only known her for a short while, and yet I missed her as if we'd been friends forever. She had saved all of us from Prince Nightshade, and although my gratitude was boundless, the guilt that came with surviving was sometimes more than I could bear.

At that moment, Nigel's voice on the talkback startled me from my thoughts. "You might want to have a look at this, sir," he said nervously.

"What is it?" Father replied.

"I don't know, but it's coming for us fast at two o'clock."

The gentlemen and I rushed out onto the balcony. The

waters were eerily still, and all the fish that had gathered around the Odditorium were gone.

"There," said Professor Bricklewick, pointing, and far off in the distance I spied what looked like the shadowy form of another conger eel snaking its way toward us. Perhaps it was a trick of the light, but the eel was actually much farther away than it appeared. Only when it kept getting bigger and bigger did we understand why.

"Great poppycock," Lord Dreary gasped. "It's enormous!"

"Yes, but what is it?" the professor asked. But before Lord Dreary could answer, the creature's massive reptilian head became visible in the searchlight—its eyes glowing yellow in the glare, its jaws smiling back at us with hundreds of copper daggers for teeth.

"Merlin's Map said nothing about a sea serpent!" Lord Dreary cried, and Father heaved a heavy sigh.

"I should have anticipated this," he said. "Even the most amateur of fortune hunters knows that magical gates are always guarded by *something*. Why should underwater gates be any different?"

"Yes, but—"

"Take heart, Lord Dreary. At least we know now for certain that the gates are nearby."

As it drew closer, the sea serpent veered sharply, and my pounding heart leaped into my throat upon seeing it from the side. The giant snake had to be at least two, perhaps even three hundred feet long, with four webbed flippers and a fronded tail that rippled behind it like a silken flag.

"It's circling us!" Nigel cried out from the talkback, and the sea serpent's head disappeared round the side of the Odditorium. Its body, however, was still visible from the balcony, and trailed behind as if it would go on forever.

Lord Dreary dragged his handkerchief across his head and said, "What was that you were saying about this being too easy, Alistair?"

Father ignored him and began flipping switches on his pipe organ. "I'm diverting all power from the Eye of Mars to the gunneries," he said into the talkback. The searchlight turned off and the water around us was green again. "We'll need to get this monster out of the way before we fire the Sky Ripper. All right, then, gunners, train your lightning cannons on its—"

Out of nowhere the sea serpent's dagger-filled jaws rose up in front of the balcony. Lord Dreary yelped with fright, and the creature bit down on the energy shield as if it meant to gobble us where we stood. The yellow window crackled and flashed—and for the briefest of moments I could see down the entire length of the monster's throat—but then the serpent let out a roar and jerked its mouth away.

"The dust bubble has shocked it," Father muttered, and

the serpent's head disappeared around the Odditorium again. Its body, however, now flush against the window, blocked our view entirely—its scales scrolling past us in a single slithering wall of green.

"Nigel, is Gwendolyn back in the flight sphere?" Father asked. "We'll need all her power to fortify the outer bubble."

"She's already there, sir," Nigel replied from the talkback. "But this slimy bugger's wrapped himself clear around the Odditorium. I can't get a clean shot at him!"

"Neither can I!" said Mrs. Pinch.

The scrolling wall of scales in front of the balcony suddenly stopped, and a low grinding sound echoed through the walls.

"The devil means to crush us!" Father cried. He furiously pressed the button for the levitation shields. The floor buzzed and the energy window flashed, but the sea serpent would not let go. "Blast it! We'll have to do this the old-fashioned way." He flicked on the talkback. "Attention, all samurai. Report to the control room at once. Cleona, get into the Sky Ripper and prepare to fire upon my command. I'm setting the proper coordinates now."

The walls creaked and groaned with the sickening sound of twisting metal. The sea serpent was tightening its grip.

"Good heavens!" cried Lord Dreary. "It's going to pop our bubble!"

"On the contrary, old friend," Father said. "The anti-gravitational properties of the fairy dust will make our bubble impervious to the serpent's pressure."

"Meaning?"

"Meaning, the fairy dust will conform to the Odditorium's shape until the outer walls are crushed or the levitation system is destroyed. Whichever comes first."

Lord Dreary and Professor Bricklewick exchanged a terrified glance, and then the whole lot of Father's samurai poured into the library behind us.

"Everyone off the balcony!" Father cried. As we scrambled out of the way, the samurai began hacking at the serpent's flank, their swords passing through the window of fairy dust as if it weren't there.

Lord Dreary cried out in protest, but Father quickly shushed him. I understood why the old man was afraid. The samurai's animus-infused swords could slice through the yellow shield because animus and fairy dust cancel each other out. At the same time, however, I also understood why our bubble wouldn't burst. The continuous stream of fairy dust through the levitation shield's expulsion vents meant that any tear made by the samurai's swords would instantly seal itself up again.

The monster roared in pain, but the samurai kept at it, the window flashing with every slice of their swords, until finally the giant serpent relaxed its grip. The entire Odditorium seemed to sigh with relief, and the serpent, its flank slashed and flayed, pulled away from us in a trail of streaming bloody ribbons.

Father commanded the samurai to fall back into the library and sat down again at his pipe organ. And as the gentlemen and I took up our positions around him, I could see no sign of the monster anywhere.

"Gunners, do you have a visual?" Father shouted into the talkback.

"The creature's below us now and slithering its way back up!" Nigel replied.

"Quickly!" Father cried. "If the serpent wraps around us from top to bottom, the samurai won't be able to get at it from the balcony. Fire at will!"

The water flickered orange for a moment, and then Mrs. Pinch's voice came over the talkback. "Something's wrong, sir. All I'm getting up here is a bunch of bubbles!"

"It was necessary to recalibrate the lightning cannons so they wouldn't tear open the levitation shield," Father replied. "What you're witnessing is a pulse of red energy surrounded by a bubble of fairy dust which, in theory, should fire like a cannonball."

"Well your theory is wrong, sir," said Mrs. Pinch. "I can't get these silly orange bubbles to go anywhere!"

Craning my neck, I gazed up through the energy shield and saw for myself what the old woman was talking about. The orange bubbles from her lightning cannons seemed incapable of traveling for more than a few yards before bursting apart completely in a shower of tiny exploding suns.

At the same time, I caught sight of the sea serpent heading upward. It was clear that Father's prediction was correct. The creature meant to wrap itself around the Odditorium in such a manner as to avoid the balcony. And as its massive head slithered up behind one of the spider legs to our left, Father shouted, "Fire, Nigel, fire!"

Nigel obliged, but almost immediately his orange bubbles burst apart just as Mrs. Pinch's had done.

"What now, Alistair?" asked Professor Bricklewick, but Father ignored him.

"Mrs. Pinch!" he screamed into the talkback. "Is the serpent close enough to the gunnery for you to get your muzzles flush with its body?"

"I can't, sir! It snapped off my starboard cannon and wedged its neck against the turret. I can't even turn round!"

Just then, the Odditorium's walls began to creak and groan—the monster was squeezing us again!

"Cleona, are you there, love?" Father shouted into the talkback.

"Where else would I be?"

"We're being attacked by a giant sea serpent."

"Yes, I gathered that from all your squawking."

"Open your porthole and tell me if you can see the creature's body. The bubble of fairy dust will prevent the water from entering your chamber."

"I'm afraid I already did that," Cleona said guiltily. "I wanted to get a look at the beast for myself but couldn't see a thing from this angle."

"Good heavens, we must be able to shake it off somehow!"

Father played some quick flourishes, causing the Odditorium to rock back and forth, but still the serpent would not let go. It was just the opposite, in fact. The monster tightened its grip on us, and underneath the endless screeching of straining metal, I heard something snap deep within the Odditorium's walls.

"You better think of something quick, sir," Nigel said over the talkback. "I don't know how much more of this the old girl can take."

"I beg your pardon!" cried Mrs. Pinch.

"I meant the Odditorium, mum," Nigel replied, and Cleona giggled.

"That banshee sounds a bit too cheery for my taste," said Professor Bricklewick, and Lord Dreary put a hand on his shoulder. For once, the old man seemed calmer than anyone.

"Chin up, Oscar," he said with a smile. "Everything's

going to be all right. Were Alistair or his son in mortal danger, that banshee would be wailing up a storm right now."

"Might I remind you that the future can be altered by even the most insignificant decisions made in the present," Father said, irritated. "Just one wrong move could—"

As if on cue Cleona started wailing—her anguished cries echoing so loudly throughout the Odditorium that the walls themselves seemed to be screaming.

"*AAAIIIEEEEEEEEEEEAAAAAAAAAAHHHHH!*"

Father shot Lord Dreary a look of *I told you so*, and the old man's face turned completely white.

"Please, Uncle!" Cleona managed to say through her cries. "Do something—*anything*—that might alter our impending doom!"

"I'm trying to think, love," Father said into the talkback. "But the serpent has wrapped itself around the Odditorium in such a manner that the samurai can't touch it. What if I sent out the wasps? They might be able to get through the bubble and—"

"*AAAIIIEEEEEEEEEEEAAAAAAAAAAHHHHH!*" Cleona replied.

"All right, then. How about we just fire the Sky Ripper and take our chances with the serpent on board?"

"*AAAIIIEEEEEEEEEEEAAAAAAAAAAHHHHH!*"

"How about the demon buggy? A magic spell, perhaps?"

"AAAIIIEEEEEEEEEEEEAAAAAAAAAAHHHHH!"

With every course of action that Father suggested Cleona's wailing only got louder and more frantic. I pressed my hands to my ears—even from down here her cries were deafening—and yet somehow, beneath it all, I could still hear the Odditorium creaking and groaning under the serpent's grip.

Finally, Father threw up his hands in exasperation and said, "Well, what shall I do then, nothing?"

Cleona's wailing instantly stopped—in fact, *everything* stopped—and once again the Odditorium breathed a sigh of relief, as if the sea monster had stopped crushing us. "So that's the plan, then?" Father asked. "Do nothing?"

"I don't know, Uncle," Cleona sniffled from the talkback. "But I *have* stopped wailing."

"The monster's released us, sir," said Mrs. Pinch. "I can turn the gunnery again. Or what's left of it."

"Well, what do you know," Nigel said. "Sir, do you see what I'm seeing?"

Gazing down through the energy shield, we could just make out the sea serpent as it sank deeper and deeper into the murky depths below—its body limp, its head streaming with blood and bands of torn flesh. Indeed, from where I stood, it appeared as if nearly half of the creature's head had been completely blown off.

"Great poppycock!" cried Lord Dreary. "What happened?"

"Could it have been Cleona's wailing that killed it?" asked Professor Bricklewick.

"Impossible," Father said. "A banshee's wailing, like the spirit who produces it, cannot travel through water."

"Then what killed that sea serpent?" Lord Dreary asked. Father shrugged, entirely stumped, and then Nigel's voice crackled over the talkback.

"Oh dear," he said. "We've got more of those baddies at two o'clock."

I gasped. Nigel was right. In the milky-green distance I could see the outlines of three giant serpents heading straight for us.

"Well, let it remain a mystery for now," Father said. He flicked some switches and began to play his organ. The Odditorium creaked and groaned a bit, but then, much to my relief, we began to move forward. "Blast it," Father muttered. "The portside damper is jammed." He flicked on the talkback. "Cleona, are you in the Sky Ripper? Are you feeling strong enough for the space jump?"

"Pshaw, it'll take more than a little wailing to wear me out."

"The steering mechanism is damaged and more monsters are approaching. We won't have time to come round for another shot should the first one miss."

"I understand, Uncle."

My heart sank with worry for my friend. Shooting the Sky Ripper really took a toll on poor Cleona. Unlike the rest of the Odditorium, which ran on the animus stored in the power reserves, the Sky Ripper drew its power directly from her spirit body. And thus, given how drained she was after our space jump from London, I couldn't imagine Cleona would have enough energy left for a second one even if we weren't being chased by a load of sea serpents.

"Very well, then, Cleona," Father said into the talkback. "Stand by to fire the Sky Ripper upon my command."

"They're getting closer, sir," Mrs. Pinch replied instead.

"I can see that, thank you very much." Father turned on the searchlight, and once again the water came alive in shimmering sheets of luminous orange. Thankfully, the three sea serpents were farther away than they first appeared. However, there was no sign of the Gates of Avalon anywhere.

"But how can you be certain you'll fire the Sky Ripper at the proper location?" asked Lord Dreary. "All I can see out there are more sea serpents!"

"I'm afraid we'll have to rely on Merlin's compass to see us through."

The serpents were closer now, their teeth clearly visible in the searchlight, but Father kept his eyes fixed constantly on the magical compass. At the same time he picked up his tune a bit, changing our course ever so slightly so that the Odditorium began heading straight for the approaching monsters.

"I hope you know what you're doing, Alistair," Lord Dreary said weakly.

"According to my calculations, we should reach the Gates of Avalon before the monsters do. If I'm wrong, then they'll block our path and we won't be able to get through."

"That is, if the gates are still there," the professor mumbled.

"Stand by, Cleona," Father said into the talkback, his eyes never leaving his compass. "Get ready to fire the Sky Ripper in five . . . four . . . three . . . two . . . *NOW!*"

A thick bolt of blue lightning shot out from the Odditorium directly above our heads. It traveled only a short distance, obscuring our view of the sea serpents, and then burst apart in the form of two colossal iron gates, the bars of which flashed and sparkled as if painted with billions of twinkling stars.

"The Gates of Avalon!" cried Lord Dreary. "You found them, Alistair!"

"Excellent shot, Cleona!" Father said. "Now get back into your charging bed. Who knows how the space jump will affect the animus reserves this time."

Professor Bricklewick steadied himself on the pipe organ. "They're even more magnificent than I imagined," he said, his voice tight with emotion.

Father pulled a lever and sped up his playing, but as we

drew closer, the Gates of Avalon suddenly vanished before our eyes, leaving only the sea serpents closing the distance ahead of us.

"Great poppycock!" cried Lord Dreary. "The gates are gone!"

"Not gone, but open," Father said. "A temporary rip in the fabric between our two worlds that is invisible to the naked eye."

"But the monsters are approaching the gates from the other side. Won't they—"

"If my theory is correct, the Gates of Avalon, like any other interdimensional portal, only open one way. Thus, we should be able to pass through from our side without the monsters following us from theirs. Not to mention that, once we're through, the portal shall immediately close behind us as it did in London."

"And if your theory is wrong, as with your bubbly lightning cannons?"

Father smiled fondly at his friend. "Then let's just say I'm sorry we never got to finish that game of chess."

Lord Dreary gulped and tugged at his collar, and as Father played on, my ears began to pound with fright. The sea serpents were coming quickly—their bulging eyes like fiery lanterns as Alistair Grim kept us on a course straight for them.

"Almost there," he muttered, his gaze locked again on

Merlin's compass, and I watched in horror as the largest of the three serpents wound its way in front of the others. Its jaws were twice the size of the monster that had attacked us earlier.

"Shall I try to lay down some strafing fire just in case, sir?" Nigel asked from the talkback, but Father ignored him.

"Almost there," he muttered again. The lead serpent was only about thirty yards away from us now—just beyond where I'd last seen the gates, I thought. But then again, as there was nothing but open water from which to get my bearings, I couldn't be sure.

"Hang on, everybody," Father said. "Here we *gooooo!*"

The gentlemen and I steadied ourselves where we stood as the sea serpent, nearly upon us, opened its mouth wide—a mouth so enormous that it appeared capable of swallowing the Odditorium whole. I winced, bracing myself for the creature's bite, but then its mouth, along with the rest of it, simply . . . *dissolved* before our eyes. There was no sign of the other sea serpents either—only the water, crystal clear and bright, and what looked like the ruins of an ancient city on the ocean floor beneath us.

"What happened?" Lord Dreary asked. "Did we make the space jump?"

Puzzled, Father yanked the old man's pocket watch out from his waistcoat and checked the time. I understood why.

Our first space jump knocked us out for five hours. It knocked out all our power reserves too. But from the looks of things back in the library, all of the Odditorium's mechanical functions appeared to be working properly.

"No loss of time," Father said. He returned Lord Dreary's pocket watch to his waistcoat and checked in with the others over the talkback. When everyone, including Gwendolyn, replied that they were all right, he ordered the samurai back to their posts and began playing his organ. The Odditorium spun in place, and a section of an incredibly wide carved stone column passed before our eyes.

"Is that what I think it is?" muttered Professor Bricklewick. As the Odditorium continued to turn round, farther off I saw another column—the bottom of which looked like a foot, and the top, at least what I could see of it, like a knee.

"Great poppycock!" Lord Dreary gasped. "We seemed to have passed through a giant pair of underwater legs!"

"The Gates of Avalon," said Professor Bricklewick. Father pressed some buttons, and immediately the water outside the balcony became a wall of frothy bubbles—the vertical thrusters again, I knew. Father was taking the Odditorium upward.

"So we're in Avalon, then?" Lord Dreary asked.

"We're definitely somewhere," Father said. "But I needn't tell you how surprised I am that it took so little effort."

"If you call nearly being crushed to death by gigantic sea serpents *little effort*," said Professor Bricklewick, and Father raised his hand in forfeit.

"Point taken, old friend. However, compared to our last space jump, you'll need to trust me when I say this time we got off light."

I had to agree with Father. I'd take a bit of damage to the Odditorium over an animus drain any day, for surely the wasps could fix us up in no time.

The Odditorium continued to rise higher and higher until finally it burst up through the surface with a loud *whoosh!* In an instant everything became nearly white with sunlight, the dust bubble a solid wall of glare, but once the Odditorium was well above the water, Father turned off the bubble and our vision cleared.

What we saw made us gasp.

There before the balcony was a giant stone eye. Father immediately backed the Odditorium away from it, whereupon we discovered that the eye belonged to a colossal statue of a warrior that appeared to be standing waist-deep in the middle of the ocean. One hand held a spear, while the other was raised as if to say, *Halt!*

"The Guardian of the Gates," Father said, and spun us away from the statue.

In the distance, across a calm blue sea, we spied a harbor

bordered on one side by a rocky coastline, and on the other by a massive breakwater. Countless flights of stone stairs rose up from it in every direction, leading to a sprawling, shining city of domes and columns and towers. Many of the buildings were adorned with colorful banners, while others were obscured almost entirely by lush hanging gardens and flowering trees. Farther still, in the forest-covered distance beyond the city, stood a gleaming, gold-domed castle on a hill.

"Ladies and gentlemen," Father said, "I give you the Isle of Avalon."

We stood there in stunned silence, and I couldn't help noticing Professor Bricklewick as he wiped a tear from beneath his spectacles. How he must have felt seeing for the first time the city of his dreams. Even for me, who by now was no stranger to such things, this odd Aquaticum of Alistair Grim's was almost beyond belief. And yet here we were, arriving safe in Avalon.

Little did we know that *someone else* had arrived along with us.

—TWELVE—

A Watch of a Different Color

As we began our approach toward the harbor, Nigel and Mrs. Pinch joined us on the balcony. Cleona, exhausted from firing the Sky Ripper, had fallen asleep in her quarters, while Gwendolyn, who insisted that she wasn't tired at all, took time out from the flight sphere for a chocolate break in the engine room. All of the Odditorium's energy systems were functioning normally, and other than the smashed upper cannon and the jammed steering damper, the damage we sustained as a result of our battle with the sea serpent appeared to be minimal.

We'd barely traveled fifty yards before an alarum bell began tolling in the distance, followed by shouts and the outbreak of a commotion in the harbor ahead. The Avalonians, alerted to our presence, were no doubt preparing to greet us. But *how* they would greet us . . . Well, that was the question, now, wasn't it?

"Are you sure this is wise, Alistair?" asked Lord Dreary. The old man had been insisting that we follow "proper etiquette" by sending an "emissary" in the demon buggy bearing gifts for the queen. Father and Professor Bricklewick, on the other hand, thought it best that we fly directly for the castle itself.

"If we're to succeed on this quest," the professor said, "we cannot risk even the slightest appearance of deception. Queen Nimue may already know why we've come. After all, not only is she over a thousand years old, but also it is said she possesses the gift of prophecy—and by some accounts, is nothing short of a goddess."

"A *fairy* goddess," said Lord Dreary. "Indeed, some legends have it that the Avalonians themselves are an entire race of fairies. And like most fairies, they have little regard for humans."

"Your counsel is much appreciated, old friend," Father said. "Which is why I think we should protect ourselves with our own fairy just in case." He flicked on the talkback. "Gwendolyn, are you there?"

"What is it, Pookie?" the Yellow Fairy replied, and she let out a long coo. Clearly, the chocolate had done its work.

"Would you care to join us on the balcony?"

"But what about this big blue banshee in the bubble before

me?" Gwendolyn asked, and then she gasped dramatically. "My, my, my, that was a lot of *b*'s." She cooed and began flapping her lips with her finger. *"Buh-duh-buh-duh-buh-duh-buh-duh . . ."*

Father rolled his eyes. I myself was quite fond of Gwendolyn after she had her chocolate, but sometimes I'd swear Father preferred her when she was quarrelsome.

"The Gallownog will be just fine," he said. "We've more than enough dust in the reserves to keep everything going for quite some time. Now please, Gwendolyn, your presence up here is required immediately."

"Whatever you say, Pookie," she said, and Father flicked off the talkback.

"You're certain you don't want Mrs. Pinch and me to return to the gunneries, sir?" Nigel asked. "I should think they'd work just fine now that we're above water. What's left of them anyway."

"We don't want to appear aggressive," Father replied. "However, having Gwendolyn close at hand would not be a bad idea in the event we need to—how shall I put it?—*lighten things up.*"

Mrs. Pinch uttered a "Humph," but I understood Father's strategy. Should we need to defend ourselves, a ball of yellow fairy dust would be much less harmful to an attacker than a blast from the lightning cannons.

"Well, it's a good thing we've got that colossus back there to show us the gates," said Mrs. Pinch. "That compass of yours is pointing us in the wrong direction."

Indeed, the needle on Merlin's compass was blinking again and pointing straight ahead.

"Remarkable," said Professor Bricklewick. "The compass must be working in reverse. It's pointing to another gateway altogether—one of the queen's shortcuts, perhaps—that's above water."

"Which means, in order to get back, we needn't travel underwater again?" asked Lord Dreary.

"At least not here in Avalon," Father said. "But we will most certainly end up underwater once we pass through into our world. Oscar, if you wouldn't mind hiding the compass in the map again, we should probably keep it a secret from our hosts for now."

The professor snatched the compass out of the air and hurried over to Father's desk. He uttered a magic spell, and in a flash the compass sank back down into the map and disappeared.

Presently, we heard what sounded like a flock of hawks screeching in the distance. "Good heavens!" cried Lord Dreary, pointing, and there in the sky above the city appeared a dozen or so dragons flying straight for us.

Of course, my only experience with dragons had been the half-human Red Dragons that had tried to kill me at Prince

Nightshade's, but I nonetheless knew what I was looking at. *These* dragons, however, appeared to be much bigger than the prince's gang, with long, slender necks and gigantic bat wings. And on each of their backs rode a single armor-clad knight.

"The Royal Guard, no doubt," said Professor Bricklewick.

The knights were upon us in an instant, their plated silver armor flashing like mirrors in the sunlight. As they began to circle the Odditorium, Father stopped his organ playing and let us drift toward the harbor. I suppose, being fairies and all, I'd expected the Avalonians to be small like Gwendolyn, but these blokes looked no different than us humans.

"Oh, look at the pretty dragons!" Gwendolyn said as she joined us on the balcony. Her eyelids were heavy, and her face was smeared with chocolate. "Hallo, hallo there, dragons!" She perched herself on my shoulder and began to coo.

"Hold tight, Gwendolyn," Father said. "We may need your assistance should the Royal Guard attack."

Gwendolyn snickered and tossed a ball of fairy dust playfully in her hand.

"We have you surrounded!" someone shouted, and a knight with a foxtail plume on his helmet reined his dragon to a stop before the balcony. His helmet hid his face, but his steel-gray eyes glared out menacingly from the slot in his visor. "Follow me directly or we shall destroy you," he said, and as if to prove it, his dragon arched back its head and spit a long stream of fire up into the air.

"We seek an audience with the queen," Father shouted back.

"She knows why you're here, Alistair Grim," Fox Tail said, and he promptly swung his dragon away and pulled out far ahead of us. The other knights swooped in behind him to form a V at our flanks, and Father began to follow them—his organ music jumbled and uneven as he tried to compensate for the jammed steering damper.

"Then the legends are true," said Professor Bricklewick. "Queen Nimue possesses the gift of prophecy—a gift bestowed upon her by Merlin himself."

Lord Dreary nodded. "And yet, even though Merlin could predict the future, he often could do nothing about it because he forgot his visions. Just think, Alistair, Queen Nimue may have foreseen our coming to Avalon long before we were even born."

"And fortunately for us, she didn't forget about it," Father said, and with his eyes fixed straight ahead he began to play faster. The damaged steering damper caused the Odditorium to wobble and sputter, but Father managed to keep pace with our dragon escort. We passed over the harbor and were flying above the city when I noticed things had grown quiet below. Gazing down from the balcony, I discovered that the Avalonians had gathered in the streets and upon the rooftops to have a look at us—their upturned faces just smudges of white amidst a sea of brightly colored clothes.

Soon the city gave way to a thick swath of ancient forest. At the far edge rose a high hill, on top of which the gold-domed castle stood at the center of a rambling complex of walls and battlements. Beyond that lay great patches of farm-land and gently sloping valleys, and then more forest stretched out to the horizon.

"Begging your pardon, sir," said Mrs. Pinch. "But what shall we do if any of these knights force their way inside?"

Father's face was like stone, his mind racing, I could tell. Should it come down to defending the Odditorium, I felt quite confident that we could hold our own against these Avalonians. In addition to all of the Odditorium's shields and weapons and whatnot, we had the samurai, the wasps, Gwendolyn and Cleona, and of course Broom, who could certainly pack a wallop—not to mention Mack, and my new friend Moral the goose.

"Mrs. Pinch is right, sir," Nigel said. "Should any of these blokes go snooping about, who knows what dangers they might find."

"Let's just hope, for their sake, it won't come to that." Father flicked on the talkback. "Attention, all samurai," he said, his voice echoing about the Odditorium. "Guard all entrances and remain on full alert."

And with that, a handful of samurai immediately took up their positions on the balcony behind us.

"Are you sure this is wise, Alistair?" asked Professor Bricklewick. "If Queen Nimue thinks we're hiding something, she'll be less apt to trust us with Excalibur."

"I'm afraid she's already made up her mind about that," Father said.

"What do you mean?" asked Lord Dreary.

"Clearly Nimue possesses the gift of prophecy, which means she'll already know whether or not we are destined to wield Excalibur. Hence, nothing we can say will sway her decision. As for defeating Prince Nightshade . . . well, wouldn't that be something if she'd tell us how it all turns out in the end?"

The professor and Lord Dreary looked at one another apprehensively, and as we flew on toward the castle, my mind began to spin with thoughts of what lay in store for us beyond its walls. Did Queen Nimue already know about Prince Nightshade? Would she welcome us as friends and help us stop him? Or would she deny us Excalibur and send us back to our world empty-handed—or worse, would she ever let us go from this one?

As we reached the far edge of the forest, Fox Tail and the

rest of the knights swooped down toward a vast, open field peppered with colorful tents. A celebration was taking place just outside the castle walls. Jugglers, tumblers, and other entertainers wove their way among throngs of revelers, all of whom wore brightly colored scarves. Mounted knights with lances pranced about on jousting lists, while more knights stood at attention in front of a long dais festooned with banners and flowers. On top of the dais sat a half dozen or so fair-haired ladies, one of whom was hidden by a silken canopy. I could not see her head, but I was certain it bore a crown.

I gasped. "Queen Nimue." I stole a glance at Professor Bricklewick. His face was frozen in amazement.

"Alistair, you don't think—" he began, but Father cut him off.

"Yes, I do, old friend. It appears all that merrymaking down there is for *us*."

The revelers cleared a wide circle in the middle of the field, and Fox Tail and his dragon-riding knights landed in a ring around its edges. Father extended the Odditorium's spider legs and touched down in the center of the circle. The crowd erupted with cheers and applause. Heralds blasted trumpets, and the knights trotted their dragons and horses into position across from one another, forming a narrow lane that led to the dais steps.

"We really shouldn't meet a queen without giving her a

gift," said Lord Dreary. "I think that'd be considered rude in *any* dimension."

"I agree with you," Father said. "But what shall we give her?"

Without thinking I said, "How about Moral's egg? I've got it here in my pocket."

"Well done, lad," Father said with a smile. "And an honorable deed, at that."

As I reached to fetch the egg, Mack began rumbling in my waistcoat. I'd completely forgotten he was there.

"What time is it?" Mack cried as I opened him.

"A *bad* time," I whispered, and was about to tap him on his XII when everything outside fell silent. The crowd dropped to their knees, the dragons and the horses bowed, and the ladies on the dais rose to their feet—all except the woman under the canopy. She was seated on a throne of some sort, but her face was hidden in shadow.

"What the—?" Mack said, whirling in my hand. "Where have we gone to now?"

Before any of us could answer, the woman on the throne called out, "Bring me the time stopper!"

A pair of attendants pulled back the canopy to reveal a beautiful fair-skinned woman with a thick golden scarf about her neck. Her chestnut hair, which fell in long ringlets to her waist, was laced with golden ribbons, and upon her head she wore a golden crown. My suspicions had been correct. It was Queen Nimue.

"With all due respect, Your Majesty—" Father said, but the queen raised her hand to silence him.

"You needn't worry about the doom dogs," she said. "Avalon exists in a realm beyond their reach. They pose no threat to us here."

Queen Nimue waved her hand and a section of the balustrade vanished. At the same time, a glowing white staircase materialized out of thin air and stretched down from the balcony to the ground below.

"Now bring me the time stopper, please," the queen said again.

Father took a deep breath and held out his hand for Mack. "I better handle this," he said, and I passed him the watch. "Follow my lead, everyone."

Father mounted the staircase, and as the rest of us descended one by one behind him, I began to wonder whether or not we'd stand a chance against these Avalonians after all. Evidently, Queen Nimue was a sorceress of great power.

Fox Tail met us at the bottom of the stairs and removed his helmet, revealing a handsome, chiseled face and a scarf like the others wore. Gwendolyn, who was still on my shoulder, batted her eyelashes and cooed at him playfully, but the knight ignored her and led us up onto the dais. My throat was parched and the blood pounded in my ears—not only because of what was happening, but also because, despite the queen's assurances, I kept expecting the doom dogs to appear at any moment.

"Your Majesty, allow me to present Alistair Grim and company," said Fox Tail, kneeling, and the rest of us followed suit.

"Thank you, Captain," said Queen Nimue. "Please rise. All of you. For surely our guests of honor mustn't spend their time in Avalon upon their knees."

As we rose to our feet, the Avalonians in the field behind us rose too. Captain Fox Tail joined his mates in the crowd, and the ladies on the dais sat down. Each one of them was lovelier than the next, and, like the queen, they all wore gold ribbons in their hair and golden scarves about their necks.

"Your Grace," Lord Dreary said with a bow. "Allow me to introduce—"

"I know who you are, Harold Dreary, as I do your companions." The queen called the rest of us by our full names too—Oscar Bricklewick, Penelope Pinch, Gwendolyn the Yellow Fairy, and, much to my surprise, *William* instead of Nigel Stout—and by the time she got to me, I felt as if I could barely breathe under the power of her all-knowing gaze. "And yet," she said, glancing around, "unless I am mistaken, it appears that one of your party is missing. The banshee called"—Queen Nimue began snapping her fingers, trying to remember—"oh, what's her name again . . . ?"

Father stiffened and shot a nervous glance at Professor Bricklewick.

"You needn't worry, Alistair Grim," said Queen Nimue. "My subjects and I have no intention of boarding that big black ship of yours in search of her. I ask merely out of curiosity. However, if you wish not to tell me, I shall respect your desire for secrecy."

"You must excuse her absence, Your Grace," Father said. "Cleona is still recovering from our journey."

"Cleona, that's it!" said the queen, tapping her forehead. "Is she ill?"

"Why no, Your Grace. You see, it is Cleona who provides the Odditorium with its power for interdimensional travel. I call this power animus, and the means by which I harness Cleona's exhausts her so completely that she must sleep to regain her strength."

"Impressive, Alistair Grim. Your powers of sorcery are greater than I imagined."

"As are your powers of prophecy, Your Grace. And so I hope you shall pardon me for assuming that you already know why we're here?"

The queen nodded. "All that Nightshade business, yes.

But first things first. May I have a look at the time stopper, please?"

Father handed her McClintock. Queen Nimue studied him closely for a moment, then smiled and wiggled his case. "Poor Dougal. How strange after all these years to see you shine so blue. And yet I must say the color suits you."

"Pardon me, Your Grace," Mack said, "but have we met before?"

"A long, long time ago, when the world was young, and the smiths of Avalon forged swords for kings and watches for wizards."

"Watches for wizards?"

"Many years ago I commissioned you as a gift for the wizard Merlin in exchange for his tutelage in sorcery. You were just an ordinary pocket watch back then—the first of your kind, as far as I can tell—until Merlin gave you the power to stop time."

Professor Bricklewick gasped, and Nigel and I looked at each other in amazement.

"However," the queen went on, "as Merlin was in love with me, he attempted to use his time stopper for—how shall I put it?—less-than-honorable purposes. As payback, I imprisoned him in a tree and secreted you away to Scotland, where I entrusted your care to the clan McClintock. And so they kept you hidden for centuries until, somehow, you wound up in the hands of Alistair Grim."

"I beg your pardon, Your Majesty," said the professor, "but nowhere in my scholarly research have I ever read anything about a pocket watch for Merlin."

"Then I am pleased to learn the McClintocks kept their secret well."

The professor made to reply, but then, seeing the sense of it, shut his trap again.

"But how can this be, Your Majesty?" Mack asked. "I have no memory of anything 'cept me old master's clock shop. And even that has gone a bit hazy."

"With the blessing of time comes the curse of forgetting," the queen said, and swiveled her eyes to Father. "This blue light is your doing?" Father looked confused. "Forgive me, Alistair Grim. Since my gift of prophecy was bestowed upon me by Merlin himself, there are details of your coming here that I have forgotten, or perhaps never knew in the first place. So do tell, was it you who gave McClintock his blue light?"

Father bowed his head slightly. "Yes, Your Grace. McClintock was damaged during my battle with the witch Mad Malmuirie, who stole him from the old clockmaker and destroyed his clan in Scotland. I tried to repair him with the animus, but could never get his time stopper working again."

The queen narrowed her eyes and leaned forward. "This . . . *witch*—Mad Malmuirie, you call her—is she still alive?"

"Very much so, I'm afraid," Father said. "A bit of a recluse, from what I gather, who, fortunately for us, has no interest in joining with Prince Nightshade."

The ladies on the dais exchanged a knowing glance, and then Queen Nimue removed a long pin from her hair and touched it to Mack's XII. "This might sting a bit," she said, and then Mack flashed and began to howl in pain. Impulsively, I rushed forward to protect him, but Nigel grabbed me by the arms and held me back.

"Please, don't hurt him!" I cried. Queen Nimue smiled and turned Mack to face me. He began to shake and talk in gibberish, and then beams of brilliant red light shot out from his Roman numerals. Blinded, I turned away, and in the next moment the light faded and Mack was quiet.

"What the—? What happened?" he said after a long silence. Queen Nimue handed him back to Father. His eyes were no longer blue, but glowed as red as those of the lion's head inside the Odditorium.

"Dougal McClintock has been restored to his former self," she said. "However, I must caution you, Alistair Grim. As Avalon exists in a dimension outside your own, the time stopper will not work here. On the other hand, should you someday choose to use him in your world, take care to use him wisely."

"Ach!" Mack cried. "You mean . . . ?"

"Yes, old friend," said the queen, but she never took her eyes off Father. "Your time stopper is repaired, and thus no longer shall you require Alistair Grim's animus to keep ticking."

Father held the queen's gaze, wherein something seemed to pass between them, while Mack, barely able to contain his excitement, sputtered and flashed with his new red light. "Oh, thank you, Your Majesty! How can I ever repay you?"

"The fulfillment of your destiny is payment enough," the queen said. I wasn't quite sure what she meant by that, but as we were now on the subject of payment, I remembered the queen's gift.

"The egg, sir," I whispered, tugging on Father's coat.

"Ah, yes," he muttered. "I beg your pardon, Your Majesty, but on behalf of all of us, my son here wishes to present you with a small token of our friendship."

Father gently pushed me forward, and I slipped Moral's egg from my pocket and held it out for the queen.

"Your gesture is much appreciated," she said. "But I cannot accept your gift. As it regards your destiny, this golden egg must serve another purpose. What that purpose is, I cannot say."

"The prophecy?" Father asked, and the queen nodded. "Then, if I may be so bold, does this prophecy tell whether or not we shall have Excalibur?"

"Once again, I cannot say."

"Forgive me, Your Majesty, but do you mean cannot or *will* not?"

"The decision is not mine to make, Alistair Grim. For you see, just as our two worlds have crossed paths, so too have we come to a crossroads in time. The outcome of your quest remains unclear, and so, like the gears of your pocket watch, your destiny depends on a delicate balance of everything working together in your favor."

"I see," Father said. "Well, then, if it is not your decision to lend us Excalibur, would you think me bold for asking whose it is?"

"Why, yours, of course."

"I'm afraid I don't understand."

"You will shortly," said the queen. "But until such time, allow me to play the humble host; join us in our castle. We have arranged a banquet in your honor."

Lord Dreary stepped forward and bowed. "The honor is indeed all ours, Your Majesty." The queen nodded, and one of

the ladies seated beside her smiled at Professor Bricklewick—
who began to blush.

"We are most grateful, Your Majesty," Father said. "However, there are matters inside the Odditorium that require our
immediate attention. We sustained significant damage during our journey, and Gwendolyn needs to recharge our flight
systems."

Gwendolyn let out a moan and shook her head. Her eyes
had returned to normal—a clear sign that the chocolate was
wearing off.

"I'm afraid I've come down with a bit of a headache," she
said. "You girls wouldn't happen to have any chocolate at this
banquet, would you?"

"I should think you've had enough," hissed Mrs. Pinch,
and she turned to the queen. "I beg your pardon, Your Grace,
but I've got just the thing for this one in my kitchen."

"Very well, then," said Queen Nimue. "I will send an
envoy to fetch you at six o'clock. Will that give you enough
time to tend to your affairs?"

"You are most generous, Your Grace," said Lord Dreary,
bowing again, and the rest of us followed suit.

"And yet," said the queen to herself, "I feel as if I'm forgetting something."

Queen Nimue racked her brain for a moment, and then,
with a smile, shrugged and rose from her throne. The ladies

rose from theirs, and with a flourish of trumpets the entire royal procession paraded their way through the crowd and disappeared behind a large gate in the castle walls. The Royal Guard and their dragons encircled the Odditorium to keep everyone at bay, and as the festivities resumed around us, we climbed back up onto the balcony. The glowing white staircase vanished and the balustrade became solid again.

Father passed me Mack and then scurried up one of the library ladders, where he began searching the bookshelves. "All right, listen up, everyone. Nigel, you get down to the engine room and set the wasps to work on that steering damper. See if you can't do something about the upper gunnery too. Mrs. Pinch, you take care of Gwendolyn's headache and get her back into the flight sphere as soon as possible. Chop-chop, all of you, we've no time to waste."

As Nigel and Mrs. Pinch hurried out with Gwendolyn, Father snatched a large leather-bound book from the shelf and slid with it down the ladder.

"What the devil are you up to, Alistair?" asked Lord Dreary, but Father ignored him and dashed over to his desk.

"Look here, Oscar," he said. "See if you can't find something in this book that might guard us against the Lady of the Lake's magic. Merlin got out of that tree somehow. Perhaps there's a clue in here as to how he broke her spell."

Professor Bricklewick took the book. It was old and

tattered, but the title on its cover was clear. *Protective Charms for the Necromancer.*

"But why this sudden paranoia?" the professor asked. "Queen Nimue has been exceedingly gracious since our arrival. She even fixed your pocket watch."

"Aye, sir, that she did," Mack said happily, and spun his hands to the proper time.

"That's precisely my point," Father said, and he reached for his notebook and began to sketch. "Given all the trouble that Merlin caused her, do you really think Nimue would trust complete strangers with a time stopper? I'm afraid the Avalonians are indeed a race of fairies after all. And as Lord Dreary so aptly pointed out, fairies have little regard for humans."

"But they don't look like fairies to me, sir," I said.

"Given your recent encounters with Prince Nightshade's second-in-command, I should think you, of all people, would remember that there are different kinds of fairies."

I shivered. Of course I hadn't forgotten that the winged demon known as the Black Fairy was just that, a fairy, but it never occurred to me that there might be other kinds of fairies too—as in, ones *without* wings.

"I'm afraid I'm with the boy on this one," said Lord Dreary. "To be sure, I didn't see a pair of wings among them."

"Of course not, because the Avalonians are *water* fairies, amphibious by nature, and thus capable of breathing both on land and under the sea. After all, why else would they wear such ornate scarves if not to hide their *gills*?"

Father showed us the page on which he'd been sketching. It was a perfect rendering of Queen Nimue in profile, but instead of a golden scarf around her neck, below her ear he'd drawn three cascading curves to represent her gills.

"Good heavens," Lord Dreary said weakly, and he fingered his collar.

"And despite her cryptic comments about the future," Father said, "I believe our Lady of the Lake has no intention of giving us Excalibur—at least not without making us fight for it."

"What do you mean?" asked Professor Bricklewick.

"All that hullabaloo out there is no mere welcome celebration, but the opening festivities of a tournament."

"A tournament?"

"Yes, Oscar. The armored knights with their lances, the jousting lists, the makeshift blacksmith forges, all of it indicating a medieval tournament of some sort—one in which I suspect our champion, whoever that may be, shall fight the queen's."

"Why of course," said Professor Bricklewick, his eyes

wide. "What the queen said about the decision being yours—whether or not you shall wield Excalibur depends on *your decision*—as in a decision awarded you by means of battle!"

"Very good, old friend." Father took out the Black Mirror from the case upon his desk and, gazing into it, said, "Show me our champion." But nothing happened. Father heaved a frustrated sigh and slipped the mirror into his inside coat pocket.

"There, you see, Alistair?" said Lord Dreary. "It's quite possible you are mistaken about this tournament after all."

"Perhaps," Father said. "However, since the Black Mirror can only play back the last reflection of someone who has gazed into it, I submit there's an even stronger possibility that our champion has never done so."

"Great poppycock, what do you intend to do?"

"Take heart, Lord Dreary. Champion or not, I have no intention of giving the queen her tournament, nor do I plan on leaving Avalon without Excalibur."

"But we've seen her magic firsthand," said Professor Bricklewick. "Magic so powerful that even the sorcerer Merlin was no match for her. How then can you expect to leave without her consent?"

"Merlin, as you'll recall, was blinded by love. We are not. You just worry about finding a protective charm in that book and leave the rest to me."

"And should the professor's search come up empty?" asked Lord Dreary. "What shall we do then?"

"I suspect there's someone else on board who might be able to help us," Father said. "Someone who is quite good at battling fairies, and of whose presence, I'll wager, the queen is entirely unaware."

"Who?" we all asked.

"The Gallownog," Father replied, and he dashed from the library.

— T H I R T E E N —

An Unlikely Ally

n intriguing turn of events," said Lorcan Dalach, and he stepped closer to the glass.

Lord Dreary, Mack, and I had accompanied Father down to the engine room, where he'd just finished explaining to the Gallownog our present situation, including the particulars of our journey to Avalon and our quest for Excalibur. Dalach had listened intently, his hazy green form barely visible amidst the sparkling yellow walls of his prison sphere. But now, as his face became clear, I could see in his eyes that Father's words had done little to break the ice between them.

"Looks like you've gotten yourself into quite a pickle," Dalach sneered.

"I'm afraid we're all pickles in the same jar," Father said. "Even if you managed to escape the Odditorium, there is no way you could ever get back to our world without my help. The kingdom of Avalon is on an island in another dimension—a dimension inaccessible to even the doom dogs."

"You're lying."

"Who ya callin' a liar, neep?" Mack said, his eyes flashing red. He hopped out of my hands and onto my shoulder. "I suggest ya take that back, or you'll find out what it means to brawl with the Clan McClintock!"

I snatched Mack from my shoulder. "Sorry, old friend, but now's not the time for picking fights." I tapped Mack on his XII, but instead of going dark, he just laughed.

"I'm afraid you'll have to do better than that, laddie!" he said. "No more fizzling out for this old ticker!"

"As you can see," Father said, "Queen Nimue has restored Mack to his former self. He no longer requires the animus to work—animus that the doom dogs most certainly would've picked up on had they been able to travel into Avalon from Tir Na Mairg. And so it stands to reason that, if not even the doom dogs can get in, not even you can get out."

Lorcan Dalach pondered this a moment. "So what do you want from me?" he asked, eyes narrowing.

"A truce and temporary alliance. Help us get Excalibur and defeat Prince Nightshade, and I'll let you out of this sphere."

"Alistair!" Lord Dreary gasped, but Father held up his hand to silence him.

Dalach snickered. "You must be joking, Grim."

"I assure you I'm not. For you see, although Queen Nimue knows much about our journey to Avalon, there are still some particulars that remain unclear to her. I am convinced that she is unaware of, or at the very least has forgotten, your presence. Therefore, should one of us have to fight her champion, we could use an ally like you—someone who is used to battling fairies and can make himself invisible."

The Gallownog fixed his eyes into Father's.

"Cleona has spoken admirably of you over the years," Father went on. "Many times has she told me stories of how you protected your clan from fairies and other supernatural threats. And thus, despite your present charge to capture her, I know that deep in her heart Cleona still admires you very much—if you take my meaning."

Father held the Gallownog's gaze until finally Lorcan Dalach looked away.

"Suppose I agree to help you," he said. "Suppose you somehow manage to obtain Excalibur and make it back to the gates. . . . How do you plan to escape the queen's magic?"

"I've got Professor Bricklewick working on that as we speak. There appears to be at least one other gateway too—a shortcut into a lake that the queen used in her dealings with King Arthur. If my suspicions are correct, we won't need the Sky Ripper to pass through it."

The Gallownog grew silent again, his mind racing.

"I hope you're not thinking of navigating this shortcut yourself," Father said. "You would disintegrate as soon as you hit the water."

"I'm well aware of that," Dalach said. "But you underestimate your enemy. Since the death of King Arthur, the Lady of the Lake has shown little interest in the matters of humans. However, should you cross her by stealing Excalibur, you'll have a war on your hands that'll make your beef with Prince Nightshade look like a game of tiddlywinks."

"Let me worry about that," Father said. "Give me your word that you'll help us, and once we defeat the prince, we can take up the fight for Cleona again as you see fit."

"Alistair, I must protest," said Lord Dreary. "Surely you're not going to trust this scoundrel at his word and set him free?"

Instinctively I glanced up at the gauge above the flight sphere. It read less than one-quarter full, which meant that Gwendolyn would need to get spinning again very soon or the field of fairy dust that kept Lorcan Dalach imprisoned would disappear and he'd be free anyway.

"The word of a Gallownog is sacred, Lord Dreary," Father said. "So what do you say, then, Dalach? Do we have a deal?"

The Gallownog was silent for a long time. "You have my word," he said finally. "You could have destroyed me but chose not to, and for that I am in your debt. However, Cleona is another matter. And just as I am bound to you by my word, so too am I bound to the Council of Elders to bring her back for judgment. So take heed, Alistair Grim. Should you defeat Prince Nightshade, you'll find my loyalty lies elsewhere."

"I understand," Father said. He turned a valve on a nearby pipe and the shield of fairy dust surrounding the sphere fizzled out. Lord Dreary gasped, but my throat felt too tight to breathe. A tense silence hung about the room as Lorcan Dalach looked us over warily, and then he picked up his spirit shackles and stepped through the glass of his prison as if it weren't there.

"Look out!" someone shouted, and we whirled around to find Gwendolyn flying down the stairs that led to the servants' hallway. She was on her way back from getting her headache cured by Mrs. Pinch, I gathered. But before Father had a chance to tell her about our truce, she hurled a ball of fairy dust straight for the Gallownog.

"Gwendolyn, no!" Father cried, but Dalach was ready for her, and as quick as lightning whipped the dust ball into a shower of sparkles with his shackles.

Gwendolyn growled and instantly transformed into her chomping shape—a massive yellow ball with razor-sharp teeth. She flew across the room, her mouth opening wide to gobble up the Gallownog, when at the last moment I jumped in between them and cried, "Don't!"

The Yellow Fairy screeched to a halt in midair with her teeth just inches from my face. "Out of my way, Grubb!" she roared. "There's only one thing left for him, and that's a good chomp, chomp!"

"Gwendolyn, you don't understand," Father said. "The Gallownog is on our side now. He's going to help us on our quest for Excalibur."

Lorcan Dalach draped his spirit shackles about his neck and bowed his head submissively. Gwendolyn just hovered there, trembling for a moment, and then in a burst of sparkles she became her tiny, dragonfly-winged self again.

"Have you gone mad?" she said to Father. "I'd rather have that demon of yours roaming about than this swine."

"I'll explain my reasoning to you later. In the meantime"— he pointed to the dust gauge—"you better get spinning again or we won't have enough power should we need to make a hasty retreat."

Gwendolyn folded her arms and floated so close to the Gallownog that their noses almost touched. "You might have fooled the others, but I'm warning you, prig: I've got my eye on you."

Dalach stared back at her coldly, and then Gwendolyn flew up into the flight sphere and started spinning—her light brightening and expanding until the needle on the dust gauge began to move.

"I'd like to speak to Cleona," Dalach said.

"She's sleeping off the effects of the Sky Ripper," Father replied. "Besides, you're needed on an invisible reconnaissance mission at present."

"An invisible reconnaissance mission?"

"Find out anything you can about the queen's plan—the whereabouts of her shortcut or even Excalibur itself—and report back to me here at the Odditorium before the banquet at six o'clock."

"Which, if I might add, is exactly three hours and thirty-three minutes from now," Mack said proudly.

"The Yellow Fairy is right," Dalach said. "You're mad if you think I'll venture outside the Odditorium alone. How do I know you won't take off while I'm gone? I'd have a bugger of a time getting back on board should you surround yourself with more of that poppet's fairy dust."

"Who you calling a poppet, ya big bamstick?" Mack said, and he hopped up again onto my shoulder.

"Please, not now, Mack," Father said. "And you have my word as a gentleman, Dalach. We're not going anywhere without you."

"I'm sorry, but after all your double-dealing for Odditoria over the years, your word carries little weight these days."

Father stiffened. "That's right. I've heard about your little quests, not to mention what you did to Mad Malmuirie. So if I'm going to help you, I need a bit of insurance."

"What kind of insurance?"

The Gallownog slipped one end of his spirit shackles onto his wrist. "Should I bind myself to a living person with these, that person can do whatever I do as long as we're chained together. They can become invisible, fly through the air alongside me, and even pass through walls as if they were a spirit themself."

Father heaved a heavy sigh. "I see," he said. "All right, then. Give me some time to instruct the others what to do in my absence, and I'll accompany you on your mission."

Dalach chuckled. "Not you, Alistair Grim. You're needed here. Besides, should the Royal Guard come calling before the banquet and find you gone, that would look a bit suspicious, don't you think?"

"I see where this is going," said Lord Dreary. "Very well, then, Alistair. *I* shall accompany the Gallownog on his mission."

"No offense, old man," said Dalach, "but I need someone with a bit more spring in his step—someone who won't hold me back should things get squirrely."

Lord Dreary sputtered and was about to protest, but Father spoke first.

"Then who do you propose to take with you?"

"The one person you'd never think of leaving behind."

The Gallownog smiled and bore his cold blue eyes into mine. My heart skipped a beat, and Father cried, "Out of the question!"

"Then it appears we're at an impasse, aren't we?" said Dalach.

"But you gave me your word!"

"Aye, and I mean to keep it, Alistair Grim. But on *my* terms."

"I'll do it, Father," I said. "I'm not afraid." That last part, of course, was a bit of a lie. Father's eyes flashed with rage and he gritted his teeth.

"You have my word, Alistair Grim," said Dalach. "I swear I shall protect your son's life as if he were my own child."

"It's too dangerous," Father said. "You're a spirit, Dalach. The queen and her Royal Guard cannot harm you. However, should they learn of your presence, there's no telling what they might do to Grubb."

"You're wrong. It's actually safer for the lad to come with me than to remain here. For as long as we're bound together by these shackles, he's a spirit just as I am. Not even Excalibur itself could harm him."

"Please, sir," I said. "It really does make the most sense for me to go. I'd have no problem keeping up with him. And certainly the Royal Guard wouldn't miss me should they come calling before the banquet."

Father raked his fingers through his hair and heaved a heavy sigh. "Very well, then," he said, and rushed over to the talkback. "Cleona, are you there, love?"

"What is it?" she said groggily.

"I've just made a decision to allow Grubb to do something very dangerous. Feeling any urges to start wailing?"

"No, Uncle, just the urge to start yawning." And she did.

"All right, then, go back to sleep." Father flicked off the talkback.

"There, you see?" Dalach said. "Your decision bodes well for everyone."

"We all know that the future can be profoundly impacted by seemingly insignificant decisions made in the present. Therefore, at the first sign of trouble, with or without Cleona's wailing, you must return to the Odditorium immediately. I warn you, Dalach, should anything happen to my son—"

"I gave you my word, Alistair Grim. I will protect your son as if he were my own child. However, what would you have us do if we find Excalibur?"

"Excalibur will be well guarded, no doubt. And we certainly don't want to risk the queen's wrath by stealing it just yet. Therefore, just locate the sword if you can." And then

Father muttered to himself, "That is, if it still resembles a sword at all."

"What's that, Alistair?" asked Lord Dreary, but Father ignored him and flicked on the talkback again.

"Nigel, how are things coming along with that steering damper?"

"It's worse than we thought, sir," the big man replied. "The outside casings are gone and its animus line is leaking and needs to be replaced. I've got Number One supervising that job herself. The rest of the wasps are working on the upper gunnery, but I wager it's going to take them some time to fashion a new cannon."

"That's the least of my worries right now. What's going on with the Avalonians?"

"Still reveling and gawking about as before. The wasps have been giving them quite a show, and when I opened the hangar doors, one of them knights flew up on his dragon and looked inside. The samurai blocked his view of the demon buggy, but since then they've been itching to have a go at one another."

"They may very well get their chance," Father muttered under his breath. He flicked off the talkback and scooped up Mack from my shoulder. "Tell me something, Dalach. Would it be possible for Mack to accompany you on your mission? After all, you'll need to keep track of the time."

Dalach held up the free end of his spirit shackles. "Aye, but I'd have to hook him onto this wrist cuff here."

"But I'm a *pocket* watch, not a wristwatch!" Mack cried. "Whoever heard of such a thing?"

"Desperate times call for desperate measures, my friend," Father said. He tossed Mack to the Gallownog, who immediately hooked the watch's single crown link onto his shackles. Mack flickered for a moment and then his form dissolved into the transparent, glowing blue light of a spirit.

"Ach!" Mack cried. "I've gone blue again!"

"Shut your gob," Dalach said, and he closed Mack's case. Mack rattled and shook, but the Gallownog ignored him.

"Now listen very carefully, son," Father said. "You do exactly as Dalach says. He's an expert at this sort of thing, and I wouldn't entrust him with your care if I didn't think you'd be safe. He's right, you know. Should the queen try anything before the banquet, you'll be better off out there than stuck inside the Odditorium with us."

"But, Alistair," said Lord Dreary, "if Queen Nimue meant to be deceptive, why would she allow you time to get your affairs in order? Indeed, why not just dispense with the banquet altogether and get on with the tournament?"

"I don't know, old friend, but if there's one thing I've learned over the years about fairies and prophecies, it's that neither of them are ever what they seem."

Father jerked his thumb at Gwendolyn, and then Professor Bricklewick's voice crackled over the talkback. "Hello, is this thing on?"

Father flicked the switch on his end. "Go ahead, Oscar."

"That chap with the foxtail on his helmet has asked to speak with you. Sounds serious, from what I can tell."

"Any luck with your research?"

"Some basic defenses against curses, some Odditoria and whatnot, but I can't see how any of it will protect us from the queen's magic."

"Wonderful," Father said, rolling his eyes. "I'm on my way." He flicked off the talkback and hugged me tight. "Promise me you'll be careful."

"I promise, sir," I said. As we parted, Dalach slapped his shackles, along with Mack, onto my wrist. My body flickered just as Mack's had done, and then all at once I dissolved into the form of a glowing blue spirit.

"Cor blimey!" I gasped, holding out my free hand in front of me. I could see right through it, but at the same time I felt no different than when I was solid. Mack, on the other hand—on the other *wrist*, I should say—would not stop shaking.

"If your friend doesn't settle down," Dalach said, "the queen will hear us coming long before we ever set foot inside her castle."

I opened Mack's case. "What time is it?" he cried, and then, catching himself, gave a chuckle and said, "Whoops! No need to ask that anymore. . . ."

"Listen here, Mack," I said. "I'm a spirit now too, but we need to keep quiet so we don't get caught."

"Say no more, laddie," Mack whispered. "Dougal McClintock is the man for this mission. And I must say, ya look a lot better in blue than that numpty standing next to ya."

Dalach sneered, and again Father put his hands on my shoulders.

"You're going to be fine, you hear?" he said, and I nodded.

"We better get moving," Dalach said, and he deliberately blinked his eyes. Our color changed from blue to white, and Father's hands passed right through me.

"Grubb?" he called, gazing round. "Are you still here, son?"

"Yes, sir," I replied. "I'm standing right in front of you."

Father and Lord Dreary turned their heads in my direction, but still they couldn't see me.

"The lad sees as I do," Dalach said. "As long as we're bound together by the spirit shackles, we appear white to each other and invisible to everyone else."

"Very well, then," Father said. "Make sure you stay no longer than a couple of hours. Good luck, all of you."

"You can count on me to have us back on time, sir," Mack said.

And with that the Gallownog dragged us down through the floor. A blurry tangle of pipes and gears rushed past my eyes, and then we were outside, flying unseen over the heads of the Avalonians and heading straight for the castle walls.

— FOURTEEN —

An Unexpected Reunion

O ver the last few weeks, I'd come to think of myself as quite the expert on flying, thank you very much. In fact, I wagered I'd done more flying than any other lad in the whole wide world. There was the coach that brought me to London in the first place, and all the flying I did in the Odditorium itself. Then there were the rides I took on Number One, the Thunderbird, and in the demon buggy. And this was certainly not the first time—nor the second, for that matter—that I'd been dragged through the air behind a spirit.

However, unlike all those other flights, there was something noticeably different about being chained to a Gallownog. I could feel no wind rushing through my hair or cold battering my cheeks—just a sense of weightlessness, as if I weren't flying at all. So this is what it's like to be a spirit, I thought. Light as a feather and one with the air.

But then, as we zoomed straight for the towering stone

battlements, I recoiled in horror—we were going to crash! I braced myself for the impact, when in the blink of an eye the Gallownog led us safely through the wall and out the other side.

"You needn't fret, lad," he said. "As spirits the two of you can go where even the light cannot reach."

We were now flying across the castle's outer ward, an immense courtyard of crisscrossing pathways and rows of cherry trees. The blossoms swirled like snow behind us as we soared over the branches and headed up a wide cobblestone road that led to the castle drawbridge. It was then that I spied the moat.

I gasped. Spirits like the Gallownog, like *Mack and me*, could not fly over water.

"It's narrow enough that we'll be all right," said Lorcan Dalach. "But it'll be painful, so steel yourselves and don't cry out."

The drawbridge was down, but it did little to protect us from the water below. And as soon as we entered the space above it, I felt as if I were being crushed by dozens of giant boulders. The pain was excruciating, but thankfully short-lived, and as we passed through the gatehouse and into the castle's bustling inner ward, the crushing sensation quickly subsided.

Dazed, the Gallownog and I fell to our knees. "Let's take

a second to recover," he said. The pain had all but left me now, but as I gazed back at the drawbridge, my thoughts drifted to Cleona. It had taken us no more than a second to fly over the moat, and so I could only imagine how Cleona must have suffered when she flew over the ocean to save me from Prince Nightshade's Sirens. My heart grew heavy with shame.

"All right, then," Dalach whispered. "Keep your wits about you and take heed: not only must we fly and disappear together, but also you must go solid when I do."

"What's that?" Mack asked. "Go solid, did you say?"

"Aye. It takes concentration and energy for a spirit to grab on to things. Fortunately, you won't have to learn how to do all that because you're chained to me." Dalach picked up a small pebble just high enough off the ground so that all the knights and servants milling about wouldn't notice. "Go ahead, try it, Grubb."

I picked up my own pebble, and then the Gallownog made both our stones drop through our fingers at the same time.

"So you see?" Dalach said. "As long as we are bound together by the spirit shackles, you have to do what I do *when* I do it. Any questions?"

Mack and I said no, and the three of us took a moment to get our bearings. The inner ward was surrounded by high battlements and towers and crammed with a sprawling

assortment of wooden buildings. Grooms tended to dragons and horses amidst a massive complex of stables, servants
hurried in and out of storehouses, and a regiment of knights
marched up the central road toward the gold-domed castle
overlooking it all.

"The humble abode of the queen herself," Dalach
whispered—when a knight trotted his horse straight through
our party as if we weren't there. The horse reared and whin-
nied, but the knight quickly gained control of the beast and
made for the stables.

"Certain animals can sense a spirit's presence," Dalach
said.

"You mean like crows do the doom dogs?" I asked.

"Aye, lad. Thus, I suggest we get moving before we attract
any more attention."

We took to the air again along the central road, past an
entire village of barracks, blacksmith shops, smokehouses,
and kitchens. Finally, the Gallownog led us up a steep ramp
and into the castle itself. We passed through a series of dimly
lit antechambers and then through a pair of high oaken doors,
whereupon we found ourselves in a dazzling throne room
leafed with silver and gold. Tall stained-glass windows shone
brightly amidst a soaring tangle of pillars and archways, all of
which converged upon a domed ceiling that was painted to

look like the sky. At the far end was a stepped dais lined with golden thrones; and on the wall behind it, a massive golden sun. The place was completely deserted.

"Why is this one so special?" Dalach asked, and he dragged me toward one of the stained-glass windows.

"What do you mean?" I asked.

"Its light is much brighter than the others."

Now I understood. The window appeared almost *too bright*, as if the glass itself were glowing. I counted six of the lofty windows on either side of the vast chamber, for a total of twelve in all, and each was cut to resemble a woman holding a sword. Their towering forms, like giants standing guard over the throne room, were dim compared to the stained-glass lady before us.

"Strange," Dalach said, gazing about. "The other windows have dates between the ladies' feet." I quickly took in some of the numbers—A.D. 816, A.D. 1107, A.D. 1645. "All of them except this one."

"I don't know about you lads," Mack said, staring at the window in question, "but lookin' up at this lass is makin' me dizzy."

Suddenly, a large wooden door opened beside the dais. Startled, I made to flee, but shackled as I was to the Gallownog, I only got a few steps before he yanked me back. Dalach raised his finger to his lips and casually moved us behind a pillar.

Silly me. I'd forgotten that we were invisible.

A maidservant, her heels echoing on the marble floor, hurried over to the brightest of the windows and waited. In one arm she carried a blanket, and in the other a towel and a golden scarf. We stood there watching her for what felt like ages, and then the window began to vibrate and glow even more brightly. Threads of white-hot lightning streaked along the metalwork that joined the countless plates of colored glass, and then a beautiful woman stepped through the window as if it weren't there. I recognized her immediately—it was the lady who had smiled at Professor Bricklewick—but she was sopping wet, and as the maidservant swaddled her in the blanket and began toweling off her hair, I noticed a row of curved slits below each of the lady's ears.

I shuddered. Father was right. The Avalonians had gills!

The maidservant wrapped the lady's hair in the towel, tied the golden scarf about her neck, and then the pair quickly disappeared through the dais door. The three of us just stood looking after them for a long time, until finally Dalach said, "I think we just found the Lady of the Lake's shortcut."

"Cor," I gasped—when something occurred to me. "Hang on. Earlier today Lord Dreary mentioned a legend about there being *two* Ladies of the Lake."

"Not just two," said the Gallownog. "Judging from how many sisters the queen has, I'd say there are at least *seven* who deserve that title."

"Ach!" Mack cried. "You mean we've got seven of those sorceresses to contend with instead of one?"

"Merlin only taught Queen Nimue his sorcery. She may have taught her sisters too, but legend has it that all one needs to pass through this window is the heart of an Avalonian. Thus, I'll wager that any of these gill people could do it."

"Father thinks that, although only an Avalonian can get in, anyone can get out."

"All right, enough of the jabberin'," Mack said. "As I am charged with keepin' us on time, I demand we resume our search for Excalibur."

Dalach ignored him and dragged us closer to one of the dimmer windows. The date between the lady's feet read A.D. 1461. The Gallownog suddenly released me from his shackles. My entire body froze in terror. I was human again. *Visibly* human.

"What the—?" Mack cried. "Are ya out of your mind, neep?"

"Hurry, lad, touch the window," said the Gallownog.
"But, sir, I—"
"As I am a spirit, even if I could pass through on my own, I would disintegrate as soon as I touched the water on the

other side. However, you, Grubb, being human, would not." Dalach grabbed my wrist. "Touch the window with your free hand. I'll pull you back if something happens. Quickly, Grubb, before someone comes."

Terrified, I reached out and touched the date between the lady's feet. But nothing happened. Dalach immediately pushed me toward the glowing window, the one *without* a date. "Now hurry, do it again."

I obeyed, but this time, as soon as my fingers touched the lady's stained-glass foot the entire window vibrated and grew brighter. Lightning danced along the metalwork, and Dalach gave my arm a gentle shove. My fingers passed through the glass as easily as they would a spiderweb—and I could actually feel the water on the other side—but then I quickly snatched back my hand. My fingers were dripping wet.

"Just as I suspected," Dalach said. "Those other windows have been closed since the date between the ladies' feet. This is the only one that remains open to our world. I'll wager it works the same as the ocean gateway through which we got here but leads to shallower water—a lake, no doubt. If only we could see what lies on the other side."

"Would someone mind telling me what's going on?" Mack cried.

Dalach lifted his shackles so that his face was level with Mack's. "Although we would need an Avalonian companion to enter Avalon, as did King Arthur, it appears that all we would need to leave is just this window and the ability to breathe underwater." His eyes flickered with an idea. "Unless, of course, you're someone who doesn't need to breathe at all."

Dalach unhooked Mack from the wrist cuff and handed him to me. "Again, Grubb," he said. "But this time, hold out the pocket watch in your hand."

"What the—?" Mack cried. "You're not stickin' me in there!"

"Only for a second," Dalach said. "We need to see what's on the other side."

"But, sir," I protested, and the Gallownog raised his hand.

"Mack is a machine. A machine that's a pain in the neck, but a machine nonetheless. He has no heart, and should be fine as long as you hold on to him."

"*Should* be?" Mack said. "That's your idea of a plan? *Should be?*"

Dalach ignored him. "You have my word, Grubb. You needn't worry about your mate. But if *Mack* is too afraid to try it, well—"

"What's that?" Mack said. "Are ya suggesting the chief of the Chronometrical Clan McClintock is a coward?" Lorcan Dalach shrugged. "Why, you— Go on then, Grubb. Let's show the numpty who wears the kilt around here."

Dalach nodded. I hesitated for a moment, and then with

a deep breath, thrust Mack through the window. The glass vibrated and flashed with lightning, and I could feel the water again on the other side and Mack trembling in my hand. I couldn't stand the thought of him being alone out there, wherever he was, so I quickly pulled him back. My heart swelled with relief. Mack was all right.

"*Brrrrrr!*" he said, shivering. He spit out a stream of water and shook himself dry like a dog. "That water's as cold as a Gallownog's rump!"

"Tell me, chief, what did you see?" Dalach asked.

"Just a bunch of cold, muddy water all around me!"

"The legends are true," Dalach said to himself. "This window must lead to a lake in our world, but you can't see it from the other side."

"And even if you could see it," I said, "according to the legend, someone from our world would need an Avalonian escort to get him through the window into Avalon. Unless, of course, he had a Sky Ripper like Father."

"But we've just proven that we won't need an Avalonian to return us to our world, nor will we need a Sky Ripper." Dalach suddenly cocked his ear. "Quickly now," he whispered, "someone's approaching outside the main gate."

The Gallownog hooked Mack and me back onto his shackles, and like the flicker of a dying flame we became invisible again. I could hear nothing but my own heart pounding in my ears, but after a tense few seconds, someone dressed in a long hooded cloak slipped in between the throne room's tall oaken doors. A lady, by the looks of her.

A shiver ran down my spine. The last time I'd seen a lady dressed like that was Mad Malmuirie. But unlike the daft witch who captured me, there was no sign of curly red locks beneath this woman's hood. Only the hint of a golden scarf. Yes, whoever this cloaked figure was, she was most certainly an Avalonian.

The mysterious woman paused for a moment by the gates, listening, and then slunk across the floor, moving briskly from pillar to pillar until she slipped out of sight through the dais door. Dalach raised his finger to his lips and we followed her—down a darkened passageway, up a spiraling stone staircase, and into another passageway, whereupon a pair of guards blocked the woman's path.

"Halt!" said one. "What business has a priestess in the royal quarters?"

The guards were answered with a flurry of blows, and before I even had time to wonder at it, the two men lay slumped together on the floor. The woman listened at a nearby door and then hauled the guards into a richly furnished bedchamber. We followed closed behind, and she quietly shut the door.

The woman rolled the guards over on their backs and

blew some powder from a small vial into their noses. Then she slipped the tiny bottle inside her cloak and dragged the men out of sight behind the chamber's large four-poster bed. As she was doing so, a long black braid tumbled down onto her breast. The woman tried unsuccessfully to tuck it back beneath her hood, and then removed the hood altogether.

I gasped at the sight of the woman's face—but it couldn't be!

"Kiyoko!" I cried, and she whirled with a dart poised in her hand. Dalach glared at me, but I ran to embrace the shinobi even as my mind told me that it could not be her. Kiyoko was dead—I had seen her fall from the sky with Prince Nightshade—and yet here she was, alive again and standing right in front of me.

The Gallownog yanked me back by my shackles.

"Please, sir, let me go!" I cried.

"You heard the lad!" Mack said. "Let him go, ya big bam!"

"Quiet, the both of you!" Dalach hissed.

"It's Grubb, miss! I'm right here!" But of course I was invisible, and Kiyoko couldn't see me. Her eyes flitted about the room and she lowered her dart.

"Where are you?" Kiyoko asked.

I pleaded again with the Gallownog to let me go. He gritted his teeth and reluctantly released me from his shackles. It must have appeared to Kiyoko as if I'd stepped out from the air itself, but her face brightened and the two of us rushed into each other's arms. She kissed me hard on the cheeks, and after a round of excited greetings, Lorcan Dalach materialized with Mack in blue spirit form.

"Well hello there, lassie," Mack said with a wink. "It's a pleasure to see you again, and looking just as lovely as ever."

Kiyoko turned to me, her eyes wide with wonder. "It seems we both have some explaining to do," she said. I introduced her to the Gallownog, and brought her up to speed on recent events and our present mission—including the revelation that Alistair Grim was my father.

"So once again we find ourselves in a castle seeking a sword," she said, smiling.

Kiyoko was referring to our earlier search for her sword

Ikari in Prince Nightshade's castle, but my mind was spinning with so many questions that it barely registered. "How did you survive your fall from the sky?" I asked. "How did you get away from the prince—how did you get *here*?"

"One at a time, Grubb," Kiyoko said with a laugh. "I should think the answer to your first question is obvious, for just as the prince's armor saved him from his fall, so too did it save me from mine. I made sure to land on top of him, you see. Had it been the other way around . . ."

Kiyoko made a splatting sound with her hands and I swallowed hard. Father had been convinced all along that Prince Nightshade had survived his fall from the sky, but hearing it firsthand from the shinobi's mouth somehow made it all the more terrifying.

"As for my escape," she went on, "I was thrown free when we hit the ground and slipped away into the forest. Soon afterward I came upon the wounded Thunderbird."

My mind flashed with images of our last battle with the prince—the fiery tip of his whip striking Gwendolyn, the sight of her and the giant bird on which she'd been riding spiraling down toward the forest below. Cleona had managed to save the Yellow Fairy, but her poor Thunderbird . . .

"I nursed her back to health with some herbs I found in the forest," Kiyoko said, "but by the time we arrived at the Thunderbirds' lair her flock was gone—fled to another location, we assumed, to escape the prince. And so, in return for saving her life, the Thunderbird agreed to help me find you."

"Cor blimey! You mean you followed us all the way from the Americas?"

"It seems Thunderbirds are quite skilled at tracking fairy dust, and so we followed the trail of Alistair Grim's Odditorium clear across the ocean to England. We caught up with you this morning on the coast, but unfortunately someone else had caught up with you too."

Kiyoko slipped out a knobby, twisted stick from under the sleeve of her cloak. I recognized it immediately. It was the magic wand that belonged to—

"Mad Malmuirie!" I cried.

"So that was her name," Kiyoko said. "It seems Alistair Grim has made more enemies than just Prince Nightshade over the years."

"But how—? What—?" I spluttered.

"Let's just say this Mad Malmuirie was not pleased to learn that I was your friend," Kiyoko said. "We fought long and hard, and I managed to steal her wand, but she flew away on her broom before I had time to finish her."

"And Mr. Smears?" I asked. "Was he with her too?"

"I met no Mr. Smears. The witch was alone when we fought."

My mind was doing somersaults now. What had become

of Mr. Smears? Did Mad Malmuirie kill him after they freed themselves from Moral's egg goo? And furthermore, how had Kiyoko made her way to Avalon?

"But now for the strangest part of my tale," she said. "The Thunderbird and I caught up with you again just as you were about to embark on your undersea voyage. Of course, I did not know that at the time, and when she dropped me off on the Odditorium's roof, I was suddenly pinned down under a bubble of fairy dust."

"Cor, you mean you traveled with us here underwater, miss?"

"That I did. And it wasn't so bad. Difficult to move, yes, but I had plenty of air. However, all that changed when the sea serpent attacked. Luckily for me I was in a position to avoid being crushed. And luckily for you, I managed to kill the beast with this." She held up Mad Malmuirie's wand.

"So it was *you*!" I cried. "You saved us from the sea serpent!"

"Quite by accident, I'm afraid," Kiyoko said, examining the wand. "As I had just avoided becoming a victim of Mad Malmuirie myself, I pierced the dust bubble with her magic wand and shot a lightning bolt straight into the serpent's head. How I did this I do not know. But a dangerous weapon this is, and much better suited for Alistair Grim's hands than mine."

Kiyoko slipped the magic wand into the sleeve of her cloak.

"He will be happy to have it, miss," I said. "And he'll also be happy to learn that you're alive. But why didn't you tell us you were here? Why didn't you come down from the roof after the levitation shield was turned off?"

"I did," she said. "However, once I overheard Alistair Grim and the rest of you talking about Excalibur and the queen's prophecy, I thought it best to keep my presence a secret in case you should need my assistance later on."

"You mean you were actually *inside* the Odditorium? You got past the samurai?"

Kiyoko smiled slyly. "The shinobi have been outwitting samurai for centuries. And so I decided to look for Excalibur myself, for if Alistair Grim was unaware of my presence, the queen could not hold it against him should I be discovered. I sneaked out of the Odditorium at the festival, and have been searching for the sword ever since."

I was about to ask her how she made it past the Royal Guard and into the castle without being seen, but immediately thought better of it. Kiyoko was a shinobi, after all, and Father told me that the shinobi were also called "shadow warriors."

"I hate to rain on such a lovely reunion," said the Gallownog, "but I suggest we resume our search for Excalibur before we're discovered."

"You're wasting your time," Kiyoko said. "I've combed every inch of this castle and can find no sign of Excalibur anywhere. The sword is not here."

"Well isn't that just peachy," Mack grumbled, and then one of the guards began to snore. Dalach quickly bound me with his shackles, and in a flash I became a spirit again.

"Pay them no mind," Kiyoko said. "The sleeping powder will keep the guards out for hours. Same for the priestess from whom I stole this disguise."

"Priestess?" Dalach asked.

"I have learned there is a temple located somewhere beyond the castle. What purpose it serves, I do not know, but I was on my way there when I ran into you."

"A temple," Dalach said. "I should think that as good a place as any to look for Excalibur. How are we doing on time?"

"We've been gone exactly forty-five minutes," Mack replied proudly.

Kiyoko smiled. "Someone has gotten himself repaired, it appears."

"Speaking of appearances, lassie, just wait till ya get a gander at me off these shackles. It's not just me case what's red these days." Mack winked and spun his hands.

"Begging your pardon, sir," I said. "I don't suppose there's room for a shinobi on these shackles?"

Dalach shook his head. "Not unless she can hook herself beside our jabbering Scotsman here."

"You needn't worry, Grubb," Kiyoko said. "There are more ways than one to become invisible."

Kiyoko took off her cloak, revealing the signature black garb of the shadow warrior underneath—a short, hooded robe cinched at the waist, a tight pair of trousers and boots, and a pair of open-fingered gloves. She slipped a stocking over her head and tied off her hood under her chin. She was now covered from head to toe in black, save for a narrow eye slit in her stocking.

My heart swelled with joy. How wonderful it was to see her like this again—and with Ikari on her back, no less!

"Shall we?" she said, eyes smiling. Lorcan Dalach blinked, and the four of us stole from the room invisible—Mack, the Gallownog, and me as spirits, and Kiyoko once again as her shinobi self.

FIFTEEN

The Writing on the Wall

As Kiyoko led us through a labyrinth of dim, torchlit passageways, it quickly became apparent why she was called a shadow warrior. At times she blended in so seamlessly with the flickering darkness that I almost lost sight of her altogether, while at other times she hid in doorways and even crawled across the ceiling to avoid the guards. Soon, however, we found ourselves outside, in the midst of a lush garden surrounded by high walls. Birds twittered and a gentle breeze rustled the leaves, but the place was deserted.

Kiyoko concealed herself behind a row of hedges and pointed to a domed structure with pillars at the far end of the garden. "That must be the temple," she said. "Go now and I'll meet you there."

Invisible as we were, the Gallownog, Mack, and I flew straight for it, while Kiyoko darted stealthily behind shrubs and clumps of trees until she joined us again behind a pillar outside the temple door. Dalach poked his head in first, and upon finding the temple empty, whispered for us to follow him.

The inside was circular and decorated in a mosaic of colored tiles. A round, glowing pool of water took up most of the floor, its light reflecting against the walls in shimmering ripples of radiant blue. Lorcan Dalach blinked us visible again and we moved to the water's edge. My heart sank. There was no sign of Excalibur anywhere.

"Well, that was a colossal waste of time," Mack said. "Of which, might I remind ya, there is less than one hour left."

"Perhaps I missed something back in the castle," Kiyoko said. "What say you, Gallownog? Shall we split up to cover more ground?"

Dalach ignored her and led us to the wall, whereupon I discovered that the tiles formed elaborate pictures that ran around the entire chamber in a series of separate panels. The panel that had caught the Gallownog's attention was a massive battle scene of knights in shining armor, but to the left of it I noticed a smaller scene depicting a knight sitting in a boat on a lake. Nearby, a maiden with flowing red hair swam underwater while thrusting a sword up through the surface. Excalibur, I knew at once—which meant that the knight in the boat was King Arthur and the woman in the water was the Lady of the Lake.

"I know this writing," Dalach said. He traced his finger over a tiled scroll at the base of the battle scene. From what I could tell, each scene had something similar—a scroll or a banner that bore its title in strange symbols that I did not understand. "'The Rise of Camelot,'" Dalach read.

"Camelot, the kingdom of King Arthur," Kiyoko said, and the Gallownog drifted to the next scene. It was King Arthur again—I could tell by his armor—but this time he was on a horse galloping away from the red-haired maiden, who knelt with a crazed expression, as if pleading with him to return.

"'The Princess's Gift Denied,'" Dalach read from the title scroll. He drifted over to the adjoining panel—another battle scene, this one depicting the fall of Camelot, Dalach informed us—but my eyes remained fixed on the red-haired maiden. I was certain I'd seen her before.

Then it hit me.

I gasped. "Mad Malmuirie!" The others whirled to face me.

Kiyoko inspected the red-haired maiden more closely. "She does bear a striking resemblance to the witch I fought."

"A coincidence," scoffed Dalach. "That picture depicts King Arthur refusing a gift from the Lady of the Lake. What this gift is I cannot say, but surely that maiden cannot be Mad

Malmuirie. That would make her over a thousand years old, not to mention an Avalonian—and not just any Avalonian, but the Lady of the Lake herself."

Embarrassed, I dropped my eyes to my shoes. I hadn't meant to suggest that the Lady of the Lake and Mad Malmuirie were the same person. That was just plain silly, now, wasn't it? But still . . .

Kiyoko placed a sympathetic hand upon my shoulder, and then Lorcan Dalach led us to the next panel. The picture was of a dark forest and a starry sky, and amidst the trees stood a hooded woman dressed in black. She appeared to be handing something to a yellow fairy who was hovering nearby—a swaddled child, I realized, who looked like a little grub worm.

My mouth gaped and my eyes grew wide.

"The title has crumbled away," Dalach said, but I didn't need the Gallownog to tell me what it might've been. After all, it was *the* Yellow Fairy herself who had told me how I came to her. Which meant that the woman on the wall was my mother and the little grub child *me*!

That's impossible, I wanted to say, but the words stuck in my throat. None of the others, not even Mack, had any idea what it all meant. How could they? None of them were there that day when Gwendolyn told me the story of my birth. And so I just stood there, frozen in disbelief, until the Gallownog dragged me over to the next panel.

The four of us gasped.

There was no question as to what *this* scene represented, for there on the wall was the Odditorium itself. And not just the Odditorium, but the entire festival from which we'd just come—the knights and maidens, the horses and dragons, Queen Nimue and her sisters—all of it spread out before me exactly as I remembered it. And there was *every one of us* from the Odditorium who had been there too. Our likenesses were uncanny—except for Mack, who for some reason hovered in the sky like a giant red sundial.

"Well, at least they got me new color right," Mack said.

"What does it say?" Kiyoko asked.

"'The Return of the Lost Princess,'" Dalach read, and upon closer inspection, I noticed someone on the dais who had not been there at the festival. It was the red-haired maiden from the earlier panels, only now she was wearing a crown and appeared much happier.

"The festival," said the Gallownog. "It was a welcome-home celebration. And for a princess, no less."

"A princess that resembles Mad Malmuirie," Kiyoko said, holding my gaze, and then she turned to Dalach. "What if Grubb is right?" she asked. "What if Mad Malmuirie really is the red-haired princess on this wall?"

"Mad Malmuirie, a princess?" Mack cried in disbelief. "Impossible!"

I expected Lorcan Dalach to agree with him, but instead he just stood there, tracing his fingers over the tiles that made up the lost princess's face. "I too find it puzzling," he said finally. "And yet my eyes tell me the boy may be right."

"So you think the woman on the wall is Mad Malmuirie?"

"I cannot tell for certain, but clearly there is much more to the story of King Arthur and the Lady of the Lake than any of us is aware."

"A love affair?" Kiyoko asked, eyeing the scene of THE PRINCESS'S GIFT DENIED.

"Again, I cannot tell," said Dalach. "But if Mad Malmuirie is both the legendary Lady of the Lake and this lost princess, then something must have happened that drove her away from Avalon all those years ago."

"And the festival should have marked her return," Kiyoko said. "But for some reason, she wasn't there."

My head was swimming, and a heavy silence fell over us as the implications of the writing on the wall came clear. Was Mad Malmuirie really the Lady of the Lake, the Avalonian princess who bestowed Excalibur upon King Arthur? And after being gone for over a thousand years, was she supposed to return to Avalon today?

"But how can Mad Malmuirie be from Avalon?" Mack cried suddenly. "I seen her up close many times, and I can tell ya she hasn't any gills!"

The Gallownog shrugged. "I myself would not have thought such a thing possible until now. But the faces on this wall, the likenesses of you and the others, prove it cannot be coincidence." Dalach stared at the lost princess for a moment longer, and then we were moving again. Kiyoko nodded at me as if to say, *Well done,* but I was too disturbed by everything I'd seen to feel even the slightest bit proud—so much so that it took a moment for the next panel to sink in.

"It cannot be," Kiyoko said. On the wall beside the castle was another battle scene, this one showing a black knight in a chariot pulled by four black horses. A cavalry of skeleton soldiers and other creatures followed close behind. My throat squeezed and my stomach felt queasy.

There before us was none other than Prince Nightshade!

"'The Return of the Black Knight,'" Dalach read from a banner below the prince's chariot. Nightshade and his minions were clearly in the midst of an attack, but their enemy had crumbled away from the wall. What followed was a twenty-foot span of nearly all brick broken up by patches of tile that appeared to have once been part of a much larger picture.

"The queen's prophecy," Kiyoko said. "It's all here."

"Not all of it," said Dalach. "Who knows how many panels are missing and what they once portrayed. . . ."

"Look!" Mack cried. We spun around to find a swirling mist of colorful sparkles forming above the pool. The four of us stepped aside, and the sparkles solidified into tiles. Faster and faster they swirled in midair until, with a great *whoosh*, the tiles flew across the room and plastered themselves in various spots along the bare brick wall.

"Well, what do you know," Mack said. "That's me again!"

He was right. In one spot the tiles had formed a small picture of Mack shooting red beams from his eyes, and in another, a picture of a golden egg—*Moral's* egg, I knew.

"What is this place?" Kiyoko asked.

"It is the future taking shape before our eyes," Dalach said. "This temple must be somehow connected to the queen. A magical record of her prophecy, perhaps, so she'll remember it."

"But these tiles," Kiyoko said. "Why are they making these pictures now?"

"Perhaps something's happened that, quite literally, has set the future in stone."

"You mean a future that cannot be changed?"

"Aye, miss," Dalach said, and he led us along the wall back to where we started, the scene of King Arthur drawing Excalibur from the lake. I, however, had become transfixed again by the scene of the hooded woman in the forest.

"We need to tell Father," I said in a daze.

"Are you all right, Grubb?" Kiyoko asked. "You look as if you've seen a ghost."

"That—that forest picture over there . . . I think it shows my mother giving me to the Yellow Fairy."

"What are you talking about?" Kiyoko asked. Gathering my wits, I told them the story as Gwendolyn had told it to me—the story of how a hooded sorceress, who turned out to be Elizabeth O'Grady, summoned the Yellow Fairy in the language of the ancients and entrusted me to her care. When I'd finished, the Gallownog knelt down with his hands on my shoulders and said:

"It appears you figure into this prophecy more than you realize, Grubb Grim. The same for you, Dougal McClintock."

"Well for the life of me I can't see how," Mack said.

"Neither can I, sir," I said.

"Your father is right, Grubb," Dalach said. "Prophecies and fairies are never what they seem. Either way, we've got to tell Alistair Grim what we've found, for I fear the next scene on this wall is about to come true—a future that has already taken shape."

"You mean Prince Nightshade is coming?" I asked.

"Along with Mad Malmuirie."

Kiyoko dashed over to the temple entrance. "The three of you will be able to travel faster without me," she said, glancing outside. "Tell Alistair Grim what we've found, and I'll try to learn more about this prophecy." I was about to protest, but

Kiyoko cut me off. "Go now. We may not have much time before we meet Prince Nightshade again."

We wished each other luck, and with a blink of the Gallownog's eyes we were invisible again and flying across the garden. Rather than travel back through the castle this time, Dalach darted upward and zoomed along the battlements. The castle grounds, as far as I could see, were deserted; the once bustling courtyard had grown eerily silent, and the drawbridge was up.

"Brace yourselves," Dalach said as we approached the moat. "The pain will be worse without the drawbridge."

I did not think it possible, but then Dalach flew us over the gatehouse and proved me wrong. As before, the pain abated as soon as we crossed the moat, but the Gallownog did not pause this time to recover, and took off across the courtyard like a wayward gunshot. The cherry trees flew past us in a smear of swirling blossoms, until finally we passed through the outer gates and landed in the field.

What I saw there made my heart freeze.

The festival had been completely abandoned. Banners and empty tents flapped in the breeze, fires still smoldered, and the ground lay strewn with rubbish, as if the Avalonians had simply dropped everything and ran.

But worst of all, the Odditorium was gone.

— SIXTEEN —

The Return of the Black Knight

ather!" I cried out in a panic, and the Gallownog took flight—up, up, up into the air until we were high enough to see the entire kingdom. In one direction lay the thick swath of ancient forest, the port city, and the colossal statue in the sea; and in the other direction, the castle, the rolling farmland and valleys, and the forest that stretched to the horizon.

There was no sign of the Odditorium anywhere.

"What's happened?" I asked. The Gallownog, his face straining, surveyed the scene a moment longer, and then dropped us back down into the field.

"The higher I go," he said, panting, "the quicker I lose my strength when shackled to a human. Give me a moment, and we'll try again."

Presently, a loud shriek shattered the silence, and from out of the forest flew Captain Fox Tail on his dragon. Dalach raised his finger to his lips—we were still invisible, of course—and the knight swooped past us and disappeared over the castle walls. The Gallownog, Mack, and I gave chase, my heart pounding so furiously that I barely felt the pain of crossing the moat again. And before I knew it, we'd followed Captain Fox Tail straight into the throne room.

The vast chamber was crowded with the Royal Guard and their dragons. The queen and her sisters sat on their thrones upon the dais, and there, standing on the steps before her, was Father.

I sighed with relief—and was about to call out to him—but Dalach clamped his hand over my mouth and flew us up onto a narrow catwalk high amongst the pillars. "Patience, lad," he whispered. "Remember, things may not be what they seem."

"I can do nothing to change your destiny, Alistair Grim," announced the queen. "For, like Excalibur itself, my gift of prophecy is also a double-edged sword. I can see the future and yet cannot remember it."

"You have my word as a gentleman, Your Grace," Father said. "I will do everything in my power to help you and your lost princess. All I ask in return is to borrow Excalibur so that I might defeat Prince Nightshade."

Dalach and I exchanged an uneasy glance. Perhaps we would learn for certain whether or not Mad Malmuirie was this lost princess after all.

"Over a thousand years ago," the queen began, "the bond between humans and Avalonians was forged by the very sword you seek. And although it was I who bestowed Excalibur upon the line of Pendragon, it was the lost princess who returned the sword to Arthur after his pride had broken it forever."

"You mean when he battled Sir Lancelot?"

"Excalibur was forged for the defense of truth and goodness, and thus cannot be wielded by one who is evil. However, even the noble Arthur was not immune to ill will. He used Excalibur in anger, and wounded Sir Lancelot after he bested the king in single combat. Ashamed, Arthur tossed the broken sword into a lake, upon which my sister, the lost princess, restored it and returned it to him. She was my apprentice, a budding sorceress who would one day rule in my place. Her name was Malmuirie of Avalon."

Father stiffened with shock. I had been right all along. Mad Malmuirie *was* the Lady of the Lake!

"Well, I didn't see that one coming," Father said after a long, tense silence.

"Malmuirie was in love with Arthur," the queen said. "However, we Avalonians are fairies from another dimension, and thus cannot remain in your world for long. So Arthur had Merlin transform my sister into a human so they could be together. The old codger was happy to do it—a devious attempt to lure me back into your world, no doubt."

"Your Grace?"

"Merlin never stopped loving me, you see, and tried unsuccessfully for centuries to find a way into Avalon. Which is why, I suppose, I always felt partly to blame for what happened. For in the end, King Arthur spurned her for the lovely Guinevere. Ashamed and betrayed, unable to face her family, Malmuirie disappeared—driven mad by a broken heart, the story goes. After all, a magical sword is one thing, but a princess's love is the most precious gift she has to give."

The Princess's Gift Denied, I said to myself, recalling the picture on the temple walls, but Father was silent, his mind clearly spinning with questions about what the queen had just revealed to him. My mind was spinning with questions too. Did Father know that the lost princess was supposed to have returned to Avalon today? Had Queen Nimue informed him about Prince Nightshade? And did he even know that the Odditorium was missing?

"So you see?" the queen said. "The true story of what happened has been lost to time—rewritten, rather, by those who wish to use history for their own selfish purposes. And thus, you humans are not only ignorant of the past, but also doomed to repeat it. You have proven yourselves incapable of wielding power without evil and corruption."

"I see," Father said quietly. "Then you have no intention of lending me Excalibur, even if I help you, Your Grace?"

"Again, that is not for me to decide, for although I am indeed the guardian of Excalibur, the end of my thousand-year reign draws nigh. Only the lost princess can take my place, and thus the fate of both our worlds hangs upon her return."

"So the decision regarding Excalibur rests with your sister Princess Malmuirie?"

"*Your* decisions, both the ones you make and the ones made for you, shall determine whether or not you are worthy of Excalibur."

"You speak in riddles, Your Grace."

"I speak the truth. We Avalonians are not like other fairies. Your world and ours are linked in ways that even you cannot fathom at present."

Father thought long and hard about this, and then sighed and raked back his hair. "Very well, Your Grace, but what about the others? I agreed to your plan because you assured me my companions would be safe. After a decision is reached regarding Excalibur, will you stand by that promise?"

"No harm shall come to your friends here in Avalon, and yet they are forbidden to interfere. When the moment arrives, you shall know why."

So Father knew that the others were safe—that was a relief—but where could they be, I wondered, and what had become of the Odditorium?

Suddenly, the entire throne room began to rumble and

shake. The dragons reared and the air grew thick with fear. Captain Fox Tail ordered his knights into some sort of battle formation, and they cleared a wide space in front of the brightest of the windows. The stained glass pulsed and flashed, lightning danced along its edges, and then from out of the window burst an enormous cigar-shaped contraption that resembled a black shark with wheels. It was dripping wet and sputtered with smoke, and as it spun out and skidded to a stop before the dais, a half dozen more of the contraptions, each one chained to the shark before it, burst through the window and skidded to a stop too.

The sharks revved and roared, and I noticed that mounted at the rear of each of them was a small engine, complete with a glass porthole through which I could see the glowing orange eyes of a demon. My guts twisted and my knees threatened to buckle. According to Father, there was only one other person besides himself who used demons in such a manner.

Prince Nightshade.

A hatch opened atop one of the sharks and out leaped the prince himself, his long black cape billowing behind him like a swollen thundercloud. I cried out in terror as he hit the floor with a thud, but there was so much noise in the throne room that no one heard me. More hatches began to open, and from out of the sharks poured the prince's skeleton

Shadesmen—axes ready and armor clanging as they positioned themselves in a wide circle around the room.

Catching sight of Father, Prince Nightshade raised the visor on his spiked helmet. His red eyes flared amidst the empty pit of his face, and the jagged red tear that was his mouth turned upward into a smile.

"Greetings, Black Knight," said Queen Nimue. "How nice of you to join us."

The queen's sisters tittered, but Prince Nightshade ignored them and gazed about the room—sizing up the situation before he attacked, it seemed. I could feel myself starting to panic, and was about to ask the Gallownog what we should do, when from out of the prince's shark climbed someone I'd never have expected in a million years.

I gasped. "Mr. Smears!" Dalach hissed at me to be quiet.

"What'd I tell ya, Your Highness?" said Mr. Smears, climbing down his shark. "Is that Alistair Grim in the flesh or is it not?"

"That it is," Nightshade purred with delight. "At long last, that it is."

Father stiffened, and I noticed that he was holding the Black Mirror by his side. He must have slipped it from his pocket during the chaos of Nightshade's arrival.

"We meet again," Father said flatly.

Mr. Smears hitched up his trousers and, cocking his top hat, swaggered over to the prince. It was instantly clear to me what had happened. The crows Cleona and I had seen in the forest had belonged to Prince Nightshade after all. He must have gotten to Mr. Smears while he was still stuck in Moral's egg goo, and in turn Mr. Smears told him about Father's quest for Excalibur. Mr. Smears knew about it from watching us in the warding stones with Mad Malmuirie!

"Looks like that daft enchantress is worth her weight in gold," he said, gazing about. "Which, from what I can tell, there's no shortage of in this place."

"Patience, Smears," said the prince. "You'll get what's coming to you."

"So you're the fiend who abused my son," Father said to Mr. Smears. "I had thought to teach you a lesson when all this was over, but no time like the present."

Mr. Smears sneered and scratched his scar. Father stepped forward to pummel him, but Queen Nimue raised her hand and stopped him where he stood. "Take heed, Alistair Grim," she said. "Yours is a fight for another day."

"Your son, did you say?" asked Prince Nightshade. "You mean the lad who stole my animus is *your son?*"

"Forgot to tell you that, I did," said Mr. Smears. "Come to find out, the little grub worm is a Grim one at that." Mr. Smears chuckled at his pun, but Nightshade's demeanor had completely changed. He glanced furiously about the room and unhooked his whip from his belt.

"Where is he?" the prince howled. "Bring me the child of Elizabeth O'Grady!"

"How dare you soil her name with your tongue!" Father cried.

The prince roared and cocked his whip, but before he could let it fly, Queen Nimue waved her hand and froze his arm in midair. Prince Nightshade's eyes flashed and he smiled.

"Extraordinary," he said, his demeanor calm again. "So the legends are true. You *are* a most powerful enchantress."

The prince lowered his whip, and with a wave of his hand, forced the queen to sit down in her throne.

"Please, use your magic on me again," he said.

"No, Your Majesty," Father said. "Nightshade is capable of absorbing magical power, and thus any spell you cast on him shall be turned back on you in equal measure."

Queen Nimue and her sisters looked at one another in confusion, and for the first time since our arrival in Avalon, all of them seemed afraid.

"Well, well, Alistair Grim," said Prince Nightshade. "It seems you know quite a bit about me."

"Likewise, from what I gather. My son tells me you're an expert on our family history, which makes me wonder why you've suddenly become so obsessed with him."

The Prince chuckled knowingly. "Where is he? And where are the others from your Odditorium? I was so looking forward to seeing them again."

"Thanks to the queen here, the Odditorium and its inhabitants are in a place where you cannot find them. You didn't think I'd risk you getting hold of my animus, did you?"

"A wise move, Alistair Grim. And speaking of moves, still fancy the odd game of chess, do you?"

"When time allows. But I can't say I've had much of that lately thanks to you."

"The secret of all good chess players, as you know, is their ability to plan many moves ahead. However, *your* problem was always worrying too much about your own moves and not your opponent's." The prince turned round and shouted, "Bring forth the prisoner!"

A hatch opened in one of the sharks and out flew the Black Fairy. Last time I'd seen the foul creature he was trapped inside a bubble of Gwendolyn's fairy dust. But now it was he who was doing the trapping; for there, struggling in the Black Fairy's arms, was Mad Malmuirie!

I gasped. "The lost princess!"

Terrified, the queen and her sisters leaped to their feet as the Black Fairy circled high above the throne room—his empty white eyes, oblivious to our invisible presence on the catwalk, passed only inches from our faces. Queen Nimue held up her hand to stop him, but her magic had no effect, and in return the Black Fairy blew apart a section of a pillar with a bolt of his thick black fire.

"You needn't bother, Your Majesty," said Prince Nightshade. "My second-in-command is immune to your magic. Therefore, if you want a fight, you'll have to do it without Merlin's trickery."

Captain Fox Tail and his knights began to scuffle with the Shadesmen, but the queen quickly commanded them to stop. The Black Fairy swooped down and, with his massive claw clamped tightly over Mad Malmuirie's mouth, landed beside the prince.

"Only an Avalonian could get Nightshade through that window," Dalach whispered to me. "He must have captured Malmuirie after her battle with Kiyoko."

"Mr. Smears," I replied. "He told the prince where to find her. He betrayed her to save his own skin!"

"Yes, Your Grace," Prince Nightshade went on below us. "I too know something about Avalonians. The Black Fairies, of which our friend Bal'el here is the last, were once your mortal enemies. And so this is sizing up to be quite the homecoming, isn't it?" The prince turned to Father. "But who'd have thought that Alistair Grim would join the party too? Something to do with Oscar Bricklewick, Mr. Smears tells me?"

Father smiled—but it was genuine, I could tell. Prince

Nightshade did not know about the professor's map and the gates off the coast of Blackpool. All that had been revealed *after* Father had disposed of my warding stone in the Cambridge sewers.

"So you're acquainted with Oscar Bricklewick, are you?" Father asked. "Know him from way back when at university? An old family friend from London, perhaps?"

Father was baiting him, looking for a clue as to Prince Nightshade's true identity. But the sly old devil didn't fall for it.

"Nevertheless," the prince said, ignoring him, "once my crows tracked the doom dogs to Mr. Smears and I learned of your meeting with Bricklewick, I temporarily set my sights on acquiring another bit of Odditoria. One that you, being the fool that you are, simply overlooked." He stroked Mad Malmuirie's hair. "The Lady of the Lake, the lost princess of Avalon. After all, who needs a Sky Ripper when you have the heart of an Avalonian to get you here the old-fashioned way?"

Mad Malmuirie squealed and struggled in vain against the Black Fairy's grip, but without her magic wand, she was no match for him.

"Dear sister, come to your senses," the queen said gently. "You have returned to Avalon. The prophecy has been ful-filled and all is forgiven. There is no more shame, only the love of your family."

Mad Malmuirie screamed something unintelligible behind the Black Fairy's hand. Prince Nightshade chuckled menacingly.

"You were always so predictable, Alistair Grim," he said. "And so I was not surprised to learn of your quest for Excalibur. However, who could have predicted that a thousand-year-old Avalonian princess would reveal her true identity to Smears here?"

"That she did," said Mr. Smears. "I overheard Malmuirie jabbering on about it in her sleep. Talkin' to herself like a regular loony, she was."

"And so," said the prince, "after Smears led me to her, the Lady of the Lake and I struck a bargain. Princess Malmuirie would bring me to Alistair Grim, and in return I would recover her stolen magic wand. A simple yet effective strategy on my part, wouldn't you agree, Alistair, old boy? For as we both know, in the game of chess the most powerful weapon is not a sword but a *queen*."

Father exchanged a nervous glance with Nimue.

"Go ahead, Your Majesty," the prince went on. "Command Alistair Grim to give me the animus-powered pocket watch and I shall return your lost princess here. After, of course, we are safely back in our world."

The Black Fairy removed his hand from Mad Malmuirie's

mouth. "My wand!" she cried, her eyes crazed and darting. "The shadow lady stole my wand!"

"Please, calm yourself, sister," said Queen Nimue. "All will be well now that you've returned to Avalon."

"Will you get a load of this one," said Mr. Smears, twirling his finger beside his ear. "Still babblin' on about her magic wand. A shadow lady stole it, she says. Gone off the deep end for good, I reckon."

"A shadow lady," Father muttered, thinking, and Dalach's entire body tensed with alarm.

"We need to tell him about Kiyoko," he whispered.

"You backstabber, Smears!" Mad Malmuirie screamed, and the Black Fairy roughly stopped her mouth. Mr. Smears laughed, and again the knights and Shadesmen began to tussle. This distracted the prince, whereupon the Gallownog flew us down to the floor and, invisible to everyone except Mack and me, whispered in Father's ear.

"We are here, Alistair Grim," Dalach said, and he quickly informed Father of Kiyoko's presence in Avalon. At the same time, the queen pleaded for the scuffling to stop. The prince echoed her command, and just as everything began to settle down, Father's eyes flashed with an idea.

"How fortunate for you, Bal'el, that your prisoner has lost her wand," Father called out loudly to the Black Fairy. "For although Queen Nimue's magic is useless against you,

Malmuirie's wand would have proven quite effective against a fairy of your kind. Your spiritual makeup is similar to the doom dogs', is it not?"

The Black Fairy's white crescent mouth bared its sharp black teeth. "*You* are the only dog here, Alistair Grim."

"Clever," Father said sarcastically.

"I haven't got all day," said the prince. "Give me the animus, Queen Nimue, or I shall tear Avalon apart—beginning with your crazy witch of a sister."

"I'm afraid you're out of luck, Nightshade," Father said. "McClintock has been repaired. He no longer runs on animus."

"Oh, well, in *that* case I'll just leave," the prince said mockingly, and the Black Fairy and Mr. Smears laughed.

"He's telling the truth," said Queen Nimue. "I mended Dougal McClintock myself, and thus you cannot use him to create your army of purple-eyed Shadesmen."

The prince heaved a heavy sigh. "I would expect such a pathetic bluff from Alistair Grim, but how unbecoming of you, Your Majesty. Now give me the pocket watch or I'll break the lost princess's neck."

The Black Fairy tightened his grip, and Mad Malmuirie squealed in pain. The knights and Shadesmen again readied themselves for a brawl, but Father held up his hand and calmly said, "Now, now, there's no need for all that." He slipped the Black Mirror into his coat and began fumbling through his pockets. "I know he's in here somewhere. McClintock, old boy, where are you?"

"Don't you dare toy with me," said the prince, but Father continued searching.

"I assure you, I'm not. Oh, McClintock? Where are you, McClintock?"

Dalach's eyes widened with understanding, and he abruptly unhooked Mack from his shackles. The watch became visible at once, but the Gallownog deftly slipped him into Father's hand and retreated with me beside a pillar.

"Ah, here we are," Father said, pretending to find Mack in his pocket.

"What the devil is going on?" Mack cried. His face flashed red and Father held him up for the prince to see. "Ach! Not you again!"

"Have a look for yourself," Father said, and he tossed Mack to Prince Nightshade. I gasped, unable to believe that Father would hand over our friend just like that, but Dalach held me by the shoulders.

"Remember Mack's picture on the temple wall," he whispered. "All will be well."

The prince turned Mack over and over, examining him closely. "Trickery," he muttered, but I could hear the anger mounting in his voice. He tapped Mack on his XII, and when all he got in return was a slew of Scottish cusswords, the prince growled, "Curse you, Alistair Grim!"

And then Prince Nightshade crushed Mack in his hand.

"No!" I cried out in terror. A brief explosion of red light shot out between the prince's fingers, and then poor McClintock was on the floor in pieces. At the same time Dalach clamped his hand over my mouth, but he was too late. The prince had heard my cries and, cocking his ear in my direction, roared:

"Bring me the son of Elizabeth O'Grady or your sister dies!"

"No!" cried Queen Nimue, but I barely heard her. My heart was breaking for McClintock, whose parts lay strewn about and crushed at the prince's feet. I began to sob.

"The temple wall, lad," Dalach said gently. "All will be well."

I glanced over at Father, who appeared entirely unmoved by Mack's demise. How could that be? Father loved Mack, and he would never do anything to hurt him. Unless . . .

At that very moment, as if reading my thoughts, Father winked in my direction. He couldn't see me, of course, but the message was clear. *All would be well.*

"You're the one bluffing now, Nightshade," Father said. "You must know that Excalibur is close at hand, and surely if you harmed the lost princess, one of her subjects would cut you down for it. So it seems you've gotten yourself into quite a pickle. Or as they say in chess, *check*." The prince stiffened. "Go on, then. It's your move."

A tense silence hung about the room, and then Prince Nightshade sighed wearily. "Oh, we are proud, aren't we? I seem to recall that being your problem. Always so pleased with yourself, always so blind to what was right there in front of you. Sadly, it was Elizabeth who paid the price for your hubris." It was Father's turn now to stiffen. "Anyhow, looks as if we're back to square one. Bring me the boy *and* the banshee, and I'll let Princess Malmuirie live."

"I'm afraid you won't find Cleona here," Father said. "Nor the Odditorium, for that matter. And so there's no chance of you stealing my Odditoria as you did Abel Wortley's all those years ago."

The jagged gash that was the prince's mouth broke apart into a smile. "You fool," said the prince. "I *am* Abel Wortley!"

Father's face dropped like a stone, and my heart along with it. Had my ears deceived me? Did Prince Nightshade just say that he was really Abel Wortley, the very man my best mate Nigel had been framed for murdering?

"And now that you know the truth," said the prince, "ask yourself if your old friend would come all this way with no moves left to get him out. Ask yourself if Abel Wortley, your old chess opponent, would leave himself open to a checkmate."

Father set his jaw and clenched his fists, but I could tell that he was distracted—his mind spinning with what the prince had just told him. How could such a thing be possible? How could Prince Nightshade and Abel Wortley be the same person?

The prince chuckled. "And so, after I tear Avalon apart and kill your son, know that I shall never rest until I find the Odditorium and your banshee. For if Cleona really was here in Avalon, then surely she'd be wailing your death by now!"

The prince whirled and, in a crack of thunder and lightning, struck Father with his whip.

"FATHER!" I screamed in horror, but Dalach held me fast as Father staggered backward and slumped lifeless on the dais steps.

"I hear you, Grubb!" the prince cried, cracking his whip again, and he turned to the Black Fairy. "Kill the witch and find the boy!"

The Black Fairy smiled and was about to snap Malmuirie's neck when a bolt of lightning shot down from above and struck him in the back. The Black Fairy uttered a deafening shriek and then burst apart in a cloud of thick black smoke. Malmuirie, collapsing to the floor, glanced about frantically, unable to fathom what was happening. The Black Fairy was gone, and she was free.

"Shinobi!" cried the prince, and I followed his gaze to find

Kiyoko perched high among the pillars with Mad Malmuirie's wand in her hand. The prince leaped for her and cracked his whip, but Kiyoko quickly disappeared down the narrow catwalk.

The ground shook as Nightshade landed. "Kill them all!" he screamed, and the throne room erupted into battle. Mr. Smears dove for cover under one of the sharks, axes and swords clanged, and Shadesmen burned in the dragon's fire. Prince Nightshade began mowing down the Royal Guard with his whip.

Queen Nimue and her sisters flew toward Malmuirie. The ladies held her by the arms as the queen slipped a long pin from her hair—the same hairpin with which she had turned Mack red at the festival. Malmuirie screamed as Nimue touched it to her forehead. A flash of brilliant white light blinded me for a moment, and then there was Mad Malmuirie, standing tall and holding a gleaming silver sword.

Dalach gasped. "Excalibur!"

Prince Nightshade saw it too. But before he could react, Mad Malmuirie was upon him—only she did not look mad anymore. Her eyes were fixed and fearless, and in a swipe of flashing steel she brought down Excalibur hard on the prince's shoulder. Nightshade cried out in pain and dropped to his knees, unable to use his whip, and then I lost sight of him as a horde of Shadesmen came to his defense.

Malmuirie quickly dispatched them with Excalibur, their skeleton bodies exploding into smoke with a single blow from the magic blade. From out of nowhere Kiyoko joined the fray, and as she and the knights set to work on the other Shadesmen, the battle escalated to a fever pitch.

It was then that I saw Mr. Smears helping the wounded prince into the hatch of his mechanical shark. It had been unchained from the others. The devils were making to escape.

"Prince Nightshade!" I cried, running after them, but the Gallownog pulled me back by my shackles. "What are you doing? We can't let them get away!"

"I swore an oath to protect you," he said. "I cannot risk you getting hurt."

Prince Nightshade and Mr. Smears were inside the shark now, its engine revving and roaring in a cloud of demon dust. And as Mad Malmuirie and the others finished off their Shadesmen, the mechanical monster skidded out and zoomed back through the window whence it came.

The throne room was now littered with fallen knights and their dragons. All of the Shadesmen were gone, their undead bodies blown to oblivion by Excalibur. As Captain Fox Tail and Queen Nimue's sisters began tending to the wounded, Kiyoko dashed over to Father and hovered with her ear close to his mouth. Dalach blinked us visible and released me from his shackles. I was human again. Queen Nimue and I joined the shinobi at Father's side, and I knelt down and cradled his head against my breast. His flesh had gone snow white and just as cold.

"Father!" I cried, the tears beginning to flow. "Can you hear me, Father?"

No response. Kiyoko rested her fingers on the side of his neck, then closed her eyes and bowed her head. There were no words for what she had to tell me.

Alistair Grim, my father, was dead.

— S E V E N T E E N —
A Resurrection of Sorts

I wept openly, unable to speak. And what would I have said if I could? For even now I cannot find the words to describe those agonizing moments wherein I held Father's lifeless body in my arms.

"His destiny is now in your hands, sister," said Queen Nimue, and through my tears I looked up to find Malmuirie standing over us with Excalibur. Her eyes were full of compassion, and before I had time to grasp what was happening, the once mad enemy of Alistair Grim touched the sword to his breast. Father's breath hitched, the color flooded into his cheeks, and he began to cough. My insides gushed with joy.

Alistair Grim was alive!

"Father!" I cried, at which he opened his eyes and struggled to his feet.

"Well, that was unpleasant," he said, dazed, and I threw my arms around his waist. "Sorry to put you through that, son, but it was necessary to gain the advantage over the prince."

"You mean you—you *planned* all this?"

"Not at first. But after the Gallownog told me of Miss Kiyoko's return, and with Malmuirie's magic wand, no less, my next move was clear. I spied her watching us from the rafters and hinted that she should fire Malmuirie's wand at the Black Fairy." Father gazed round. "And so, Miss Kiyoko, once again we find ourselves in your debt."

Father gave a slight bow, and Kiyoko pulled down her stocking to reveal her face. "The Black Fairy and the Shadesmen are dead," she said. "However, the prince was wounded by Excalibur and escaped through that window there with Mr. Smears."

"Unfortunate, to be sure," Father said, thinking. "But at least we know now where he's headed. Hang on—where *is* the prince headed, Your Grace?"

"That particular window leads to your Lake Ullswater," said Queen Nimue. "It is the last of our windows into your world, but you needn't fear. The prince cannot return to Avalon without the heart of one of us to guide him."

"I thought as much," Father said. "Nevertheless, now that Prince Nightshade thinks I'm dead, we will have the element of surprise on our side."

"But I'm afraid I don't understand, sir," I said. "You mean you got yourself done in on purpose?"

"You can thank the prince himself for giving me the idea.

After all, in chess one must often sacrifice a piece or two in order to gain the advantage. However, the rules of the game clearly state that if you can get one of your pawns to the far side of the board, you may exchange it for a more valuable piece." Father turned and bowed to Princess Malmuirie. "A queen, perhaps, if you've lost one."

"Well done, Alistair Grim," Malmuirie said. "It was because of your sacrifice that I am returned, both in mind and body, to claim my rightful place here in Avalon. And thus you and your friends have proven yourselves worthy of Excalibur."

She handed the sword to Father. It was somewhat smaller than I imagined, its blade plain and unblemished, its hilt ordinary and unadorned. And yet I shivered in awe at seeing it up close. After all . . . Well, if you've stuck with me this far, I needn't remind you that the most powerful Odditoria are often those things that, on the surface at least, appear to be ordinary.

Father examined the sword and tested its balance. "It was the hairpin, wasn't it?" he asked, and Queen Nimue smiled. "I suspected as much after you mended Mack at the festival. Excalibur was forged to unite armies rather than destroy them. To heal rather than to hurt."

"So you knew Excalibur would bring you back to life, Father?" I asked.

"I'd hoped so, yes, and decided in the end—as do all good chess players—to trust in the power of my queen."

"It was the Lady of the Lake, sir," I said. "Princess Malmuirie—she was the one who wounded Prince Nightshade and brought you back to life with Excalibur."

"You have my undying gratitude, Your Grace," Father said. "No pun intended."

"The gratitude is all mine," said Princess Malmuirie, the soon-to-be queen of Avalon. Her voice was gentle and kind, her eyes clear and content, and despite everything that had happened, it did my heart well to see her so. Father's too, I could tell, and with a smile he bowed to her and Queen Nimue.

"And now I beg your pardon, Your Majesties, but we do have an evil necromancer to catch."

"I will dispatch the Royal Guard into Ullswater to pursue the prince," said Queen Nimue.

"That will not be necessary, Your Grace. Prince Nightshade will undoubtedly have more of those mechanical sharks waiting to ambush us. Besides, the prince thinks I'm dead. And although he's wounded, he will no doubt set out to destroy the Odditorium and capture Cleona for her animus. First, however, he will need to take care of that business with his armor." Father smiled. "And I know just where he intends to do it."

The queen closed her eyes and pondered this—and for a moment I thought she was trying to foretell our future—but in the end all she said was, "Very well. I bid you good fortune on your quest. However, aren't you forgetting someone?"

"Good heavens!" Father said, spying Mack's scattered parts on the floor, and he held out Excalibur for Princess Malmuirie. "If I might trouble you one last time, Your Highness?"

Princess Malmuirie took the sword and touched its tip to Mack's crumpled case. There was a great flash and a pop, and then all Mack's pieces began to join back together of their own accord. His case straightened itself out and his eyes flickered to life, and there was the chief of the Chronometrical Clan McClintock, beaming red and hopping about as good as new.

"Wha-wha-what time is it?" he sputtered, hands spinning.

I scooped him up off the floor and hugged him close.

"Mack!" I cried with tears of joy. "You're all right now!"

"What the—?" he said, squirming about. "What's all that blubbering for? And where's that devil what tried to squash me?"

"I'll explain it to you later, old friend." I closed Mack's case and slipped him into my waistcoat, where he promptly began shaking up a storm.

Princess Malmuirie handed Excalibur back to Father. "When your quest is over, you must return Excalibur to Ullswater. Toss the sword far out into the lake and one of my sisters will be there to catch it."

"After which this window to your world shall be closed forever," said Queen Nimue, and she touched Malmuirie's cheek. The other princesses joined them, their shimmering white gowns like a curtain of loving light around their sisters. Kiyoko passed Father the magic wand and he offered it to Malmuirie.

"Keep it for your collection," the princess said. "A gift of Odditoria for bringing an old witch back to her senses."

"I shall cherish it always," Father said. He slipped the wand inside his coat and turned to Queen Nimue. "And speaking of gifts, Your Grace. That prophecy of yours—it wouldn't happen to say anything about our defeating Prince Nightshade, would it?"

Queen Nimue smiled. "That story has yet to be written."

But something *had* been written—or pieced together, I thought—on the temple walls. Fragments of the future that were unalterable—the battle with Prince Nightshade, the pictures of Mack and Moral's golden egg. But now was hardly the time to tell Father about all that, nor did I think it proper to ask him about what was sure to be the most mind-boggling revelation of them all:

Prince Nightshade was really Abel Wortley!

"Very well, then," Father said. "This Aquaticum of ours is not over yet."

We said our good-byes to Princess Malmuirie and her sisters, and then, with Excalibur in hand, Father and I mounted one of the dragons behind Captain Fox Tail, while Kiyoko rode on a dragon behind Queen Nimue herself. And with an escort from the Royal Guard, the queen led us from the castle and out over the walls.

The sun was low in the sky, alarum bells rang out at us from every direction, and the Avalonians, who had come out from hiding, cheered as we flew overhead. The entire kingdom had come alive with music and dancing. And as we passed over the port city, the inhabitants spilled out onto the rooftops to give us a hero's welcome.

The lost princess had returned, the prophecy had been fulfilled, and the whole of Avalon was celebrating.

When we reached the harbor, Queen Nimue waved her hand and the Odditorium rose up out of the water. Its protective dust bubble dissolved, revealing Professor Bricklewick and Lord Dreary at the organ and Nigel and Mrs. Pinch in the gunneries. Father held up Excalibur and the professor's mouth hung open in disbelief. Lord Dreary dragged his handkerchief across his head and steadied himself against the balustrade. The old man appeared on the verge of collapse—from relief, I reckoned.

"But I thought the Odditorium was no longer in Avalon," I said.

"A bit of a fib, that was," Father replied. "Queen Nimue insisted on hiding it underwater, but I wasn't clear why until I realized I needed to die in order to trick Prince Nightshade. After all, if we were going to convince the old devil that the source of his animus had left Avalon, we needed to hide Cleona someplace where he wouldn't hear her wailing."

"Cor. That queen is a crafty one, eh?"

"Well, as I mentioned earlier, fairies and prophecies are never what they seem. Fortunately for us, it all turned out well—so far, at least."

The dragons dropped us off on the Odditorium's balcony, while Number One flew out to shore to pick up Lorcan Dalach—her black paint would protect him from the sea, of course—and once the Gallownog was safely inside we said our good-byes to the queen. Father handed Excalibur to an awestruck Professor Bricklewick and spun the Odditorium around to face the Guardian of the Gates. I barely had time to wonder at the colossus again, for Father quickly activated the dust bubble and plunged us back beneath the waves.

With evening fast approaching, the ocean depths had grown dark. Father flicked on the searchlight to illuminate our path and continued on with his organ playing. His fingers moved across the keys like lightning, and with a violent lurch the Odditorium headed for the Guardian's legs.

"Listen up, everyone," he said into the talkback. "We won't need to fire the Sky Ripper again, but who knows what will be waiting for us on the other side."

Cleona yawned. "I'm happy to hear that. I'm still tuckered from that first jump, not to mention all that wailing you caused me. What about Lorcan? Is he all right?"

"He's fine, love," Father said. "In fact, it was Lorcan's quick thinking that saved us. Had he not told me about Kiyoko, I'm not sure what I would have done."

Father, his expression suddenly grave, fixed his eyes on the Gallownog. Dalach pressed his lips together tightly and dropped his eyes to the floor. He looked almost guilty, I thought.

"Great poppycock, man!" cried Lord Dreary. "Aren't you going to tell us what happened? What with the way Cleona was carrying on we feared the worst!"

"I'll explain the details to you later, but this should give you an idea." Father handed Lord Dreary the Black Mirror. "Show me Abel Wortley," he said.

The mirror flashed and swirled with sparkling color, and then in its glass appeared the image of Prince Nightshade greeting Father in the throne room. Indeed, Father had secretly captured nearly their entire confrontation, and as the Odditorium pressed onward through the water, Lord Dreary and Professor Bricklewick watched the scene unfold before them in stunned silence.

"So it's true, then," I said when it was over. "The prince really is Abel Wortley."

"But how is that possible?" Lord Dreary asked. "Abel Wortley is dead. We both saw him buried with our own eyes!"

"I have my theories," Father said, and he lowered his voice. "But, if you wouldn't mind, I'd rather break this news to Nigel myself. No telling how he might react."

Father returned the Black Mirror to his coat and my heart sank. Poor Nigel. Somehow, it was Abel Wortley who'd framed him for his own murder. Abel Wortley, the old man for whom he sometimes worked, who kept William Stout from his daughter all these years. And even though I couldn't fathom how such a thing was possible, I swallowed back a sob at the thought of everything my dear friend had suffered.

"All right, listen up, everyone," Father said into the talk-back. "We'll be through the gates momentarily. Everyone keep an eye out for sea serpents."

"I had Number One recalibrate the cannons, sir," Nigel replied from the lower gunnery. "But I can't guarantee they'll work."

"You needn't worry about that," Father said. "We've got something much more effective now." He removed Malmuirie's magic wand from his coat and handed it to Kiyoko. "You *will* show me how to use this one day, won't you?"

The shinobi smiled. "I think I've got the hang of it now."

And then, as Father steered the Odditorium past the Guardian's massive stone legs, the statue simply dissolved before our eyes.

"It worked!" said Lord Dreary. "We made it to the other side!"

The ocean had grown dark in our world too, I imagined, but I could hardly tell in the gleam from the searchlight. Nevertheless, I shivered at the thought of what lay in the murky depths beyond its reach. And as if reading my thoughts, Mrs. Pinch cried out over the talkback, "The monsters are back, sir!"

"Good eyes, Mrs. Pinch," Father replied. He steered the

Odditorium to face them, and the monsters' eyes flared up like torches in the searchlight. They were close too, the largest of the three once again leading the charge. But before the beast could open its jaws to chomp us, Kiyoko fired the magic wand through the dust shield. The bolt of white lightning found its target smack between the eyes, and then the monster was sinking, its head streaming with blood and bits of flesh until it disappeared from view.

Undaunted, the pair of remaining serpents kept coming. Kiyoko made quick work of them too, and soon the Odditorium was heading for the surface. Finally, we burst out of the ocean and rose high into the air. Father turned off the dust bubble, and what a beautiful sight there was to behold. The setting sun had painted the sky in low-hanging strips of pink and orange. The sea was calm and smooth as glass, and far off on the horizon I spied the jagged silhouette of the coastline.

"Blackpool," Father muttered. His eyes had grown sad. He's thinking of Mother again, I thought. There was something more in his gaze, though, as if he were searching for something out there in the distance. And perhaps because of what I had seen in the Avalonian temple, I began to wonder if he was asking the same questions I was. Why, of all places, should Elizabeth O'Grady's body have been found so close to the Gates of Avalon? Did she know of their existence, and had she journeyed to the North Country with some purpose other than leaving me with the Yellow Fairy?

"Don't mind if I conk out for a bit, do you, Uncle?" Cleona asked from the talkback. "I can barely keep my eyes open."

Startled, Father was about to answer, but Dalach spoke up in his place. "Might I have a word with you first?"

A long silence crackled back, and then Cleona said, "Aye, you might."

As Dalach turned to leave, Father rose from the organ and reached out for the spirit's arm. His fingers passed right through him, but their eyes held, and this time the Gallownog did not look away.

"I had hoped you might reconsider your business with Cleona," Father said. "We couldn't have gotten this far without you and . . . well . . . let's just say my offer to join our family here at the Odditorium still stands."

Lorcan Dalach's eyes were hard and unblinking. "I gave you my word that I would help you defeat Prince Nightshade. After that, you're on your own."

Father nodded solemnly, and then the Gallownog drifted into the library and disappeared up through the ceiling. Flicking on the talkback, Father ordered Nigel to remain on lookout in the lower gunnery and asked Mrs. Pinch to fix us supper. Then he plotted our course into the organ, set the helm to autopilot, and rushed over to his desk with the rest of us following close behind.

"Begging your pardon, sir," I said, "but you don't really think the Gallownog will try to capture Cleona again, do you? It's obvious they still care for one another."

"I have every faith that Lorcan Dalach will keep his word—both to us and the Council of Elders." Father began flipping through the book he'd loaned to Professor Bricklewick earlier—*Protective Charms for the Necromancer.* "However, we'll need the Gallownog on our side if we're going to stop Wortley before he gets to London."

"London?" asked Professor Bricklewick.

"How do you know Wortley's headed for London?" asked Lord Dreary.

"You recall how the old man and his housekeeper were murdered?" Father asked.

"A dastardly deed if ever there was one," Lord Dreary said with a shiver. "Stabbed to death, they were, with one of Abel's antique daggers."

"A *transmutation* dagger, to be exact," Father said, and he held up the book for all of us to see. The page to which he'd turned showed an illustration of a long, thin dagger with a cluster of strange symbols scrawled beside it.

"Good heavens!" cried Lord Dreary. "That looks just like the murder weapon!"

"That's because it *is* the murder weapon."

"But of course," said Professor Bricklewick. "The transmutation dagger is the only one of its kind known to exist. Its origin remains a mystery, but according to legend, the transmutation dagger is said to have the power to transfer a person's spirit into a magical receptacle that will shelter it."

"Shelter? You mean from the doom dogs?" Kiyoko asked.

The professor nodded. "Precisely. The technical term for such a receptacle is solphylax, and it can be anything, really—an urn, a chest, even jewelry and such. But its purpose is always the same. A solphylax allows a person's spirit to exist outside its body without being drawn into the Land of the Dead."

"The prince's armor!" I cried. "That's his solphylax!"

"Very good, my young apprentice," Father said. "Wortley used his transmutation dagger on *himself*. He transferred his own spirit into his suit of magical armor, after which he framed Nigel for his murder and slipped away from London reborn as Prince Nightshade. What a fool I was not to have recognized the murder weapon as Odditoria—not to mention that the answer has been right here in my library all these years!"

Father slammed the book shut and rubbed his eyes in frustration.

"It makes perfect sense," said Professor Bricklewick. "And as Wortley was getting on in years, I'll wager he initially acquired the transmutation dagger with the hopes of capturing a spirit and using its animus to prolong his life. Little did he know that he would need a spirit like Cleona—a spirit pure of heart and uncorrupted by its own intentions—for such a thing to work."

"Yes," Father said. "No telling how many people fell victim to his little scheme before he realized their spirits would not give him the animus he desired."

A heavy silence hung about the room, all of us shuddering at the thought of Abel Wortley gadding about London offing people with his transmutation dagger.

"But this armor of his," Lord Dreary said finally. "Where did he get it?"

"Perhaps our resident Regius Professor of Modern History would care to handle this one," Father said.

Professor Bricklewick cleared his throat. "Well, judging from the queen's comments and what I saw in the mirror, I would venture to guess Prince Nightshade's armor once belonged to the Black Knight himself."

"The Black Knight?" asked Lord Dreary. "You mean the archenemy of the Knights of the Round Table?"

"That I do, old friend. The Black Knight appears in one form or another throughout Arthurian legend, invariably possessing some sort of supernatural power. Indeed, according to one legend, the Black Knight's armor held the ghost of an ancient Roman gladiator. Regardless, as we all know Abel Wortley was a collector of antiquities, it's clear that one of his early finds was the armor in question—fortified, no doubt, by a bit of his own black magic."

"The Return of the Black Knight," I mumbled.

"Something more to add, son?" Father asked, and Kiyoko and I related what we'd seen in the temple—including the panel of my mother handing me over to the Yellow Fairy and the tiles forming themselves into pictures of Mack and Moral's egg.

"An intriguing turn of events," Father said. "And given the fact that prophecies are never what they seem, I would submit that all this fits into the mix in ways that—how did the queen put it? Ah, yes—in ways that not even I can fathom at present."

"But this temple," Kiyoko said. "What purpose does it serve?"

"I cannot say for certain without having a look at it," Father said, rising. "However, as we will not be traveling back to Avalon anytime soon, there's no point in speculating ourselves silly."

Father mounted the ladder and returned the book of charms to its shelf.

"Yes, but that scene you played for us in the mirror," said Professor Bricklewick. "I saw for myself how Wortley reacted when he learned that Grubb was your son. He specifically called him the child of Elizabeth O'Grady. Don't you think that odd, Alistair, especially in light of what the boy just told us?"

"Yes," Father replied.

"Do you think it's possible, then, that Wortley could've known about Elizabeth giving up a child? Do you think he might have had something to do with her disappearance, or at least knows why she left?"

"I don't know."

"Yes, but don't you think—"

"I don't know what to think!" Father snapped, and the room grew silent. My heart was pounding. Clearly Father had been entertaining the same idea that Wortley knew more than he was letting on—but then he sighed and descended the ladder.

"Forgive me, Oscar," Father said. "That little outburst was more about me than you. I've played over Elizabeth's disappearance a thousand times in my mind and watched her in the Black Mirror a thousand more. This revelation about Wortley being alive changes nothing—at least not at present. After all, it was my preoccupation with my own troubles that blinded me to all this transmutation business in the first place."

Professor Bricklewick adjusted his spectacles. "My apologies, Alistair. I shouldn't have been so insensitive."

"Stuff and nonsense. You've been nothing but the good friend you've always been." Father gave him a pat on the shoulders and then began rummaging through a nearby cabinet. "But now on to more pressing matters, the first of which is surprising Wortley before he can get to the transmutation dagger."

"The transmutation dagger?" asked Lord Dreary. "You mean the very same weapon that he used to transfer his spirit into the Black Knight's armor?"

"That I do. Ah, here we are." Father removed a large rolled document from the cabinet and unfurled it onto his desk. It was a map of London.

"But why do you think Wortley will go after the transmutation dagger?" Lord Dreary pressed.

"I'm surprised at you, old friend. Given your knowledge of Arthurian legend, I should think the answer would be as plain as the sword in the good professor's hand."

"Of course," said Professor Bricklewick, examining the blade. "Although Excalibur has the power to heal, anything it cuts cannot be mended—neither armor nor the flesh beneath it."

"Sir Lancelot!" Lord Dreary exclaimed, the light dawning. "Arthur wounded him with Excalibur, and as I recall, his wound never healed!"

"Very good, old friend," Father said. "And now that the Black Knight's armor is damaged, Abel Wortley will once again need the transmutation dagger to transfer his spirit into another solphylax that will protect it."

"Another suit of magical armor?" asked Professor Bricklewick.

"Perhaps. But after seeing those mechanical sharks first-hand, who knows what other nasty tricks Abel Wortley has up his sleeve. Which is why we need to get to him before he gets to the transmutation dagger."

"And where is this dagger?" Kiyoko asked.

"The same place it has been ever since William Stout's murder trial ten years ago." Father pointed to a spot on the map. "In the evidence room at Scotland Yard."

Lord Dreary gasped. "Good heavens, man! You're not saying you intend to break into Scotland Yard, are you?"

"No, but I intend to prevent Wortley from doing so. After that crack from his whip back in Avalon, the old devil will think I'm dead—our little chess game, over—and thus he'd never expect me to counter his next move. After all, in chess, the best defense is a good offense, which is why I intend to first attack Wortley where he lives—in his castle in the clouds."

Lord Dreary gasped. "Great poppycock, Alistair! Have you gone mad?"

"Forgive me, Alistair Grim," said Kiyoko. "I know the prince's castle well. It is fortified with lightning cannons powered by his Eye of Mars, not to mention an entire army of Shadesmen and evil creatures ready to do his bidding. Should you choose to attack with your Odditorium, I fear the prince will prevail."

"I have no intention of attacking his castle head-on, Miss Kiyoko—quite the opposite, actually. In fact, I should think a clandestine, targeted strike inside the castle's engine room would prove much more effective."

"The demon buggy!" I exclaimed. "You said Prince Nightshade's engine room runs on a flight sphere filled with a hundred demons. He uses their dust just like we use ours for the demon buggy!"

"Very good, my young apprentice. If one of us could get inside the prince's castle undetected, he could render it flightless from within, thus ensuring the castle's destruction when it runs out of demon dust and plunges to the ground." Father gazed up at the lion's head above the hearth and began muttering to himself rapidly. "Yes, yes, Wortley's Eye of Mars will no doubt be continuously activated. And when crushed under the weight of his falling castle, it should incinerate everything and everyone inside. The castle's black paint should help contain the blast, but to be safe we'll make sure we sabotage it somewhere remote—in the countryside where no innocent bystanders can get hurt. Consequently, Wortley, with nowhere to retreat, will be vulnerable to Excalibur. . . ."

Father trailed off, his mind racing with the beginnings of his plan. Lord Dreary dragged his handkerchief across his head. After a long silence, he cleared his throat with a loud *"Ahem!"* Startled, Father just looked at him as if he'd forgotten he was there.

"But just how do you plan to *do* all this?" the old man asked.

"I haven't worked out all the details yet," Father replied, "but it involves someone else Abel Wortley thinks is dead— someone very powerful who, quite literally, he let slip through his fingers."

Father pointed to my waistcoat pocket, which appeared to be alive from Mack's shaking. I'd been so wrapped up in all the excitement that I hadn't even noticed.

"The time stopper!" I cried.

And Father smiled.

— E I G H T E E N —

On the River Thames

That evening at supper Father laid out his plan. Given our present location, even at full speed the earliest we could hope to arrive in London was just after midnight. Father calculated that Wortley, coming from Lake Ullswater, farther north, would arrive a little later, and so he planned to intercept his castle over the marshlands outside the city.

"I understand the geography of it all," said the professor. "However, regardless of whether or not Abel Wortley thinks you're dead, he will no doubt be expecting an attack on his castle sometime soon—either by those of us left at the Odditorium or by the Avalonians themselves."

"I agree, old friend," Father said, munching away. "But what the old devil will *not* be expecting is the demon catcher transported invisibly into his engine room. The Gallownog and his spirit shackles will make such an operation possible—virtually foolproof, in fact. You won't even need the protection of the warding stones. The demons cannot possess you if you're spirits."

"You?" the professor asked. "As in *me too*, you mean?"

"Of course. Being that you're a sorcerer, I'll need you to operate the demon catcher. And while you and the Gallownog are busy crashing Wortley's castle into the marshlands near Shepherd's Bush, the rest of us will be waiting for him with the time stopper in London."

"But what if you're wrong?" the professor pressed. "As Wortley is wounded, what if he sends one of his minions after the transmutation dagger instead? I should think a seven-foot, black-armored knight gadding about Scotland Yard would be sure to attract attention."

"Given that his very existence depends on it, Wortley would never trust the theft of the dagger to anyone else."

"And his demons? What do you suggest we do after we catch them?"

"Well, since you'll be meeting us in London, dump them off in the River Thames on your way back. That will destroy them just as it would any other spirit."

"But, Alistair," Lord Dreary said, "I still don't see how you can be certain that Wortley is headed for London in the first place. How do you know he didn't steal the dagger back years ago?"

"A simple matter of calculated risk," Father said with a swig of ale. "Although Abel Wortley had no idea about my interest in Odditoria until fairly recently, he would nevertheless assume that the theft of his murder weapon, were it made public, would arouse my suspicions. Besides, if Wortley had thought the transmutation dagger would be of use to him after his murder, he would never have left it for the authorities to find."

"In the stables where William Stout had been employed," said Lord Dreary.

"That's correct. Not to mention that Wortley did take some of his other magical objects along with him. Objects that, to the average eye, appeared to be worthless, but to one with a knowledge of Odditoria . . . well . . . If only I'd recognized that dagger, I might have been able to put a stop to all this before it began."

"Don't beat yourself up about it," said the professor. "It really does look like just an ordinary dagger. Not to mention that it's much easier to frame someone for murder when you've got the weapon to show for it."

"Poor Nigel," said Mrs. Pinch. "To think that Abel Wortley would allow a gentle soul like him to hang for murder—to leave his little girl without a father—oh, blind me, what a cruel, cruel man!"

Mrs. Pinch began sobbing into her napkin. Father had broken the news about Prince Nightshade's true identity to Nigel earlier, upon which the big man asked to be left alone in his quarters. All of our hearts were breaking for him, but Mrs. Pinch seemed to be taking it harder than anyone.

"There, there, Penelope," said Lord Dreary, patting her hand. "We need to be strong for him now."

"Begging your pardon, Father," I said, "but if it's all the same with Mrs. Pinch, might I be excused to bring Nigel his supper? He hasn't had a bite since this morning, far as I can tell."

"Good idea, son. He'll need a full stomach for what's coming."

"Speaking of which," Kiyoko said, "do you not think it wise to test the time stopper before confronting the prince?"

"Queen Nimue wasn't being cryptic when she cautioned me about using him, for I'm afraid old McClintock is good for stopping time only once every few hours, and even then only for a minute or so. He's over a thousand years old, after all. And should we test him now, there's a good chance he won't have the strength when we need him."

"But, Alistair," said Lord Dreary, "how can something speed up time for one person and virtually stop it for another?"

"It's quite simple, really, given the laws of interdimensional physics," Father said. I too was still a bit confused about all that time stopper business, but I didn't care to listen again to Father's explanation. My thoughts had been on Nigel ever since he'd heard the news about Abel Wortley. And as Father blathered on with a load of big words that I didn't understand, I slipped into the kitchen, fixed Nigel a plate, and hurried up the lift to the third floor, where I met Lorcan Dalach in the hallway.

"Oh, hello, sir," I said. "We missed you at supper."

"I am a spirit, and thus have no need for food."

"Oh, I know that, sir. I just thought that . . . well . . . being as you're on our side now, I just expected to see you there, is all. Cleona almost always joins us for supper." Dalach stared at me blankly. "She's still asleep, I take it?"

The Gallownog nodded and an awkward silence passed between us.

"Er—uh—I never got a chance to thank you, sir," I stammered. "For looking out for me, of course, but for everything else too. Father's right, you know. We couldn't have done all this without you."

"Your father is right about a lot of things," Dalach said. "Tell me, lad, is he right to trust me with his plan instead of sticking me back in that sphere?"

"You gave him your word that you'd help us defeat Prince Nightshade."

"I also gave my word to the Council of Elders that I'd

bring back Cleona for trial. Do you know what happens to a Gallownog who breaks his word? That's right, lad. Eternal torment amongst the doom dogs in Tir Na Mairg."

I swallowed hard. I hadn't forgotten the Gallownog's offer to take me to the Land of Sorrow. But whereas before I could chalk up his proposal to desperation, now that I knew him to be honorable, the possibility of seeing my mother, of getting the answers to all my questions from her myself, suddenly weighed upon my mind like a mound of soot.

Dalach read my thoughts. "I told you the truth about your mother. I did see her once, but only from a distance, through the mists of Tir Na Mairg. I'd hoped to learn more about what happened the night Cleona tried to save her, but your mother didn't heed my call." I stared back at him, confused. "How all that works is a story for another time, but unfortunately, I found out nothing to help Cleona. Or you, for that matter."

"And after everything that's happened, you still believe Cleona is bewitched by Father? You still believe you must take her away from him?"

Lorcan Dalach's eyes flitted to the floor. "What I believe matters not. I swore an oath to the Council of Elders to bring Cleona back, but I also swore to prove her innocent and keep her from Tir Na Mairg."

"But even if you convinced your Council of Elders that

she had been bewitched, if you took her away from her family here, do you really believe she could ever love you again the way she does now?"

"You underestimate me if you think that will sway me from my duty."

"Forgive me, sir, but I don't believe that. You're at the Odditorium, and if there's one thing I've learned about all the magic round here, it's that love truly is the most powerful of them all. I reckon not even your Council of Elders could stand up to that."

Dalach's expression softened. "You're a good lad, Grubb, and a brave one at that. Were you in the Order of the Gallownog, I should be proud to call you brother."

"Well, should you change your mind and join our family here, I'd be proud to call you the same."

Dalach smiled at me fondly. "Your friend's supper is getting cold." He held my eyes for a moment longer, as if he were contemplating saying more, and then sank down through the floor and out of sight.

I crept over to Nigel's chamber and tapped on the door. He bade me enter, whereupon I found him in a chair reading some papers by the hearth. The grate was ablaze, the entire room alive in a flickering dance of red and shadow, and as I approached him with his plate, the big man crumpled up one of his papers and tossed it into the fire.

"I brought you some supper, Nigel."

"Thank you, Grubb," he said, his goggles never leaving the flames. "You can leave it on the desk there and I'll get to it later."

I did as he asked, and noticed that all his books and the newspaper articles about Abel Wortley were gone. My heart sank. So that's what he was burning.

I slipped round the demon buggy and the evil spirit's eyes flashed hatefully at me from the engine. I shivered. How Nigel could spend so much time in here with that thing was beyond me. The room felt unusually cold too, despite the fire, and I could hear the wind whistling through the Odditorium's steelwork outside.

"Did you come to gawk at our friend there in the buggy?" Nigel asked.

"Er—no, sir," I said, and was about to leave when I spied the miniature portrait of Maggie on a small table by his chair. "I'm sorry about the news, Nigel," I said after a long silence, and he crumpled up another paper and tossed it in the fire. "Are you feeling all right?"

"I don't know what I'm feeling, to be honest," Nigel said blandly.

I stared down at the portrait of his daughter. Nigel told me once that he sometimes would see her from a distance when he drove Mrs. Pinch out to the country bearing gifts from Father. He also told me that he sent out the bats regularly to check up on her. Unfortunately, being on the run as we were, he'd been unable to do so for some time now. I imagined he'd been missing her something terrible long before he knew it was Abel Wortley himself who had kept him from seeing her all these years.

"You should have seen the way her face used to light up when she saw me," Nigel said, touching Maggie's portrait. "Used to call her Bright Eyes, I did. I ever tell you that?" I shook my head. "Bright all around, she was. Only three years old and she could write her name. That's more than I could say before I come here."

"Chin up, Nigel. Remember what you once told me? You said that, perhaps when Abel Wortley's murderer was brought to justice, it might be safe for you to see Maggie again as her uncle Nigel. Well, now that we know Prince Nightshade is actually Abel Wortley himself—"

"And just who's going to explain all that to the authorities?" Nigel said bitterly. "Me? You? The boss? You forget, the lot of us are fugitives now, wanted dead or alive for all that trouble we caused back in London. And even if we succeed in sending Wortley's spirit to hell, you really think anyone's going to believe our story about magic daggers and sorcerers and whatnot?"

"Yes, but—"

"For ten years I'd thought to clear the name of Stout, but now I know any hope of that is lost."

"Don't say such a thing. I just know in my heart that you and Maggie will be reunited someday. I just know it."

"I know you mean well, Grubb, but my cards have been dealt. I'll never be able to see my daughter again." Nigel tossed another wad of paper into the hearth. "You run along now and rest up a bit. We've still got hours to go before London, and you'll need your wits about you come midnight."

I left Nigel there by the fire and traveled down in the lift to the shop. Somehow, someday, I would make it right for him, I swore to myself, but for now my heart was so heavy that all I wanted to do was sleep.

"Why the long face, Grubb?" Mack asked from the worktable.

"Just a bit tired, I suppose. If you'd be so kind as to wake me in a couple of hours, I'd be much obliged to you, Mack."

"That'll be a piece of cake, laddie," Mack said proudly. "And being that I'm such an important part of Mr. Grim's plan, he wants me to rest too. No telling how long after he uses me time stopper that I'll be able to do it again. It's been a while, and I'm afraid I'm a bit rusty."

Mack chuckled and I rolled over on my side. Half of me wanted to ask him more about his time stopping, but the other half just wanted some peace and quiet. The latter won out, and soon I was asleep.

The clocks in the library were chiming half past eleven as Mack and I joined Lord Dreary and Kiyoko round Father's desk. They were studying his map of London.

"Great poppycock, Alistair," cried Lord Dreary. "You mean you intend to confront Wortley along the River Thames?"

"Wortley would be a fool not to use those submarine sharks of his. Thus, the most likely spot at which he'll land is this wharf here"—Father pointed to the map—"just a hop, skip, and a jump from Scotland Yard."

"But, Alistair, the River Thames has become a cesspool of filth and disease, not to mention home to some of the worst cutthroats in London!"

"The perfect cover for Wortley and his minions, wouldn't

you agree? And so I believe the old devil will attempt to slip into London under cover of the Thames, retrieve the trans-mutation dagger as inconspicuously as possible, and then slip away downstream along with the rest of the filth."

Lord Dreary dragged his handkerchief across his head. "Well, I shudder to think what might happen if you're wrong. And should Oscar and the Gallownog fail in their mission—"

It was then that I realized Lorcan Dalach and Professor Bricklewick were gone.

"They shall not fail," Father said, studying a book of tide tables. "Number One will get them to the proper altitude, and once they're on the castle grounds, shackled together and invisible, the rest will be child's play."

"Cor," I said. "You mean they've left already?"

"We dropped them off near Hammersmith while you were resting," Father said. "And after Oscar and the Gallownog capture and dispose of Wortley's demons, Number One will fly them back to the Odditorium here in London."

"We're in London already?" I asked, running out onto the balcony. Far below, through the wisps of scattering clouds, I spied a patchwork of tiny lights with a thin black ribbon through its center. London at night was certainly a beauti-ful sight to behold, and yet all I could think about was the Gallownog and Professor Bricklewick in the bowels of

Nightshade's castle. During our escape, Kiyoko and I had not ventured into the engine room, but I could see it as clearly in my mind as if we had—a cavernous dungeon and an enormous flight sphere filled with a hundred churning demons. I shivered.

Kiyoko stood beside me with her hand on my shoulder. "Do not fret, Grubb. As long as our friends are spirits, not even Prince Nightshade himself can harm them."

"And his castle?" I asked. "What will happen to all his minions when it crashes to the ground?"

"The explosion from the prince's Eye of Mars, crushed under the weight of his castle, will obliterate Nightshade's army at once."

"Judge Hurst too?"

I'd nearly forgotten about Alistair Grim's old enemy these last few weeks, never mind the fact that the prince had turned him into a purple-eyed Shadesman. However, unlike the rest of the evil creatures that inhabited Nightshade's castle, Judge Mortimer Hurst hadn't chosen to ally himself with the prince. And even though he had tried to betray me while we were being held captive, I still couldn't help feeling sorry for the old codger.

"It is for the best, Grubb," Kiyoko said with a hand on my shoulder. "I should think being a purple-eyed Shadesman is a fate far worse than death."

"Are you there, sir?" came Mrs. Pinch's voice from the organ's talkback, and Father and Lord Dreary joined us. "I've poured the professor's potion in the prison sphere as you requested, but blind me if I can say it'll work."

"Thank you, Mrs. Pinch," Father said. "Now please take your station in the upper gunnery. What about you, Nigel? Did you adjust the levitation shield's output settings?"

"I did, sir," Nigel replied on the talkback. "I rerouted everything to the Odditorium's belly, but as for the invisibility mist, I can't say how long it'll last."

Invisibility mist? I had no idea what Nigel was talking about, and yet it did my heart good to hear him sounding like his old self again.

"Very well, then, Nigel," Father said, flicking some switches. "I'm releasing the invisibility mist now. Load up the egg blaster and I'll meet you in your chambers. Oh, and wake Cleona, will you? She should be more than rested by now."

"Right-o, sir," Nigel said.

"Invisibility mist?" Lord Dreary asked. "Good heavens, Alistair, what on earth is going on?"

"It seems the professor's research wasn't a waste of time after all. I had Mrs. Pinch whip up an invisibility potion that he found in the old protective-charms book. When released through the Odditorium's levitation system, the potion should create an invisibility mist that will conceal our descent and subsequent surveillance in London."

"You mean you actually intend to land the Odditorium in London?" Lord Dreary asked, aghast. Father nodded, and my jaw hung open. He hadn't mentioned anything about taking the Odditorium itself into London! "But, Alistair," Lord Dreary cried, "we're wanted men! Should the authorities—"

"The invisibility mist will take care of all that," Father said, cutting him off. "And should Wortley choose to make as grand an entrance as last time, we'll need the Odditorium's lightning cannons to take care of his army."

"Great poppycock," Lord Dreary said weakly, and he dragged his handkerchief across his head.

"Very well, then—here goes nothing." Father flicked a switch, and the outsides of the Odditorium flashed, blinding all of us momentarily.

"Well?" Lord Dreary asked as our vision cleared. "Are we invisible?"

The answer was no, I thought. Everything looked exactly the same as before.

"Go ahead, Broom, have a look," Father said, and she took off into the air. I'd been so bewildered by what was happening that I hadn't noticed she'd joined us. Broom flew out a short distance then circled back, upon which she bumped into the outside walls a couple of times before landing again on the balcony. She gave a brief curtsy and then set about tidying up the library.

"Splendid," Father said. "Although everything looks the same to us on the inside, from the outside we are entirely invisible. I've also managed to dampen the organ a bit, but let's just say it's a good thing we'll be close to Westminster Abbey."

Father played and we began our descent into London. The organ was noticeably quieter, but still, I could hardly imagine what anyone who heard it might have thought, what with this strange music seemingly coming from nowhere. However, as the thin black ribbon that was the River Thames grew wider and wider, my mind quickly shifted to the terror at hand. Father was taking us down into the river itself!

"I told you our Aquaticum wasn't over," he said, sensing my fear. "Luckily for us there's hardly any traffic this time of night."

And with that we touched down into the river with a splash. At the same time, the stench churned up by our entrance was almost unbearable. Father went on to explain how Nigel had rerouted the levitation shields to waterproof only the Odditorium's belly, leaving us free to enter and exit through the upper floors, but I was trying so hard to keep from retching that I didn't get it all.

Father changed his tune and we began to travel upstream. The lower part of the Odditorium was entirely submerged, the balcony just a few feet above the water, and had we not been invisible, I imagined we must have looked like an enormous fishing float that had broken free from a giant's pole. And yet, I could hardly believe that any fish could survive in such a foul river; and as the city whipped past us in a jumble of lights and shadow, I remembered Father's promise to take me fishing and prayed he would choose a different spot.

Soon, we passed beneath an archway to an enormous stone bridge—Waterloo Bridge, Father called it—and then, a short distance upstream, Father deployed the Odditorium's spider legs and docked beside a tall, brick-pile buttress to another bridge that appeared to be under construction.

"Why, this is to be the new railway bridge at Charing Cross!" Lord Dreary exclaimed. In the gloom I spied the shadowy shapes of mooring posts, wrought-iron girders, and scaffolding, and beyond that, a cluster of boats and a flight of stairs leading up to more construction on the embankment.

"Although it's high tide, I daren't moor the Odditorium closer to shore," Father said. "Don't want to get stuck in the mud or be seen should the invisibility mist run out."

Presently, a pair of samurai stepped out onto the balcony, and next thing I knew, Lord Dreary, Kiyoko, and I had followed Father upstairs into Nigel's chamber. The big man and Gwendolyn were already in the back of the demon buggy with a handful more samurai standing nearby. Father threw the lever on the wall and the hangar doors hissed open, filling the room with the river's cold, putrid air. Kiyoko climbed into the buggy's front seat with Excalibur, but as I tried to slip in beside her, Father held me back.

"Not so fast, son. You're staying here with the others."

"But, sir, I want to come with you!"

"I'm afraid not, Grubb. I'm leaving you in charge of the Odditorium in my absence."

"Me?" I gasped.

"That's right, so listen carefully. There are still plenty of samurai on board, and as long as you don't go flying, there's more than enough fairy dust in the reserves to keep you buoyant. However, should something go wrong, if for some reason we don't make it back, you're to get the Odditorium as far away from London as possible."

"But, sir, I can't play the organ well enough to—"

Father held up a hand to shush me. "Yes, you can. But no matter what happens, Abel Wortley must never get his hands on Cleona. Do you understand me?"

I nodded numbly. Everything was happening so fast that I couldn't speak. Father held out his hand and I passed him

Mack. "Remember, Grubb," Father said as he slid behind the steering wheel, "fairies and prophecies are never what they seem."

"Chomp, chomp!" Gwendolyn said with a smile, and then the buggy's engine roared to life in a cloud of demon dust. The samurai who couldn't fit in the backseat stood along the running boards, and then Father zoomed out the hangar door and splashed into the river a good ten feet below. I stood in the opening watching after them in amazement—I'd had no idea that the demon buggy was also a demon *boat*—and yet, as soon as Father sputtered round the Odditorium and out of sight, I found myself choking back tears. I wanted to go with them.

Lord Dreary put his hand on my shoulder. "Chin up, lad. There's no shame in holding down the fort."

I dashed past him without a word, all the way back downstairs and out onto the balcony, where, squeezing past the samurai, I caught sight of the demon buggy through the scaffolding on the river. They were close to the landing stairs, their faces like vague yellow phantoms in the glare of Gwendolyn's fairy light. She was protected from the water by the buggy's magic paint, of course, and could easily hold her own against the worst of the prince's minions. But still I worried that her glow might give them away.

As if reading my mind, Nigel tucked Gwendolyn under his coat, and the whole lot of them, demon buggy and all, faded back into the darkness. I searched for them for a long time afterward until, ever so briefly, I saw their shadowy forms skulking along the embankment before disappearing again amidst the wharf upriver.

"'Chin up' is right," I said, puffing out my chest. I was in charge of the Odditorium now, which meant I had no business feeling sorry for myself. Besides, I thought as I gazed down at the organ, my playing wasn't all that bad. I knew how to move the Odditorium's spider legs, didn't I? Not to mention its vertical thrusters, so perhaps I was the right bloke for this job after all.

"You can count on me, Father," I whispered in the dark.

There was no way he could hear me, of course, but if he had, not even Alistair Grim could have predicted just how soon I would make good on my promise.

NINETEEN

A Change of Plans

I'll wager it was Lorcan who put that bug in his ear," Cleona said. She had joined me on the balcony just after midnight, and the two of us stood gazing out across the Thames. The clouds had parted, and the river looked like molten silver in the moonlight.

"What bug in whose ear?" I replied.

"The one in Uncle's about your staying here. Lorcan told him what he saw in the Avalonians' temple."

"What does that have to do with anything?"

"You don't understand. While you and the others were flying back here on your dragons, Lorcan slipped away to have another look. There were more tiles, he said, rising up from that pool of glowing water and plastering themselves against the wall."

"What sort of pictures did they make?"

Cleona shrugged. "Lorcan said it was for Alistair Grim's

ears only, but I gathered from the look in his eyes that it had something to do with me."

"You mean the tiles formed a picture of *you*?"

"Lorcan refused to speak about it. He's strange that way—a bit superstitious. Then again, who isn't when it comes to prophecies?"

Perhaps that was why the Gallownog looked so out of sorts when we returned to the Odditorium. Unbeknownst to everyone, he had gone back to the temple and seen more of the queen's prophecy. Had the tiles really formed a picture of Cleona? And if so, what exactly did Dalach tell Father he had seen?

"Did he tell you about the other pictures?" I asked. "The ones of my mother and me? Of Mack and Moral's egg and all that lost-princess business?"

"He told me everything that happened, including that little bit about Abel Wortley. Pshaw, I didn't see that one coming, did you?"

I shook my head. "Neither did Father."

"Anyhow, Lorcan was very impressed with your bravery. He's grown quite fond of you, in fact. Then again, no accounting for taste, is there?" Cleona giggled.

"You can say that again. Look who he's been sweet on all these years." Cleona laughed heartily. "Speaking of which," I said, "you don't really think he'd ever take you back to Ireland, do you?"

"Lorcan talks a good game, but in my heart I can't see it happening."

"Neither can I."

Cleona and I gazed out at the wharf, its mooring posts and ship masts black as ink against the moonlit river. There was no sign of Father and the others, but the wind had picked up some, bringing with it the dull toll of dinghies and laughter from the darkened shore. A violin played somewhere in the distance, and despite the gravity of our circumstances, a strange feeling of peace came over me.

The moment was quickly cut short, however, when in the distance we saw a light break the surface of the water.

"There," Cleona said. The light winked off, revealing one of Wortley's black, cigar-shaped sharks floating in the river. Almost immediately another light surfaced and then winked off nearby. And then another. And another. My breath hitched and my knees felt weak. Father had been right about Wortley's next move after all, as well as him not coming alone.

"How many of those big black fish does the devil have?" Cleona asked. More sharks, at least a half dozen of them, had surfaced and were now heading for the wharf.

"I've got them in my sights," Mrs. Pinch whispered from

the organ's talkback. She and Lord Dreary were in the upper gunnery.

"Remember, Penelope," said Lord Dreary, "don't fire unless it's absolutely necessary. We don't want to give away our position."

Cleona held my hand and we watched the sharks slip silently, one by one, into the wharf. For a few tense moments we lost sight of them behind what looked like a coal barge in the foreground, and then I spied the silhouettes of the prince's minions clambering along the docks. I recognized Shadesmen and goblins and a troll or two, and there was the towering form of Prince Nightshade himself lumbering slowly behind them. Judging by the way he was moving, he must have been wounded worse than we thought.

Suddenly there was shouting, followed by the clash of metal and a bolt of brilliant white lightning from Kiyoko's magic wand. Gwendolyn, who remained onshore, expanded into her bright, toothy ball—her light illuminating the entire wharf as the battle began. Kiyoko and the samurai clashed with the Shadesmen while Gwendolyn chomped up the goblins and trolls. At the same time as Nigel hit the prince with the egg blaster, Father ran along the dock straight for him. In one hand he held Excalibur, and in the other, the time stopper.

Then, without warning, everything just . . . *shifted*. The

evil minions were gone, the prince lay on his back, and Father stood over him with Excalibur. It was as if the entire scene had jumped forward in the blink of an eye.

"Mack," Cleona said. "Uncle used his time stopper on the prince."

"And he killed him with Excalibur!"

"So that's it, then?" Cleona said after a moment. "Just like that, it's over?"

Cleona had echoed my sentiments exactly—I too had expected something much more dramatic—but still we watched with bated breath as Father passed the sword to Kiyoko and knelt down beside the prince's lifeless suit of armor. He lifted the visor on his helmet, and then suddenly shrank back onto his feet. Everyone looked around in confusion, and then Father grabbed Excalibur and raced for the embankment.

"I knew it," Cleona said. "Something's wrong."

The others followed Father from the dock, and as Gwendolyn took her normal shape again, I lost sight of them behind a mass of buildings along the wharf.

"Hang on," Cleona said. "I'm going to have a look from the roof." She quickly disappeared up through the ceiling.

"What's happening?" Mrs. Pinch said from the talkback. "I can't see anything now." An eternity passed in which all I could hear was my heart pounding in my ears, and then a police whistle shattered the silence. "Stop, thief!" someone cried. "Murderer!" cried another. A handful of lanterns, their lights bobbing up and down, began moving along the darkened embankment, and then Mrs. Pinch was on the talkback again.

"Cleona, what are you doing in the gunnery—?"

"It's another one of those submarines!" Cleona shouted over her. "Wortley must have slipped into it somewhere behind us. He means to get away upriver!"

"What are you talking about?" I asked. "We just saw Father kill him on the—"

"I can see Scotland Yard clear as day from up here," Cleona said with the gunnery gears grinding behind her—Lord Dreary, I could tell, was steering them to the opposite side of the roof. "They're up in arms and crying murder. Which means all that business on the wharf was a distraction while Wortley stole the transmutation dagger!"

I was entirely bewildered. I'd seen Prince Nightshade fall to Excalibur with my own eyes. In fact, I could now see a crowd of locals gathering round his armor on the—

"His armor." I gasped, and my heart froze as I replayed Father's reaction in my mind. Could someone else besides Abel Wortley have been inside the prince's armor?

"Quickly now, Mrs. Pinch," Cleona cried from the talkback. "Target your cannons over the port side."

"I am, I am," said Mrs. Pinch. "But I don't see— Well, blind me, there he is!"

"Fire when ready, Penelope," said Lord Dreary, and the Odditorium trembled with the cannon's blast.

"He's moving out of range," said Mrs. Pinch.

"Grubb, you've got to get us closer," Cleona cried. "If he gets past Waterloo Bridge we'll lose him for good!"

"But I can't—"

"Hurry, Grubb, there's no time to lose!"

And just like that my hands were on the organ. The music, if you could call it that, was jumbled and discordant, and yet somehow it did the trick. The spider legs creaked and groaned, and before I knew what was happening, the Odditorium had turned completely around and began to crawl upriver.

"Well done, Grubb!" Cleona said from the talkback. Yes, I was doing it. I was piloting the Odditorium just as Father had taught me. I could see the submarine shark directly ahead of me now, cutting fast through the water. I played faster, and the Odditorium responded by speeding up. Mrs. Pinch rained down a barrage of red lightning from the upper gunnery, but we were still too far away, and her cannon blasts fizzled out in the water just short of her target.

"Faster, Grubb!" the old woman cried. "You need to get me just a little closer."

The Odditorium rocked clumsily under my control, but

still I managed to keep the spider legs splashing forward with a *thwomp, thwomp, thwomp!* through the riverbed. Then, out of the corner of my eye, I saw something flash. The Odditorium sputtered a bit, and the organ music grew louder.

"Grubb, you've turned off the invisibility mist!" Cleona cried—how she could tell, I had no idea—but I kept my eyes fixed on Wortley's shark. My fingers raced along the organ with a mind of their own. And then, much to my amazement, Beethoven's "Ode to Joy" began blaring out across the Thames.

"That's it, Grubb!" Mrs. Pinch called from the talkback. "Just a little closer!"

"A regular prodigy!" Lord Dreary cheered in the background.

I could hardly believe my own ears, but there I was, playing "Ode to Joy" almost as well as Alistair Grim himself. The Odditorium's spider legs now crawled steadily, almost effortlessly under my command—*thwomp-th-thwomp-th-thwomp!* they trudged in time with the music. I was getting the hang of it now and closing in on Wortley fast—so close that I could make out the submarine's demon glaring back at me from its engine porthole. If only Father could see me now, I thought.

"Steady, lad, I've got him in my sights," said Mrs. Pinch. The notes continued rising and falling—my fingers racing, my eyes locked on the demon in the submarine's engine. *Got you now, you devils,* I said to myself. But then, at the precise moment I was certain Mrs. Pinch would fire, Wortley's shark sank beneath the churning water and disappeared from view.

I inhaled sharply and snatched back my fingers from the organ. The Odditorium lurched to a stop, and the river below became smooth and silvery again as if nothing had happened. "No," I moaned, unable to believe my eyes, but there was no denying it. Abel Wortley was gone.

"We've lost him," Lord Dreary said quietly from the talk-back. My heart sank and I buried my face in my hands. If only I had played better, Abel Wortley might not have gotten away. *But he* did *get away,* said a voice in my head. *And with the transmutation dagger, at that.* My throat grew thick as the tears began to rise. Alistair Grim's plan had failed—and it was all my fault.

"I'm sorry, Father," I whispered. "I let you down."

Then, all at once, it seemed, there were shouts coming from every direction, more police whistles, and people crying, "The Odditorium!" and, "Get them!" My stomach squeezed and my tears subsided. At the same time, Cleona dropped back down through the ceiling and onto the balcony beside me.

"You've got to turn on the invisibility mist," she said, and I immediately flicked the switch on the organ to activate it. But nothing happened. I flicked the switch again and again, but still, the invisibility mist would not turn on.

"It must have run out," I said.

"It's the lightning cannons," Father said, startling me, and I looked up to find him and the others hovering in the demon buggy outside. "They must have short-circuited both the prison sphere's induction unit and the organ damper."

"Pshaw, even the most amateur of inventors would've anticipated that," Cleona said sarcastically.

"All right, then, everyone out," Father said, and the others scrambled from the buggy and onto the balcony. "Nigel, get down to the engine room and see if you can't get the invisibility mist working again. Gwendolyn and Cleona, to your stations; Kiyoko, you stay with Grubb. We've got a mob on our hands, so let me dock the demon buggy and I'll fly us out of here."

As everyone scattered to his or her place, Kiyoko put her arm around me and I gazed out guiltily at Father. "That shark, sir," I said. "I tried to stop it, but—"

"It's not your fault" was all Father said, but his eyes spoke volumes. Abel Wortley had the transmutation dagger, and the thought of it terrified him.

A chill ran up my spine, but before I could ask Father what had happened, he zoomed off to dock the demon buggy. The samurai took up defensive positions on the balcony, while

Kiyoko led me into the library and handed me McClintock. The old pocket watch was snoring up a storm.

"We tried using his time stopper a second time," Kiyoko said. "But it only seemed to tire him further."

I tapped Mack on his XII to wake him, but the poor fellow just muttered some gibberish and went right on snoring. I slipped him into my waistcoat.

"What happened?" I asked. "And who was that in the prince's armor?"

"It wasn't the prince's armor," Kiyoko said. "Similar, yes, but not fortified with black magic. And inside was your old friend Judge Hurst." I gasped. "Your father saw him only for an instant, and then his body vanished—disintegrated by Excalibur, along with the rest of Nightshade's minions."

My head was swimming. Judge Hurst? Why Judge Hurst? Last I'd seen of him, he'd just been turned into a purple-eyed Shadesman. So what was he doing in London dressed like the prince?

Just then a scuffle broke out on the balcony, and in a matter of seconds the samurai were ripped to pieces—their armor flying into the library as if they'd been blown apart from the inside. Kiyoko and I ducked for cover behind Father's desk, and when we looked again, there on the balcony, with the transmutation dagger in his mouth, was Prince Nightshade!

"EEEEYA!" Kiyoko cried, and in a blur of whirling black

she flew at him with Ikari. She brought the sword down hard, but it was no match for the Black Knight's armor. And with a single swipe of his massive arm, the prince knocked Kiyoko clear across the room, where she slammed against a bookcase and crumpled limply to the floor.

"Kiyoko!" I cried, rushing to her side. The prince had bashed her out cold—or worse!

Prince Nightshade chuckled and removed the transmutation dagger from his mouth. He appeared to still have some use of the arm below his wounded shoulder, but the gash where Malmuirie had struck him with Excalibur was red and smoking.

"We meet again, young Grubb," he said, gazing about the room. His voice sounded weak, and he was panting. "Inside the Odditorium at last, where the doom dogs cannot save you."

"You devil!" I screamed, cradling Kiyoko's head. I was on the verge of hysterics, unable to tell if she was breathing.

"Sentimental fool," the prince sneered. "Just like your father."

At that moment someone called to him from outside. "Is everything all right, Your Highness?"

My breath hitched. I recognized the voice immediately—it was Mr. Smears. He must have helped Wortley escape in his mechanical shark and then the two of them circled back underwater, unseen by Father and the others, whereupon

Wortley climbed up the side of the Odditorium and onto the balcony.

"Hold tight, Smears!" the prince called back, and then he turned to me and smiled. "A man after my own heart, your old master. Pity, though, he didn't finish you off years ago. Would've saved me so much trouble."

The prince's eyes flashed and he raised his dagger. Without thinking, I ran for the parlor door. Nightshade blocked my path, so I turned on my heels and made for the balcony—I would take my chances in the river, I thought—but as I went to leap over the balustrade, I found Mr. Smears gazing up at me from his mechanical shark down below. I froze, giving the prince just enough time to clamp his hand down on my collar.

"Leaving so soon?" he said, dragging me into the library. He lifted me off my feet with his good arm and turned me round to face him. The transmutation dagger was in his other hand, and as he strained to raise the blade to my throat, the glowing red features of his face twisted with pain.

"I don't think you'll ever realize how much trouble you've caused me," he said, out of breath. "Nevertheless, do give your parents my regards when you see them in the Land of the Dead."

"Let him go, Wortley!" Father shouted, and we spun round to find him standing in the parlor entrance with Excalibur.

The prince gasped and pulled me close. A long, tense

second passed in which all I could hear was the mob outside along the riverbank, and then the prince laughed and, with noticeable effort, raised the dagger again to my throat.

"Well played, Alistair Grim," he said. "I knew something was amiss when everyone in Scotland Yard just froze as if time had suddenly stood still." Father stiffened and set his jaw. "Oh dear. Yes, I'm afraid whatever magic you used to make that happen had no effect on me. My armor again, don't you know. So I do owe you a bit of gratitude for making my business here much less arduous."

"That body double of yours on the wharf," Father said. "You wanted to frame Judge Hurst for your crimes, is that it?"

"Well, when you've got a purple-eyed Shadesman lying about, you might as well use him."

"Just as you used William Stout?"

The prince chuckled, and suddenly I understood. Abel Wortley had not only planned on using Judge Hurst and the others to distract the authorities while he escaped, but he was also *hoping* for the judge to get caught. That way he could frame him for all his crimes, while at the same time throwing the *rest of us* off his trail!

"You got what you came for, now let the boy go," Father said. "You're weak and need to use that transmutation dagger."

"An excellent deduction," said the prince. "But you know very well you'd never have figured out all this transmutation business had I not told you my true identity. Then again, who knows? It appears I've underestimated you for quite some time now. Your strategy is quite impressive—I see it all so clearly now. Allowing yourself to be killed in Avalon? Only to be resurrected by Excalibur and return to London invisible? Well, not even I would have expected such a move. Brilliant, man! Simply brilliant!"

"There's more to this game, I assure you," Father said, inching his way into the library. The prince, afraid of Excalibur, pressed the dagger to my throat and backed away with me toward the hearth.

Then, out of the corner of my eye, I saw Number One buzz past the balcony. She had returned from the prince's castle. But where were the Gallownog and Professor Bricklewick?

"Aren't we confident now that we've got the big bad sword," said the prince. "And yet, Excalibur or not, if you take one more step your son will feel the wrath of a very different kind of blade."

Father stopped and lowered his sword. "Tell me, Wortley, why this obsession with my son? If I didn't know you better, I'd swear you were afraid of him."

The prince laughed. "Oh, Alistair. However clearly you see the future, you are still so blind to the past. Nevertheless, your arrival in London with Excalibur has thrown a wrench in my works, and so it appears I'll have to change my plans."

"Hurry, Your Highness!" Mr. Smears called up from outside. "There's a regular mob gathering round here!"

"Very well, then," said the prince. "As much I'd love to kill you now, I'll have to save it for some other time—must find another solphylax, as I'm sure you've guessed. And please don't try any tricks, or your son here gets it."

Father cocked his ear as if someone had whispered to him and his eyes flickered.

"And just where do you plan on going, Wortley?" he asked with a sly grin. "The demons in your castle's flight sphere have been disposed of by Professor Bricklewick. Thus, whatever Odditoria you were planning on using to house your spirit will soon be incinerated when your castle crashes into the marshes outside of London."

"Nice bluff," the prince said, and then a distant rumbling explosion shook the walls. Father slipped his pocket watch from his waistcoat and checked the time.

"Ah, right on schedule," he said, snapping it shut. "For you see, while you were busy pinching the transmutation dagger, our old friend Oscar Bricklewick was busy snatching up your demons. What you just heard was your Eye of Mars exploding under the weight of your crumbling castle."

"You're lying," said the prince, but I could feel him tensing behind me.

"I assure you, I'm not," Father said. "After all, being an

expert on Odditoria, I should think you of all people would recognize a demon catcher when you saw one. Go ahead, Oscar, show him."

Oscar? I said to myself, and then a nervous Professor Bricklewick materialized next to Father with the demon catcher clutched tightly to his breast. Prince Nightshade gasped. It must have appeared to him as if the professor had blossomed out of thin air, but of course I knew that Lorcan Dalach had simply released him from his spirit shackles, which meant that the Gallownog was here in the library with us too.

Everything next happened so fast that it seemed over before it began. Professor Bricklewick unlatched the demon catcher, and while the prince was distracted, Lorcan Dalach materialized directly in front of us and pulled me from the prince's grasp. At the same time, Father rushed the prince with Excalibur, and in a whirl of flashing steel, thrust the sword deep into his chest. Prince Nightshade howled in pain, then stumbled backward and slumped down heavily against the hearth.

"I'm afraid it's checkmate, Wortley," Father said, yanking his sword free. The prince clawed at his chest, and the gash in his armor sparked and smoked through his fingers. "Your castle home is in ruins, your armor destroyed. There's nowhere left for your spirit now except the pits of hell."

The prince's glowing red eyes darted frantically about the room until they found me. I was far away from him now, behind Father's desk with Dalach and the professor, but still I trembled under the terror of his gaze.

"It's all for the best, Grubb," he said, and the jagged gash of his mouth parted into a smile. "Heaven forbid you should ever grow up to be as big a fool as your father."

And with that Prince Nightshade uttered a strange incantation and plunged the transmutation dagger into his chest wound. The blade sparkled and flashed, and then a stream of red liquid light flowed upward from the pommel and into the lion's mouth above the mantel. The prince twitched and jerked about, and then the stream of light vanished and his armor lay lifeless on the floor.

"Oh no," gasped Professor Bricklewick. "The Odditorium—it's the perfect solphylax in which to house his spirit!"

Suddenly, the blue animus exploded out from the sconces with a *whoosh*, and in its place burned a bright red fire. Laughter echoed from the walls, and the lion's mouth began to move, began to *speak* with the voice of Abel Wortley!

"Home at last!" he cried. "The animus, the Odditorium—all of it is *MINE*!"

Every muscle in my body froze. Abel Wortley had transferred his spirit into the Odditorium!

The library doors slammed shut of their own accord and

the organ began to play madly by itself. The floor trembled and shook, the spider legs creaked and groaned, and red lightning began raining down outside the balcony. Father just stood there, stunned, and Professor Bricklewick shook him by the shoulders.

"Snap out of it, Alistair!" he shouted.

"What's happening, sir?" Mrs. Pinch cried from the talk-back. "The cannons are firing by themselves!"

Lord Dreary screamed something unintelligible, and then Cleona cried out over the talkback too. "I'm trapped in my charging station, Uncle! I cannot move!"

"But this is impossible . . ." Father muttered.

"No, it's sorcery!" screamed Professor Bricklewick. "Wortley is binding his spirit to the Odditorium! We've got to get him out!"

The professor yanked the transmutation dagger free from the prince's chest, and his empty suit of armor crumbled into dust upon the hearth. Professor Bricklewick gave it only a passing glance as he made to stab the lion's head, when a bolt of bright red fire shot out of its mouth and struck his hand. The professor yelped in pain, and the dagger went flying out over the balcony and disappeared into the river below.

The lion, its eyes flashing, roared triumphantly, and then Wortley's deafening laughter filled the chamber. The

Odditorium rocked to and fro, knocking books from the shelves and throwing me out onto the balcony, where, in the flash of the lightning cannons, I could see buildings exploding and people running for their lives. We were heading up the embankment—the boats, the docks, the very wharfs themselves crushed beneath the Odditorium's massive spider legs.

Abel Wortley was steering us straight for the streets of London.

Coming to his senses, Father rushed to the organ, but when he tried to play, tiny bolts of red lightning shot out at his fingers and shocked him backward onto his bottom. Abel Wortley laughed, and another burst of red fire shot out from the lion's mouth.

"I AM IN CONTROL NOW!" he boomed. *"THE ODDITORIUM IS MINE!"*

Father scrambled to his feet and tried the talkback on his desk. "Nigel, Gwendolyn—can anyone hear me?" he screamed, but only Abel Wortley's voice came crackling back at him.

"Have a seat, Alistair, and enjoy the show!"

Wortley turned the Odditorium toward the Thames and fired again and again on Waterloo Bridge. The stone exploded in great showers of rubble and dust, and then one of the archways crumbled into the river. Wortley howled with laughter, and yet somehow, through the mad drone of the organ music and the chaos outside, I heard Father say, "He's won. There's nothing I can do."

Lorcan Dalach looked down at his shackles, then leaned in close to me and said, "Tell Cleona I love her." And before I realized what was happening, the Gallownog streaked up into the hearth and Cleona started wailing high above us in her chamber.

"AAAIIIEEEEEEEEEEEEAAAAAAAAAAHHHHHH!"

I pressed my hands to my ears, and was vaguely aware that the organ music had stopped, when in the next moment the lion roared, and from out of the hearth Lorcan Dalach emerged with Abel Wortley's smoky red spirit bound by his shackles.

The old man, more of a withered corpse than a man, was bald with hollow eyes and sunken cheeks. And where his mouth should have been there was only a ghastly, gaping black O. And yet he seemed to struggle with the strength of twenty men, hissing and clawing at the Gallownog like a feral cat that had been snared by the tail.

"Lorcan, no!" Father cried. But the Gallownog ignored him and dragged Abel Wortley's spirit out onto the balcony. As they passed Professor Bricklewick, the old man shrieked and swiped at the professor's face, and in a desperate attempt to grab on to something, snatched the demon catcher from his grasp. Lorcan Dalach gave his spirit shackles a final pull, and together he and Wortley tumbled from the balcony and plummeted toward the river below.

I screamed in horror—the Gallownog would surely disintegrate as soon as he hit the water. Wortley cried out something that I didn't understand. The demon catcher flashed in his hands, and then the spirits were gone, swallowed up in a violent burst of bubbling black.

After that, Cleona stopped wailing.

— T W E N T Y —

Odditoria That's Given Back

THE MYSTERY DEEPENS!

Despite circumstantial evidence to the contrary, The Times has learned that the authorities in Shepherd's Bush have officially labeled their recent claim to fame "a natural disaster resulting from a meteoric impact," thus dismissing once and for all any connection between the strange events there and the brief, albeit devastating, appearance of the Odditorium in London earlier this month.

Readers of The Times will recall how, just after midnight on the third of November, an unidentified flying object smashed into the marshlands between Hammersmith and Shepherd's Bush. One eyewitness to the event reported seeing what looked like "a castle falling from the sky," and another, "a blinding flash of brilliant red light." However, as all that remains at the impact site is a water-filled crater thirty feet deep and one hundred yards wide, The Times has been advised by both the local authorities and a representative from the Royal Observatory to consider the matter closed.

Readers of The Times will also recall how, after wreaking havoc along the Thames on the very same night as the "Meteorite on the Marsh," the Odditorium simply vanished into thin air, leaving in its wake a path of destruction even worse than that of its exodus from London early last October. In addition, The Times has recently learned that the wreckages of at least a half dozen underwater boats, or "submarines," have been found amidst the rubble near Charing Cross, thus delaying construction of the new railway bridge and deepening the mystery as to why Mr. Alistair Grim—inventor, fortune hunter, and, some say, mad sorcerer—has once again seen fit to lay waste to our fair city.

Speaking on condition of anonymity, a source for The Times reports that, simultaneous with the Odditorium's appearance on the Thames, a forced entry occurred in the evidence room at Scotland Yard. What items, if any, were stolen, the source could not say. However, as there can be no doubt that the aforementioned submarines are another example of Mr. Grim's mechanical wizardry, it is the proposal of The Times that the title of "river pirate" be added to the growing list of Alistair Grim's dubious professions.

Nevertheless, despite Mr. Grim's continued disregard for the welfare of his fellow man, it is nothing short of a miracle that no deaths have been reported in the aftermath of his most recent visit. However, it is the opinion of The Times that, unless the unhappy man and his Odditorium are quickly found, Londoners will not be so fortunate the next time Alistair Grim rears his villainous head.

The afternoon light hung heavily in the library as Professor Bricklewick finished reading the newspaper and laid it on Father's desk. All of us were there except for Cleona and Gwendolyn, and upon hearing the news that Alistair Grim had been blamed for both the theft at Scotland Yard and the invention of Wortley's sharks, what little hope we had that the truth might someday be revealed was shattered in an instant.

Ever since our escape from London, Professor Bricklewick and I had been fetching newspapers for Father. Excalibur had disintegrated Judge Hurst's body and the prince's minions during the battle on the wharf, but we were certain that the authorities would find *some* evidence that would shed light, or at least cast doubt, on what really happened that night. However, it now appeared that any such evidence, except the sharks, had been blown to bits when Wortley's spirit took over the Odditorium. Even Mr. Smears had vanished—either drowned or got away, we wagered. My gut told me it was the latter, for like all rats, my old master had a knack for surviving.

As for that business near Shepherd's Bush, Professor Bricklewick and I had seen the crater up close a week earlier, along with hundreds of others who'd traveled there to gawk at the "Meteorite on the Marsh." Father had been right. The explosion from the Eye of Mars incinerated Prince Nightshade's castle and its contents upon impact, while at the same time its magic paint helped contain the blast so that the damage wasn't too widespread.

"So now you're a pirate, eh?" Lord Dreary said. "Well, as long as you don't start sporting an eye patch and ask us to call you captain, I can live with such a title." The mood in the library lightened. Mack, who was sitting on my shoulder, gave a hearty chuckle, and Father smiled and leaned back in his chair.

"Pirate indeed," he said. "It appears old Wortley has a knack for framing people even in death."

My eyes darted to Nigel. The big man stood in the very spot where Nightshade's armor had crumbled into dust. Broom had long since swept all that up, but I kept expecting it to appear again at any moment with Abel Wortley back inside. Professor Bricklewick, however, had assured me that both the armor and its former occupant were gone for good.

"As is often the case with supernatural entities," he told

me earlier, "fairies, Shadesmen, goblins, and trolls—as well as Odditoria like the Eye of Mars—usually vanish once they cease to function. Thus, since Wortley's spirit had been bound to the Black Knight's armor, once it was released, the armor no longer served a purpose and disintegrated. Just as the old man's spirit did when it hit the water."

The professor still felt awful about losing the transmutation dagger, but given the circumstances, not to mention the burn on his hand, one could hardly blame him.

"But come now, sir," said Mrs. Pinch. "Can it really be there's no evidence to implicate Abel Wortley in all this? No chance of you clearing your name or Nigel's?"

Father shrugged and smiled sadly. "I'm afraid that, at least for the time being, any hope of vindication seems to have vanished into the Thames along with the Gallownog."

Again, a heavy silence fell upon the library. And while the rest of us hung our heads in sorrow, Father poured us some brandy to honor our friend.

It had been nearly two weeks since Lorcan Dalach sacrificed himself to save us, and yet in my mind I could see the moment when he hit the water as clearly as if it was happening again before my eyes. A sob rose in my throat. That Cleona should have wailed the Gallownog's death as if he were part of our family meant only one thing: Lorcan Dalach, in his heart, had joined us at the Odditorium after all.

Our glasses now full and in hand, Father raised a toast and said, "To Lorcan Dalach. May his memory live on forever here at the Odditorium."

"Hear, hear," said Lord Dreary, and we drank. This wasn't the first time we'd toasted our friend, and whereas I had once been quite fond of brandy, in the days since his passing its taste had grown bitter with mourning. Our grief, however, could not compare to Cleona's, and although most of the time she managed to keep a stiff upper lip for the rest of us, on more than one occasion I'd heard her weeping alone in her chamber.

Poor Cleona, I thought. I really should check up on her.

"Begging your pardon, sir," I said, setting down my glass. "May I be excused?"

Father took my meaning, and with a glance at the clock, said, "Just be mindful of today's lesson, my young apprentice. The hour draws near."

Before I could answer, Mack said, "You can count on me to keep the lad on time, sir." I snapped his case shut and tucked him inside my waistcoat.

"Yes, blind me, will you look at the time," said Mrs. Pinch. "I'd better get cracking on supper if it's to be ready when you get back."

"Jolly good," said Lord Dreary, and as the old folks hurried off to the kitchen, Kiyoko rose unsteadily from her chair.

"There, there, miss," said Professor Bricklewick, and he held her elbow. Kiyoko had suffered quite a blow to the head, and even after a steady diet of Mrs. Pinch's magical remedies, had yet to fully recover. Father insisted that she stay on at the Odditorium until she was better. The professor agreed to stay on with us too. After all, there was more work to be done, he said, and how could one go back to teaching after an adventure like that? I, however, suspected an even bigger part of his reasoning had to do with Kiyoko. The professor had been assisting in her recovery the entire time and had clearly grown fond of her—and she of him, from what I could tell.

"Some fresh air is what you need," said the professor. "Would you do me the honor of accompanying me onto the balcony?"

"I would," Kiyoko said with a smile, and as the two of them strolled arm in arm outside, Father crossed to Nigel and put his hand on his shoulder.

"Take heart, old friend," he whispered. "We're closer now than ever."

Nigel was about to reply, but upon noticing my presence, jerked his chin at me. Father glanced back over his shoulder and was surprised to see me still standing there.

"Well, what are you waiting for?" he said, and without a word I dashed from the room.

As I traveled upward in the lift, I began to wonder at the

meaning behind what Father had said to Nigel. *"We're closer now than ever."* He must have been reassuring him about seeing Maggie someday, I concluded, and by the time I reached Cleona's door, the matter was forgotten.

I found Cleona gazing out the chamber's single porthole from high above in the Sky Ripper. The room was cold and drafty, and yet her mirror-paneled walls gleamed warmly with amber twilight.

"Father and I will be off shortly," I said. Cleona nodded, her eyes never leaving the sky. We'd been flying in and out of the clouds for most of the day, due north above the English countryside, so heaven only knew how long she'd been sitting there. "Just checking to see if you needed anything," I said after a moment.

Cleona turned to me, and I noticed her normally crystalblue eyes had grown gray from weeping. "Do you know why Uncle's library is always so warm?" she asked.

"Begging your pardon, miss?"

"Of course, we spirits do not feel temperature. But you, Grubb, did you ever wonder why, especially on a cold day like today, the library stays warm even when the balcony wall is raised?"

Her question caught me off guard. Oddly, in all my time at the Odditorium, I'd never asked myself that. "I'm afraid it never occurred to me, miss," I said, thinking. "But now that you mention it, I suppose it has something to do with the Eye of Mars."

Cleona shook her head. "Years ago, when Uncle started building the Odditorium, often I'd find him working in the library with the balcony wall wide open. This was before the Eye was hooked into everything, when there were screens and curtains up outside, hiding what the wasps were doing. And there was Alistair Grim, in the dead of a London winter, tinkering away in just his shirtsleeves. 'Aren't you cold, Uncle?' I asked him, and he just smiled and said, 'How could one be cold amidst all this magic?' Of course, him being Alistair Grim, I thought he was having me on. But then, at some point over the years, I came to realize he was telling the truth." I furrowed my brow in confusion. "Don't you see, Grubb? It's the books. Alistair Grim had been speaking quite literally. It's the magic in his books what keeps the library warm."

"Cor," I gasped as my mind began to spin. Even though what Cleona was saying sounded impossible, I knew it to be true. After all, if the odd was the ordinary at Alistair Grim's, that meant the impossible was the possible too.

"The warmth," Cleona said, her eyes distant. "Why is it, I wonder, we always take magic like that for granted? And yet, only when it's gone—when it's cold—do we realize how magical it truly was?"

I knew what she was driving at, but didn't quite know how

to answer. "Sort of like the loss of a loved one, you mean?" I said in the end, and Cleona nodded. "I don't rightly know, miss. But I suppose that's why people give gifts to one another. So, when they're apart, they can feel close to the person who gave it to them."

Cleona sighed and turned again toward the sky. It pained me to see her so sad, and without thinking, I reached into my pocket and pulled out Moral's egg. Its polished shell shone like a tiny golden sun in the light from the porthole.

"I'd like you to have this, miss."

Cleona's eyes widened and she floated down to the floor. "I can't accept that," she said. "Moral laid that for you. And Lorcan told me he saw a picture of it on the temple wall."

"Good, because I'm giving it to you on his behalf."

"But the queen's prophecy—"

"I don't care about that. Lorcan would want you to have something to remember him by. Besides," I said, pointing at her egg-shaped Sky Ripper and bed. "I should think one more egg is just what this place needs." Cleona hesitated. "Please, miss. It would mean the world to me if you'd take it."

Cleona smiled and took the egg. "I shall cherish it always," she said, and kissed me on the cheek. Her lips were ice-cold, and yet a bolt of warmth shot through my body as if she'd touched me with the Eye of Mars itself.

Blushing, I dashed from the room and down the hallway

into Nigel's chamber, where I waited for Father in the front seat of the demon buggy. Despite Queen Nimue's prophecy, I knew that giving Cleona my golden egg was the right thing to do. In fact, upon seeing her smile like that after so many days of sadness, I decided that I had received the greatest gift of all.

Soon, however, my mind drifted to another gift. The Black Mirror. Father told me that my mother had given it to him upon their engagement—a gift of love, powerful in its own right. Now that Prince Nightshade was defeated, I wondered, would Father once again embark on his quest to rescue his long-lost love from the Land of the Dead? Would he ever learn the reason why she ran away all those years ago, why she left his son with the Yellow Fairy, and why, of all places, there was a picture of that night in an Avalonian temple? Clearly, Abel Wortley had known more than he was about to tell. Which is why I suspected that, even in death, the fiend still had a few surprises left in store for us.

Suddenly, I felt a rumbling in my waistcoat.

"It's five o'clock!" Mack cried as I opened his case. "Time for your lesson, lad."

"Thank you, old friend, but I'm already here."

"As am I," Father said, entering with Excalibur. He threw the lever for the hangar doors and the room was instantly freezing. Shivering, I slipped Mack into my pocket and buttoned my overcoat. I was tempted to ask Father about what Cleona had told me regarding the library, but given that my lesson had officially begun, I resolved to broach the matter another time.

Father slid into the buggy beside me and handed me Excalibur. "Are you ready?"

"Yes, sir," I replied, donning my goggles. Father donned his, and a moment later we were off.

My ears were numb by the time we reached the lake, and as we splashed down, a brace of ducks scattered noisily from our path. Father turned off the buggy's engine, and an eerie calm settled over us as we began drifting upon water. In the waning twilight, all but the center of the lake appeared black from the towering mist-ringed fells reflecting down on us from shore.

"Go ahead," Father said, pointing to Excalibur.

I swallowed hard and stared back at him, unsure if I should proceed. Father nodded encouragingly, at which I stood up and, grasping the sword's ice-cold grip, hurled Excalibur out over the lake. The sword tumbled end over end, and just as it was about to hit the water, a hand—delicate and feminine— exploded up through the surface and caught the hilt. The blade flashed with an unearthly light, and then the hand drew the sword straight down, where it disappeared beneath the water.

Alistair Grim had kept his promise. Excalibur was on its way back to Avalon, and the last window in the queen's castle would soon be closed. I gaped at Father in amazement. *How could Nimue have known that we'd return Excalibur today?* I wanted to ask, but the question froze in my throat.

"Our worlds are linked in ways that not even I can fathom at present," Father said, reading my mind. "Given what you saw in her temple, I should think you'd understand that better than anyone."

A wave of guilt rippled through me. Of course, given what I saw in the queen's temple, I still had loads of questions about how my mother and I were connected to Avalon. I'd asked Father about it more than once over these last two weeks, but he always just shrugged and seemed to grow sad. No, now was not the proper time to ask him again. Besides, I was beginning to have doubts about giving Cleona my egg.

"Begging your pardon, sir," I said as I sat back down. "But I should probably tell you that I gave Cleona Moral's egg." Father's face dropped in shock. "On Lorcan's behalf," I added quickly. "To cheer her up."

"Did the Gallownog put you up to this before he died?" Father asked.

"Why no, sir. I done it on my own." Father gazed out over the water and quickly became lost in thought. "Please don't be cross with me, sir," I said after a long silence. "I only done it—*did* it, I mean—to make Cleona happy."

"You misunderstand me," Father said quietly. "Before he died, Dalach confided in me about what he saw when he returned to the temple a second time. It seems the tiles had formed a picture of Cleona holding Moral's egg."

"Cor," I gasped. "But what could it mean, sir?"

"Only time will tell, I'm afraid. And thus, although our Aquaticum appears to be over, I suspect our business with the Avalonians is not."

Father and I pondered this a long time. An owl hooted in the distance, a nightingale began twittering onshore, and then the frigid wind joined them, whistling along with their twilight song. I shivered.

"Begging your pardon, sir," I said, rubbing my hands together, "but now that we've returned Excalibur, shouldn't we be getting back to the Odditorium?"

"Not yet. We've still got your lesson."

Father lit a lamp, hung it alongside the buggy's windshield, and then retrieved a pair of fishing poles from the backseat. He handed one to me, and my insides swelled with excitement. Father quickly checked our lures, showed me how to cast my line, and then, with the last of the afternoon light quickly fading, we watched our floats disappear amidst the blackened water. A fish splashed somewhere close by, but when I asked Father what I should do if I caught one, he shrugged, and with a smile said:

"Why, give it back, of course."

Alistair Grim's eyes twinkled in the lamplight, and the nub of his lesson came clear. There was more magic in moments like these than in anything at his Odditorium. For even though the wind was blowing quite fiercely now, I wasn't cold at all.

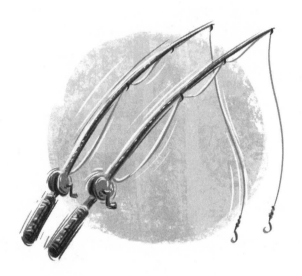

— TWENTY-ONE —

Just a Bit More

I f the odd was the ordinary at Alistair Grim's, then I suppose it came as no surprise that I should find magic in the most unexpected of places: on a lake in the middle of nowhere, fishing with my father. Such magic, I learned, was more powerful than anything Abel Wortley could dish out.

And yet, the old devil had certainly dished my family a lot of sorrow, much of it dating back to before I was born. I just knew in my heart that he'd had something to do with Mother's flight from London. But as all that was still a mystery, there was no use in speculating myself silly about it. We had other problems, and soon I would learn just how important—and how *magical*—my gift of Moral's egg truly was.

However, if the word *Odditoria*, at once both singular and plural, is used to classify any object living, inanimate, or otherwise that's believed to possess magical powers, perhaps the biggest lesson I learned back then is that friends and family are the most magical gifts of all.

And who am I to speak of such?

Why I'm Grubb Grim, of course. Son of Alistair Grim—inventor, fortune hunter, and, some say, mad sorcerer and river pirate. But *I* say he was the greatest father in the world. I know there's many a lad who feels that way about his father, but how many can say theirs saved them from a man-eating rabbit?

Good heavens! There I go getting ahead of myself again.

My apologies, but I'm afraid you'll have to take my word on all that rabbit business for now. Kiyoko is calling. Time for my sword-fighting lesson, you see.

After all, now that the whole world had heard of Alistair Grim, there were loads more baddies coming after him for his Odditoria.

An intriguing turn of events, wouldn't you agree?

Character List

Some relevant persons at the Odditorium:

Grubb: Name spelled like the worm but with a double *b*, Grubb is twelve years old and the narrator of our story. A former chimney sweep, he is both the long-lost son and newly found apprentice of Alistair Grim.

Alistair Grim: Fortune hunter, purveyor of antiquities, and, some say, mad sorcerer. He is the inventor of the Odditorium, a flying house of mechanical wonders, and thus the chap after whom these stories are named.

Nigel (a.k.a. William) Stout: The Odditorium's jack-of-all-trades, he is big and bald and wears a pair of thick black goggles to hide the fact that Mr. Grim brought him back from the dead.

Mrs. Pinch: Mr. Grim's nearsighted housekeeper and resident witch.

Lord Dreary: Mr. Grim's business partner and longtime family friend.

Professor Oscar Bricklewick: Mr. Grim's former schoolmate and rival for the hand of Elizabeth O'Grady, Bricklewick is an expert on Arthurian legend.

Kiyoko: A fierce shinobi warrior and friend of Grubb.

Some baddies, human and otherwise, who'd like to see the above folks done in:

Prince Nightshade: Mr. Grim's nemesis and archaeological rival, the prince is an evil necromancer obsessed with finding a source of animus so he can build an army of purple-eyed Shadesmen.

Mad Malmuirie: A fetching but mentally unstable witch from whom Mr. Grim "acquired" some Odditoria.

Mr. Smears: Grubb's former master, Mr. Smears is fond of drink and blaming others for his troubles.

The Black Fairy (a.k.a. Bal'el): An evil winged demon who excels at blowing up things with his bolts of nasty black fire.

Shadesmen: The long-dead armies of Romulus and Remus resurrected by Prince Nightshade.

Judge Mortimer Hurst: A former enemy of Mr. Grim's, Prince Nightshade turned him into a purple-eyed Shadesman with Mack's animus and a magic spell.

Doom dogs: A pack of vicious shadow hounds charged with fetching escaped spirits back to the Land of the Dead.

Sea serpents, dragons, and other **monsters,** many of which have allied themselves with Prince Nightshade.

A few people who are either dead or just talked about:

Abel Wortley: An elderly philanthropist, purveyor of antiquities, and dear friend of Alistair Grim's, Mr. Wortley and his housekeeper were murdered in London ten years before Grubb arrived at the Odditorium.

Maggie Stout: Nigel's/William's daughter, Maggie was sent to live with Judge Hurst's sister after her father was hanged for the abovementioned crime.

Elizabeth O'Grady: Mr. Grim's long-lost love and Grubb's mother, she died under mysterious circumstances twelve years ago.

Glossary of Odditoria

Not to be confused with Mr. Grim's Odditorium, the word *Odditoria*, at once both singular and plural, is used to classify any object living, inanimate, or otherwise that is believed to possess magical powers.

Some Odditoria relevant to Mr. Grim's Aquaticum:

Cleona: A mischievous banshee, she is the source of the Odditorium's animus, the mysterious blue energy that powers its mechanics.

Lorcan Dalach: A soldier in the Order of the Gallownog, Dalach is charged with enforcing banshee law and assassinating their enemies.

Gwendolyn, the Yellow Fairy: A wood nymph who is very fond of chocolate and gobbling up nasty grown-ups, and whose dust enables the Odditorium to fly.

Dougal "Mack" McClintock: Chief of the Chronometrical Clan McClintock, Mack is a salty Scottish pocket watch that Prince Nightshade wants for his animus.

Nimue, Queen of Avalon: Also known as the Lady of the Lake, she is a beautiful water fairy capable of great feats of sorcery and forgetfulness.

Moral: A temperamental goose that lays exceedingly messy colored eggs.

Broom: The Odditorium's maid, she is just that, a broom.

The Eyes of Mars: A pair of magical orbs that the Roman god of war gave to his twin sons, Romulus and Remus. Alistair Grim has one Eye, and Prince Nightshade has the other.

Demon catcher: A wooden box that . . . Well, you get the idea.

The Black Mirror: A silver-handled mirror with dark glass that Elizabeth O'Grady gave to Mr. Grim upon their engagement.

Excalibur: The legendary sword of King Arthur Pendragon.

Map of Merlin: A magical map that shows the location of entrances into Avalon.

Number One: A large mechanical wasp.

Samurai: Legendary Japanese warriors; Mr. Grim uses their magic-infused armor to guard his Odditorium.

Solphylax: A general term used to classify any receptacle capable of housing a disembodied spirit or demon.

Acknowledgments

At the risk of déjà vu, I must first thank my dear agent, Bill Contardi, as well as my brilliant editors, Emily Meehan, Jessica Harriton, and Elizabeth Law. Ladies, as always, I find myself in awe of your collective insight, and I cannot thank you enough for your assistance on this project. Boundless gratitude also to the people at Disney Hyperion who once again helped bring the world of the Odditorium to life: Laura Schreiber for first believing in this story; Whitney Manger, Su Blackwell, and Colin Crisford for another amazing cover; copy editor Alix Inchausti; and my incredible illustrator, Vivienne To, whose imagination never ceases to enchant. In addition, a load of thanks to my crackerjack publicist, Mary Ann Zissimos; the delightful Dina Sherman, director of school & library marketing; and the indefatigable Marianne Merola (Brandt & Hochman) for hustling those foreign rights deals.

As always, I am eternally grateful to my wife, Angela, and the rest of my family for their love and support—especially my mom, Linda Franco, who must have bought at least a hundred copies of the first book. Much appreciation goes out to all the readers who offered critiques on the first draft: Michael Combs, Michael and Anthony Funaro, Jill Matarelli Carlson, Grace and Ellie Hamashima, Libby and Isabelle Snyder, Debbie and Sophie Lee, Paul and Jack Schneider, Jessica Purdy, and Holli Staats. Thanks also to the legion of friends, colleagues, and students (past and present) who helped promote the first book on social media. Your names are too many to list here, but each has been written in my heart.

Finally, my undying gratitude goes out to you, dear reader, for joining Grubb and his family on their adventures. Then again, I am not surprised. After all, you are Odditoria, too!